WITHDRAW

CHILDISH
THINGS

ALSO BY MARITA VAN DER VYVER

Entertaining Angels

CHILDISH THINGS

Marita van der Vyver

cu

Translated by Madeleine Biljon

A DUTTON BOOK

DUTTON
Published by the Penguin Group
Penguin Books USA Inc., 375 Hudson Street, New York, New York 10014, U.S.A.
Penguin Books Ltd, 27 Wrights Lane, London W8 5TZ, England
Penguin Books Australia Ltd, Ringwood, Victoria, Australia
Penguin Books Canada Ltd, 10 Alcorn Avenue, Toronto, Ontario, Canada M4V 3B2
Penguin Books (N.Z.) Ltd, 182–190 Wairau Road, Auckland 10, New Zealand

Penguin Books Ltd, Registered Offices: Harmondsworth, Middlesex, England

First published by Dutton, an imprint of Dutton Signet,
a division of Penguin Books USA Inc.
Distributed in Canada by McClelland & Stewart Inc.

First Dutton Printing, August, 1996
10 9 8 7 6 5 4 3 2 1

 REGISTERED TRADEMARK—MARCA REGISTRADA

LIBRARY OF CONGRESS CATALOGING-IN-PUBLICATION DATA
Van der Vyver, Marita.
    [Dinge van 'n kind. English]
    Childish things / Marita van der Vyver ; translated by Madeleine
Biljon.
        p.   cm.
    ISBN 0-525-94148-7
    I. Biljon, Madeleine.   II. Title.
PT6592.32.A517D5613   1996
839.3'635—dc20   96–26030
                                                      CIP

Printed in the United States of America

PUBLISHER'S NOTE
This is a work of fiction. Names, characters, places, and incidents either are the products of
the author's imagination or are used fictitiously, and any resemblance to actual persons,
living or dead, events, or locales is entirely coincidental.

This book is printed on acid-free paper. (∞)

For all those who were there

The town, Black River, like all characters in this novel, exists only in the author's imagination.

When I think back on all the crap I learnt in high school, it's a wonder I can think at all.

Paul Simon, 'Kodachrome'

Acknowledgements

Flight 605

I had resolved never to write about my youth. After all, what can you say about the seventies – except to wish you hadn't been there?

The sixties produced hippies and sex, the eighties yuppies and money. But the seventies? What can you say about platform shoes and trousers with absurdly wide legs, David Bowie's hacked hairdo, John Travolta's disco dancing and Abba's music?

It was probably the most ephemeral decade in the history of the world. Disposable fashion, disposable dances, disposable music. And disposable lives in the warm country where I grew up. Young white boys shot on the Border for the good of the nation and the country. Black schoolchildren shot in townships for another nation in the same country.

But eventually I realized what all storytellers have to realize before they can break free from the past: it's not what you want to tell, it's what you have to tell.

So here I am travelling through time, in more ways than one. Rushing towards a child I have never seen, while remembering the child I used to be. With another child next to me. And I am writing about my youth, about the seventies, about that country of contrasts.

You'll Have Fun on the Way

When I looked up she was standing in the door, two suitcases like coffins under her arms and a funereal cloud on her face.

'*Yesterday, all my troubles seemed so far away,*' she sang in a gruff boy's voice and kicked one suitcase across the bare floor so that it slammed against the opposite bed. 'Damn.'

I was so flustered that I forgot to wipe away the tears on my cheeks. She dropped the other suitcase heavily on the floor and flopped back on the bed, shoes and all. Not the regulation lace-up shoes but the prettier, prohibited ones with a strap across the instep. She folded her arms behind her head, sighed, and stared at the ceiling.

'I'm Dalena,' she said without looking at me. 'I'm your roommate and I'm as disgusted with this dump as you are, so cry away.'

'I'm Mart,' I sniffed and gave my eyes a quick wipe. 'Sorry, I'm not used . . .' A vague gesture encompassed it all – the bare hostel room, the bars in front of the window, the unfamiliar trees in the garden, the humid closeness so early in the morning. 'I'm not used to this.'

'Never mind, neither am I.' She turned her head and smiled at me over her elbow with the widest mouth I'd ever seen. 'And I've been here for three years.'

Her eyes were a strange colour. Greyish-green. Or greeny-grey? Athletic legs, slender ankles and knees, decently curved calves. Muscular thighs under a school dress which had ridden up to the elastic of her panties.

She wasn't wearing the prescribed large, grey bloomers, either.

'In the hostel?'

'Yep. But I schemed to be out of it this year. I talked my father

3

into letting me lodge with the PT teacher in town. She's nice, she would've given me more freedom than this place. I convinced my father that I planned to take my schoolwork "seriously". Told him I was aiming for a few As in matric but that I didn't have enough time to swot in the hostel. And he fell for it. But the teacher unfortunately has a dish of a brother . . . and yesterday my father caught us in the shower . . .'

'You and . . .' I couldn't believe my ears.

'Yep.'

'*Naked?*'

She looked at me as though I was mentally deficient.

'Do you shower in your clothes?'

Long ago, I remembered, Simon had a marble, shot with green and grey and almost as translucently bright as her eyes. When the light caught it in a certain way, there were yellow flecks in it as well.

'And then?'

'And then there was a helluva scene and I was disinherited – not for the first time – and here I am, back in the hostel!'

And I had been under the impression that children on the platteland were innocent.

'The worst of it is that I can't have my old room! It's been given to someone else!'

When the breakfast bell shrilled unexpectedly, I immediately jumped up, but she remained lying on the bed. Stretched out. 'Now I've got to sleep in this stupid room with you. You've probably discovered it's right under the bell. No one else wants it, that's why they give it to new pupils.'

She swung her legs down and sat on the edge of the bed, stretched arms resting on the palms of her hands like guy ropes to keep her upright while she looked me up and down. I felt as though I was facing a headmaster. But then she smiled, a smile that literally spanned her face from ear to ear like a long, beautiful bridge.

'Whose table are you sitting at?'

I was so entranced by the smile that I forgot the matric girl's name.

'She has . . . huge boobs?'

'Oh, Laurika. With that bunch of drears? Sheesh, no, you've got to get away from them.' When she adopted a serious look her face was nothing special. Except for the colour of her eyes, perhaps. 'Would you like to sit with me?'

I could only nod enthusiastically.

'Stick with me, baby.' As soon as she smiled, as she did now, her face became one you would notice in a crowd. 'I can't promise to make you famous. But you'll have fun on the way.'

That's how I got to know Dalena van Vuuren. And nothing would ever be the same again.

Since my arrival the previous day I had felt like a wild animal locked up in a zoo for the first time. Later I realized that an Afrikaans school hostel in a conservative platteland town could, in fact, be described as a kind of zoo. The windows were barred to keep inmates in and outsiders out. There were feeding times and visiting hours and sleeping times and even times when pupils were gated. Sometimes we behaved like animals, too.

Hideous, I'd thought when I first saw the hostel room.

A grey blanket on a grey iron bed, greyish linoleum on the floor and a greyish-white clothes cupboard. Empty, but with a musty smell emanating from its interior. The smell of lost dreams, I thought with the poetic licence of an almost sixteen-year-old. Actually, it was only the smell of stale food, I realized later: of cake and rusks and other edibles hidden behind clothes and gobbled in silence.

Even the walls had a greyish tinge. And bare, bare, bare. Not a poster or a painting or a postcard, not even a hole where a nail had been or a mark where sticky tape had stripped away the paint.

A cheap wooden table, grey with age, under the window. Wire mesh against mosquitoes in front of the window. And bars behind the mesh, even though the room was on the second floor.

Slowly I'd sat down on my bed and stared at my knees under my new grey school uniform as if they belonged to someone else. Golden brown legs after a holiday at the sea.

My mother suppressed a sigh and sat down on the other bed in the room. I hadn't wanted to look at her, afraid that I would start crying. Or even worse, that she would cry.

'Only three days,' she'd said in a thin, unfamiliar voice, 'then it's the weekend.'

I looked away, through the mesh in front of the window, to where orange flames burned in a tree. I didn't know what kind of tree it was. Where I came from, trees behaved in a dignified manner, green in summer, bare in winter. Oak trees, weeping willows, fig trees. Not gaudy pink and purple and orange like the frangipani and the jacaranda and the tree-with-flames in this hot, feverish country.

But now we had come to live in the Lowveld because my father had made a mint with one of his schemes and for the first time had been able to afford a small farm. Because he wanted to play at being a farmer even though he was an attorney. Because he'd seen too many cowboy movies, as my mother had mumbled when she'd heard of this plan. Because he saw himself as a pioneer in the Wild West.

The idea was that my mother would run the small banana farm while my father and a few partners developed a kind of health farm in the vicinity. A place where wealthy people could stay when they wanted to stop smoking or drinking or to lose weight or simply to rid themselves of aches and pains. Stupid, I thought, like all my father's schemes. To expect adults to pay large sums of money to stay in a glamorous concentration camp! To get a bowl of lettuce for lunch and do PT three times a day!

And it was as a result of this fantastic idea that I, at almost sixteen, was sitting in a hostel room for the first time in my life. A few years ago, when I was still reading the Afrikaans version of Angela Brazil's books, I wouldn't have minded. There was a time, not too long ago, when stealthy midnight feasts and silly pillow-fights sounded more fun than the wildest party in the darkest of garages. There was a time when I could eat tins of boiled condensed milk down to the last lick without worrying about whether my jeans would still fit me.

Now I felt too old.

'Well, I suppose I have to go.' My mother's face was shiny with perspiration. This was her first acquaintance with the greyness of a hostel room as well. She looked at me as if she would never see me again. 'Your father's waiting in the car and it's hot.'

He was the one who wanted to come and live here, I thought.

'Will you manage the unpacking?'

She looked at the new nylon suitcase on the floor. Grey – as though we'd had a premonition when we bought it the previous week – with its handle and binding as extravagantly orange-red as the flowers in the unfamiliar tree.

'Yes, of course, Ma. Do go.'

She got up and hugged me briefly, frightened of an emotional outburst. She smelt as she usually did, of baby powder and cigarette smoke and the sickly sweet hairspray ('For Firm Hold') which made her hair stick to your fingers. But her smell mingled with the strange odours in the room – stale food, disinfectant, Peaceful Sleep mosquito repellant – and I drew away because I felt sick. She thought it was because I didn't want to kiss her.

It was only when she had left the room that I cried.

(Years later she told me that she had cried too, all the way home. While my father tried to convince her that I would learn team spirit and obedience and good table manners in the hostel – plus all the other decent attributes which, according to him, his four children seriously lacked.

'This is what happens when you try to rear children in the modern manner,' he had accused her, and not for the first time. 'From Dr Stock's books.'

'Spock,' Ma had sighed.

'You know perfectly well what I mean. If I've told you once, Marlene, I've told you a dozen times that you mustn't come crying to me if they turn out to be drop-outs or drug addicts.')

My holiday by the sea felt like something in the distant past. I couldn't even remember the colour of Nic's eyes.

Brown, of course, I thought in a wave of panic, but what kind of brown? Brown like bitter chocolate or brown like milky coffee or brown like gingerbread or . . . ? I realized that I was hungry and wondered whether hostel food was as awful as everyone said it was.

The bed opposite me was empty, the sheets and pillow case a dirty white with the faded letters for the Transvaal Education Department, in both languages, T.O.D. T.E.D. T.O.D. T.E.D. T.O.D, in their serried ranks as the only decoration. 'We always keep a couple of beds open,' the matron had explained. 'Newcomers are often a day or two late.' Her voice sliced through my marrow like a butcher's saw. I hoped that the newcomer on her way here had been involved in a car accident. I didn't want to fall asleep next to a girl I didn't know from a bar of soap.

The bell rang so shrilly that I was startled, and ran to the door. Outside, in the passage and above the door, hung something that looked like a giant's bicycle bell – a stainless-steel serving dish which made an indescribable noise. Of all the rooms in the long passage, I had been given the one directly below the bell. I shut the door and burst into tears.

That was the supper bell, the first of many bells I would learn to distinguish in my new life as a boarder.

The dining hall was even more hideous than the bedroom. There were eight girls at each long table, seated on hard wooden chairs with high backs. While Matron said grace some stared at a bowl of brown bread in the middle of the table, faces as strained as a sprinter's in the blocks. The moment the saw-like voice said 'Amen', everyone made a grab for the bowl.

There were twelve slices of bread in the bowl, I realized later, which meant that only the four fastest eaters could have a second slice.

It was even worse than I had imagined, I thought, while the girl next to me swallowed her bread in great, greedy bites and shot out her hand for the second slice. It was like something from Charles Dickens!

At the head of each table sat a matric girl who was allowed to serve herself first. Then the stainless-steel dishes were passed back and forth until they eventually reached the end of the table where the losers sat. The unpopular ones, the ugly ones, the stupid ones, the newcomers, like me. By the time I'd served myself the last of the food, the matric girl's plate was virtually empty.

The evening meal was mealie porridge and sausage with a sauce of baked tomatoes. Where I came from we had mealie porridge for breakfast, with milk and sugar and a lump of butter. And even for breakfast I wasn't mad for it.

The matric girl at the head of the table had the face of a young child: a button nose, her hair bunched in pony tails above her ears; but her breasts were two majestic mountain peaks which overshadowed everything in their vicinity. I stared at them unashamedly.

Perhaps this area was so fertile that it wasn't only the vegetation that grew faster than in other places? Maybe the people too were affected. I looked at my seven table companions. Naturally they didn't all have big breasts, but the one next to me, the one who had grabbed the bread, had hands almost as big as my father's. And the one opposite had a plait as long and thick as a child's arm.

'What did you say your name was?' the one with the incredible plait asked when she saw I was looking at her.

'Mart.' The porridge stuck to my teeth like wonder glue. 'Mart Vermaak.'

Now all seven were looking at me. Where do you come from? Which school were you in? Do you know . . . ? But as suddenly as the chorus of questions started, they forgot about me. Seven heads turned away from me. Seven voices chatted enthusiastically about the recent holiday.

I stared at the baked tomato peels on my plate – as horrid as skin on a cup of coffee – and tried to remember exactly what it sounded like when a wave broke on a rock.

Another grey tiled floor in the bathroom, two rows of dirty-white basins opposite one another, two rows of lavatories and baths behind closed doors, and a few open showers against the furthest wall. What had happened to all the colours in the world? Even the girls around me seemed colourless, off-white in their summer nightgowns as though I were looking at an over-exposed photograph.

I brushed my teeth and thought about my holiday. Tried to recall the smell of suntan lotion, the screech of gulls carried away on the wind, the sticky feeling of sand against a wet body. Anything to get away from this unreal reality.

But all I could smell was the Clearasil ointment the girl next to me was using for her pimples. Looking at herself in the mirror with open-mouthed concentration, she was unaware that I was staring at

9

her. All I could hear was water rushing out of taps and showers. If I closed my eyes, perhaps I could imagine it was the sound of waves.

When I closed my eyes, the sharp, foamy taste of toothpaste was on my tongue and I suddenly remembered that Nic's mouth had tasted of peppermints and tobacco with a lingering aftertaste of salt.

A bell rang – another one – and everyone rushed out of the bathroom like cockroaches when a light went on in a dark room. I also changed into a cockroach.

In my new bedroom my unpacked suitcase and my empty school rucksack lay on the bed. On top of the suitcase were balls of crumpled newspaper in which I had wrapped a mug, a porcelain doll and a few other pathetic ornaments to remind me of home. I sat down on the bed and read one of the newspaper reports because I didn't know what else to do until the next bell rang.

Our enemies must know that every single one we lose on the Border, binds us more closely to our country, South Africa. So said the Minister of Police, Mr Jimmy Kruger, at the funeral of a young constable shot in Rhodesia.

I crumpled the newsprint and looked for a waste basket. Under the table there was a wire waste basket. Grey, what else?

When I looked outside, through the mesh and the bars, the unknown tree still flamed orange. Hundreds of tongues of fire licked at the deepening dusk. Further back an orange bougainvillaea poured over the wire fence surrounding the hostel garden. And almost in front of the window grew a green shrub as high as a tree, with great white flowers which hung from the branches like inverted crinkle paper cups. I wondered whether it was these cups which gave off the heartbreaking odour.

I had to turn away from the window because my eyes were smarting with tears again.

So I sat and stared at the bare wall in front of me, absently stroking the coarse sailcloth of my rucksack. A grubby rucksack on which the names of friends and silly messages had been written with various coloured felt-tipped pens. I looked down and drew in my breath sharply. Next to me on the bed lay something which looked like a small heap of spilt salt. Carefully, because it was far more precious than salt, I tried to gather it into my cupped hands.

I let the sea sand flow back and forth between my hands while my holiday unreeled like a movie in my head. Actually much better than a movie because I could even *smell* the suntan lotion.

I had used the rucksack as a beach bag, packing it each morning with my towel, book, dark glasses and purse before I went looking for Nic. Don't run after him, my mother warned endlessly, as mothers have always warned. But I didn't run after him. I merely made sure that I was in the right place at the right time. There's a difference.

I learned to read the weather and the waves. That's what you do when you're stupid enough to fall in love with a surfer. I knew when I could find him and where.

In the end I had to admit that he was more interested in the waves than in me. But at least he was more interested in me than in any other girl.

When the lights-out bell rang, I remembered the colour of his eyes. It was like those damp blisters you saw on kelp, blisters which burst with a soft plop when you trod on them.

London, 16 June 1992

Dear Child

You have just turned sixteen, I realized today. As old as I was the day the photograph was taken at the Pretoria Zoo.

I dug it out – the only picture I have of all four of us – after I had read my son to sleep with Roald Dahl's scary little verses. No, they don't seem to frighten him. The crueller they are, the wider his smile. My innocent, bloodthirsty little boy.

He doesn't know the date nor what it means. In the cool green land where his forefathers starved, it's called Bloomsday by readers who know who Leopold Bloom was. In the hot country where his mother's forefathers hunted and plundered – where politics have always been more important than books – it's remembered for other reasons. He doesn't know about the children who died or about the child who was born a short while before that day.

And now I'm staring at a photo of four terribly white teenagers on a yellow lawn, a cageful of monkeys in the background. The boys' haircuts are brutally short, their bodies are awkward in army uniforms. The girls are dressed according to the fashion pages in the Afrikaans *Sarie* and the American *Seventeen*. One is wearing a halter-neck smock which bells out at her hips over jeans which hang even more widely over high cork soles, rather like an old-fashioned layered wedding cake draped in denim. The other one's hair is hidden under a kerchief, her body under a patchwork pinafore dress, as if she had borrowed a maid's outfit for the occasion. A rich man's child in the clothes of the poor.

I wish I'd spent my teens in a more elegant age!

I have begun to write a story about that terrible time which I would like to dedicate to you, if ever I finish it. But I don't even know your name.

Happy birthday, my nameless child. I hope your seventeenth year is better than mine was.

M.

We Will Fight and Go Forward with Faith

'So it *is* getting a little better?' my mother asked, her eyes worried. Opposite her my young brother was sucking up the last of his chocolate milkshake so noisily that he could be heard in the street. She wore her usual martyred what-have-I-done-to-deserve-this expression but apart from that ignored him.

'I didn't say that,' I muttered, the straw clamped between my lips.

We sat in the Portuguese café next to the local movie house, the walls around us covered in old film posters. In front of me there was a grease mark on the red and white checked tablecloth, a large red plastic tomato filled with ketchup and a menu covered in plastic like a schoolbook. After three weeks in this dull town I had accepted the fact that there were no elegant coffee houses in Black River.

'*Doctor Zhivago*,' my mother sighed. 'It was the only love story your father ever liked.'

My eyes wandered to the posters on the wall while I fought the temptation to suck up the last of my milk shake as Niel had done. *Love Story*, I saw, and remembered how I had cried when Ali McGraw died so beautifully and giggled every time she said *bullshit*. Opposite me my twelve-year-old sister stared open-mouthed at Niel, which encouraged him to suck even harder.

'*Wow!*' she said with an American accent.

'Shaddup,' I hissed and tried to hide behind my mother as one of the matric boys at a table in the corner turned to look at us.

'Children,' my mother tried saying in my father's voice. But it never worked.

'Ma, he's wearing his school uniform and he's behaving like an elephant in a zoo!'

'Tcha, old Mart is just scared one of her boyfriends at the table there at the back will think her brother doesn't have any manners.'

'Well, he doesn't.' I grabbed the glass away from him so fast that the straw hung in his mouth like a long, soggy cigarette.

'Sheesh, where'd ya learn to grab so fast?' he asked with something like admiration in his voice.

'At table in the hostel. If you don't grab you go hungry.'

I enjoyed the slightly shocked expression on my mother's face. She touched her bottle-blonde hair, stiff and sticky with spray as usual, and looked over my head at the posters. Niel burped, looking me straight in the eye. Lovey giggled behind her hand and my mother looked more martyred than ever.

'You should've kept him back a year, Ma,' I said. 'Any idiot can see he shouldn't be in high school yet.'

He looked at me as if I'd slapped him. I almost felt sorry for him. He was the smallest in his standard-six class and his biggest fear was that he wouldn't grow much taller.

'Never mind,' Ma comforted as usual. 'Simon only started growing when he'd almost finished school.'

Hearing Simon's name made me feel depressed all over again. My elder brother had started his National Service a month ago. Now I was the eldest in the house with this poison dwarf of a baby brother, and a sister who believed that life was a movie in which she played all the leading roles.

The Portuguese café owner was leaning forward behind the counter, resting on his elbows, between the cash register and a fan which swung to and fro like a human head. Every three seconds a breeze blew through his dark hair. There were two similar fans in the far corners of the café, high above the tables, but they seemed to make no difference. My grey school uniform clung to my thighs and there were damp circles of perspiration under my arms.

Behind the owner's head hung the only poster which didn't advertise a movie. It was the kind you saw in travel agents' windows: a big colour picture of a deserted beach with palm trees. Like somewhere overseas, I thought longingly. *Lourenço Marques*, it said in heavy black letters across the blue sky. That was where LM Radio broadcast from.

The man had sad eyes. He reminded me of the café owner in a book I'd read during the holidays, *The Heart is a Lonely Hunter*. The name caught my attention in the bookcase at the beach house between all the other books which had stood there for years, fading in the sun. I had wanted to tell Dalena the plot but she lost interest when she heard that it didn't have a happy ending.

'*Gone with the Wind*,' Ma sighed again, her eyes on an old poster.

'They don't make movies like that anymore,' Niel and Lovey said quickly before Ma could say it.

Ma didn't even seem to hear.

'Have you heard from him again, Ma?'

'Simon?' My mother ferreted in a crocheted bag with wooden handles and took out her pack of Cameos. 'Two letters in one week! He must be terribly homesick.'

'I miss him.'

'So do I, Mart.'

Ma swallowed the last of her tea and lit a cigarette. *Equality?* asked the woman in the Cameo advertisement peering at the camera through thick false eyelashes. *Only men are born equal. We're different. Like our cigarettes.* She was beginning to look a little bored. Ma, not the girl in the ad.

Actually, all four of us were a bit bored. It was Friday but because the school was holding a sports meeting on the following day, the hostel children weren't allowed to go home on the Friday afternoon. Ma felt sorry for us and had come to see us. But when she and Lovey drove to the farm later on, Niel and I would have to remain behind.

'A Friday in the hostel!' *We will not give up the fight against terrorism and Communism*, I read in the newspaper lying in front of my mother. *We will fight and go forward with faith until we have achieved a just peace.* The Minister of Police had spoken at the funeral of an adjutant who had been killed with three other policemen on the Rhodesian border. 'It's terrible!'

'It's going to be fun!' Niel smiled with Ma's dark eyes, adult eyes in a pointed little-boy's face which made him look even more like a poison dwarf.

'I wish I was a year older,' Lovey sighed. 'Then I would've been in the hostel too!'

'I wish I was two years older, Lovey, then I need never see a hostel again!'

'My name is not Lovey,' she said as usual.

'Sorry, Lovey,' I said as usual.

Pat Garrett and Billy the Kid, I read on a poster in the corner where the matric boys were sitting. Now that was a smart movie. Bob Dylan's music.

'If you want to go to Stellenbosch, Mart,' Ma said and drew an ashtray set in a miniature tyre towards her, 'you'll have to stay in a hostel.'

'No ways, Ma! I'd rather go to an English university. Then I can do as I like even if I have to stay in residence.'

'You'll break your father's heart if you don't go to Stellenbosch.'

'He broke mine,' I replied, 'the day he dropped me in front of the hostel.'

'Don't always exaggerate, Mart. It's not that bad.'

'How do you know how bad it is, Ma? You've never been in a hostel!'

It sounded sharper than I'd meant it to but Ma didn't react, simply tapped her ash neatly into the little car tyre. *Goodyear* was written on the rubber. A good year for whom?

'Well, I listen to you talking . . . about your roommate, the way you . . .'

'If it wasn't for Dalena I'd have committed suicide by now!'

This time she reacted.

'Don't say things like that, Mart.' A forefinger tap-tapped the cigarette. This was a sure sign that you had to watch your step. She didn't lose her temper easily, my father was the quick-tempered one, but the day she did lose her cool . . . Don't push me, she always said. *Don't push me.*

'If it wasn't for Dalena I'd probably have run away.'

'*Lady and the Tramp!*' Ma's petulant mouth opened, her eyes pleased. 'Do you remember it?'

She knew I wouldn't run away. I would moan and groan, I would threaten and sulk, I would cry every evening until my eyes were sore. But I would endure and persevere.

I was nothing if not her daughter.

*

17

'This is wild country,' Pa said with the pride of a pioneer in his voice. 'Wild but beautiful.'

They were standing on the veranda, grilling meat and looking out over banana trees which stretched as far as the eye could see. Closer to the house, next to the swimming pool where I lay reading in the sun, the thin trunks of a few pawpaw trees towered above the pinks and purples of the bougainvillaea and the scarlet flowers of the hibiscus. I turned on to my back to catch the sun on my front.

'Look, way across there, where it's hazy, lies the Kruger National Park.' Pa gestured, a beer bottle in his hand and a silly little cloth hat on his head. *Prisoner of Love* was printed in red on the white material. He swallowed a mouthful of beer and deftly turned the grill. 'You can hear the lions roaring at night.'

'I'll be damned!' said his friend from the Cape.

'I kid you not,' my father confirmed. 'Sometimes the hippos come and drink at the swimming pool.'

The man from the Cape gave an uncertain laugh. I turned up the radio so that I wouldn't have to listen to my father's tall tales. Wiggled my bottom to the beat of Mick Jagger unable to get no satisfaction. Tried to concentrate on my book again.

Dalena had told me to read it. Which should have made me suspicious immediately because my roommate wasn't the world's greatest reader.

'Has it got sex in it?' I'd wanted to know.

'It'll make your teeth curl.'

'In Afrikaans?'

'Man, André *P.* Brink is not like other Afrikaans writers.'

The way in which she accented the *P.* made the name sound elegant and exotic. 'I'm telling you, it's hot stuff. Nude scenes.'

I didn't want to show any interest. But when my mother took us back to the hostel on the Friday afternoon, after our visit to the Portuguese café, I asked her to stop at the library.

'Have you got *Ambassador* by André P. Brink?' I asked the old lady behind the counter.

'*The Ambassador.*' She looked at my grey school dress and her heavy eyebrows rose like twin helicopters above her spectacle frames. 'Aren't you a bit young for such a difficult book?'

'It's for my mother.' Without turning a hair. Sometimes I took after my father.

So here I was lying in my holiday bikini next to the swimming pool, sweatily searching for the first nude scene.

'This place is alive with snakes,' Pa said. 'As thick as my upper arm. Mambas. Green ones in the trees, black ones on the ground.'

'What do you do if you come across one?' The man from the Cape was beginning to sound sceptical.

'You wet your pants!' my father laughed. I peered towards the veranda over my dark glasses. Pa shook his head and bent down to turn the grill again. 'No, the black people here know how to deal with snakes. Never Die – he's the boss boy – always carries a long stick. He can crush a snake's head with one blow.'

'That's probably why his name is Never Die,' said Pa's other friend who came from Pretoria.

Silently I sang along with Mick Jagger. I didn't know what I would've done without LM Radio.

'Mart, you must be careful of the sun!' My mother warned from the edge of the veranda where she had appeared with a bowl of salad in her hands. 'Else you'll be crying in a vinegar bath tonight.'

'Oh, Maa!'

'It's just a thought.' Ma was wearing a trilobal skirt over a matching floral bathing suit. Her dark glasses could have belonged to Jackie Onassis. The clusters of red cherries hanging from her ears looked real enough to eat. 'But remember it's not the Cape sun.'

I placed the open book over my face. The black letters swam in front of my eyes. I felt the sweat running down my stomach and filling my navel.

'Gosh, but the water looks good.' The voice of the Pretorian sounded closer, as though he were standing next to my mother. Ma's high-heeled cork sandals creaked as she walked away. It was quiet for a few moments but I had the feeling that someone was watching me. I peered past my book and saw the man leaning on the railing of the veranda. 'Nice hills on the horizon.'

'Yes.' My father gave an embarrassed laugh. 'I'll have to buy a shotgun one of these days to keep the boys at bay.'

'I'd like to see her in a few years' time.'

Did the bastard think I was deaf? I lay without moving as though I'd fallen asleep.

'Mart is a quiet child,' my father said, 'always has her nose in a book. Lovey is going to give me grey hairs, I can see that already. She's the wild one.'

'My name's not Lovey!' Lovey called out from somewhere, ran down the stairs and jumped into the swimming pool with a splash which sounded like applause.

I was so grateful for the distraction that I didn't even mind getting wet, just tried to keep the book dry by holding it above my head. I turned my back to the veranda and watched my sister bursting through the surface of the water like a glittering trout.

'I caught her in the bathroom the other day, shaving her legs,' my father said, sounding annoyed. 'With my razor! And she's not even in high school!'

Lovey climbed out of the swimming pool, straddled me and shook herself. The drops of water scorched my skin like dry ice.

'Come on! Look what you've done to the book!'

'What are you reading?'

'Nothing you'll be able to understand.'

'How do you know?'

She sank down on the wet paving next to me. Her skin was as brown as a nut, her body still unformed but her nipples already showed darker under the tight bikini top. She winked at me as if she knew what I was thinking.

'You must ask Ma to buy you a bra.'

'I already have.' Not ashamed about it at all, as I had been. 'I wear it to school.'

I pulled the damp book towards me, tried to read again. The frangipani tree behind me smelled as stickily sweet as Ma's hairspray. All around me on the paving, the creamy-white frangipani flowers had been dropped as though the scent had become too much even for the tree. It was difficult to concentrate on a book – even one with sex in it – when the trees around you smelled of hairspray and the sun burned your bare legs and the plants were so green that it seemed as if you looked at the world through dark glasses even when you took them off. Now I understood why everyone always said people overseas read more than people in Africa.

That was yet another reason for living in an attic in Paris one day: to read lots of books while eating long loaves of French bread, drinking cheap French wine and smoking strong French cigarettes. And when I wasn't reading, I would write romantic Afrikaans poetry which I would declaim with great feeling to madly attractive Frenchmen with black eyes and sunken cheeks who naturally wouldn't be able to understand a word . . .

'I've thought up a name for myself.' Lovey's voice broke into my dreams of the future.

'You've got a name,' I said irritably.

'How would you like it if everyone called you Lovey?'

'I can't imagine anyone ever calling me Lovey,' I sighed. 'I probably don't look like a Lovey.'

'Well, I wasn't stupid enough to tell the kids at my new school that you call me Lovey.'

'And now they call you Loulene?'

'Hm-mm.'

Slowly she shook her head while she drew patterns on the wet paving with her forefinger. Bit her full lower lip as Ma did when she wanted to hide her feelings. But it had always been easier for Lovey to show her feelings than to hide them.

'What's wrong with Loulene?'

'Nothing. It just doesn't suit me. A name is like a dress, it has to suit you.' She dropped her voice to make the most of the dramatic moment. 'I told them my name is Bobby.'

'*Bobby?*'

'Yes. Like that song Simon always sings. "Me and Bobby McKay".'

'McGee.'

'Yes, that one.' A blinding smile lit her face. 'Don't you think it suits me?'

'Bobby Vermaak!' I muttered and turned on my stomach to read again.

'Better than Lovey Vermaak, don't you think?'

*

'The Army is a strange place,' Simon wrote from Potchefstroom. 'I wanted to be a parabat, remember, so I'll have to go to Bloemfontein when I've done basic training, but now I'm beginning to wonder whether it's such a great idea. I mean I've got this picture in my head of a paratrooper all the girls will fall for but perhaps I'm the only one who's going to fall, hard, out of an aeroplane. No, I'm not becoming a pansy. I'm just wondering.

'I'm reading a book Pierre lent me. *Catch-22*, I think you'll like it. I told you, didn't I, that Pierre is the guy who grew up in Black River? He was expelled in standard nine, I heard the other day, because he told the headmaster that he was an old fart, can you believe it, so his parents sent him to a private school in Pretoria and he did standards nine and ten in one year. And last year he hitch-hiked across the country. I've never met a guy who asks so many questions. Or has so many strange opinions.

'He says the Americans saw their assholes in Vietnam. Solidly. He also says the whites have seen their assholes in Africa, but we're still arguing about that.'

'Here a man eats meat,' Pa said. 'Beef, venison, lion . . .'
'Snake?' asked the man from the Cape who was beginning to grasp the game.
'Snake,' my father said. 'Only last week we had a snake barbecue.'
'No, really, Carl, now you're talking shit.'
'Not so loud, there are children around,' Pa said primly. 'Come and have a piece of sausage meanwhile.'
'I saw a monster of a snake next to the road this morning,' said the Pretorian and swallowed some beer. 'Easily six feet long. A car had driven over its head but its body was still wriggling when I stopped.' Another swallow. The man knew how to expand a story. 'I put it into the boot. Thought I could play a little joke this evening. Leave it under Jake's bed with just the tail showing . . .'
'No, dammit, man!' One could almost hear the sigh of relief in the Capetonian's laughter. 'What would you have told my wife if I'd had a heart attack?'
My father joined in the laughter.
'But now I've had a better idea,' the Pretorian said. 'I think we

should grill the snake this evening. Then Carl can show us how he does his thing.'

'I second the motion!' laughed Jake-from-the-Cape, even more relieved.

My father was no longer amused.

'We can do that,' Pa said, his eyes on the grill, 'but I'll have to inspect the snake first. You can't throw any old snake on the coals.'

'Come on, Carl, it's too late to chicken out now!'

Jake-from-the-Cape slapped my father on the back. My throat closed as though I were choking on a piece of snake meat. The man shouldn't have said that.

'Chicken!' My father's voice rose as it did when he was losing a court case. 'Ha! You'll swallow your words tonight, Jake my man! Along with a nice mouthful of grilled snake!'

'*Bye, bye, Miss American Pie,*' Don McLean sang over the radio. '*Drove my Chevy to the levee but the levee was dry . . .*'

I sang along, moved my shoulders and kicked my feet as if I wanted to swim through the music.

'Why did the guy take his car to a lavatory?' Lovey asked, lying next to me with her eyes closed.

'I've also wondered.' I thought she'd fallen asleep. 'But Simon says when you sing, the words don't have to make any sense. He says if everyone sang more and said less the world would be a better place.'

'Not if everyone sings as off-key as you do,' Lovey mumbled.

I pretended not to have heard. Just listen to old Bob Dylan, Simon said. *Oh, but I was so much older then, I'm younger than that now.* It was actually better if the words were a bit jumbled, Simon said. Then it sounded *deep*.

London, 14 July 1992

Dear Child

I hate zoos. But I was so homesick today that I dragged my child to a zoo. Since I started writing my story last month, I've been homesick all the time. Or heartsick, as I prefer to call it. (There's an Afrikaans word that describes the feeling better, but I can't bring it to mind.) I thought I would feel better if I saw a few other exiles from Africa but that depressed me even more.

A rhinoceros behind bars in a London zoo is a pathetic sight. It simply stood there, immobile, staring crossly with its small eyes at the visitors. Its rough, dirty-grey skin reminded me of the heels of the children at Cape Town's traffic lights, those begging hands and drugged eyes which used to appear behind my closed window like visions from hell. I couldn't take it. It was one of the reasons why I fled. I didn't want to live in a country where children looked like that. And yet, when I stood in front of the rhino today I wondered which one of us felt less at home here, in the heart of London.

I grabbed my child's sticky hand and walked unseeingly to the lion cage. In the innocence of his two-and-a-half-years, he, in any case, was more interested in the packet of dinosaur sweets in his other sticky hand than in any of the pathetic animals his mother wanted to look at. Children are supposed to like zoos but I wonder whether that isn't just another myth adults want to believe.

In the souvenir shop, at the end of our visit, he asked me to buy him a plastic dinosaur. They don't sell dinosaurs here, I snapped at him, unnecessarily impatient, fed up to the back teeth with this passion for a species that died out ages ago. Zoos are for *living* animals, I tried to explain more patiently. Why? he wanted to know.

Why, indeed?

I offered to buy him a plastic rhino. Or an elephant or a lion. He wanted a plastic dinosaur. Sometimes my son is stubborn – like any other toddler – but sometimes it seems as if his whole body becomes one solid unyielding mass. Then he becomes far heavier than he appears to be, totally immovable. That's when he reminds me of Pierre.

The lion walked endlessly back and forth behind the bars, its mane tattered. It looked even worse than the rhino.

'*Leeu*,' I said to my son.

'Leo,' my English son repeated as though speaking of an astrological sign.

'Roar, Young Lion!' I ordered the lion but it stared at me as uncomprehendingly as my son. 'Rrroaaa! Rrroaaa!'

My son's munching jaw stilled for a moment before he clapped his hands in excitement. Applause for a mother who behaved like an idiot.

Years ago there was a zoo below Rhodes Memorial in Cape Town. I don't know if I ever saw it. Perhaps it was before my time. Perhaps my mother told me about it. But I swear I can remember an emaciated lion in a dirty cage near a freeway.

That is my earliest memory of a zoo. The others are even worse.

In junior school I went on an expedition, with a crowd of fellow pupils, to the Tygerberg Zoo. All I can remember is a bunch of wriggling snakes in a snake pit. I dreamt about snakes for months on end, woke up screaming night after night. My mother was at her wits' end.

And then, of course, there was the visit to the Pretoria Zoo, the day the photo was taken which I told you about last month. I was a teenager, all long legs and private parts, sweating in a small cable car high above a hippopotamus enclosure with only the thin floor of the cable car and a helluva long drop between me and the hippo. With his skinny body in his ugly brown army uniform, Pierre made the car swing back and forth, laughing defiantly. I squeezed my eyes shut and prayed to be in another place – any other place – when I opened them. When I dared to peer through my lashes again, I hung right above the rhino enclosure. It was probably the start of my perpetual doubt about the power of prayer.

'Which is worse?' I asked my son, a game I regularly play with him. 'To be squashed by a hippopotamus or impaled by a rhinoceros?'

He squealed with laugher and even offered me one of his dinosaur sweets. He loves such horrible possibilities. Give him a story with a violent ending and he smiles from ear to ear. Dwarfs who tear themselves in half through sheer rage. Witches in burning shoes, forced to dance until they drop dead. Where did this bloodlust originate?

His African ancestors' hunting spirit? Or the fighting spirit of his Irish forebears?

Only an hour ago I sent him to sleep with another pitiless fairy tale. So that I can continue my own pitiless story.

What does it feel like to be sixteen? I would like to experience that feeling again – really experience it, not just recall it superficially – so that I can tell my tale the better.

I would also like to believe that you are well and happy, wherever you may be.

M.

Nights in White Satin

It was dark in the hostel and as oppressively hot as it was every night. Not quite as dark as every night, I realized, after lying with my eyes open for a while. The moon had to be nearly full.

Simon would've known. His moods always became stranger as the moon grew. It was inexplicable, Ma said, it should actually happen to me because the moon was my ruling planet but she thought it might have something to do with his rising star. Ma took things like that seriously. Simon only laughed and said he didn't believe in the stars, it was because he was a werewolf that he was affected by the moon.

I turned on my side so that I could see Dalena's bed. She was also lying on her side. Probably as soaked in sweat as I was. The smell of Peaceful Sleep hung stupefyingly in the air. As it did every night.

I was startled when I saw the whites of her eyes.

'I thought you were asleep,' I whispered.

'Too hot,' she whispered back.

'Don't you ever get used to it?'

'To the heat?'

'To everything,' I whispered, 'I've been in the hostel for almost two months and it feels as if I'm never going to adapt!'

'You're simply not a hostel child.'

'Are you?'

'I never had a choice.' She sighed and turned on her back, folded her hands behind her head. Like the first morning she'd walked in here and thrown herself down on the bed. Bent her knees so that the sheet looked like a white tent in the dark. 'We farm children had to go to boarding school from the start.'

We were quiet for a long time until I asked carefully: 'What do you think of Ben?'

'He's all right.' She turned her face towards me so that the moon shone on her cheek like a searchlight. Her skin looked as white as the sheet. 'A bit too sweet for my taste.'

'What do you mean . . . too sweet?' Yesterday Ben had asked me, stuttering and stammering, to go to Heinrich's party with him. I would have been at the party over the weekend in any case – but suddenly everything had changed. I didn't know what to wear, I didn't know whether I should borrow my mother's curlers to put up my hair, I didn't know whether my short hair would look stupid with a bunch of curls, I didn't even know whether I still wanted to go to the party. 'Can he dance?'

'Not half bad.' Her teeth were a white flash in her wide mouth. 'But if you want to move beyond dancing . . . he's terribly shy, you know.'

'That's OK,' I said quickly.

'I don't think he's ever kissed a girl properly.'

'Oh, that shy?' I couldn't hide the disappointment in my voice.

'Perhaps you can teach him something,' Dalena comforted. 'There's always a first time.'

A few more moments of silence while I digested the information. 'When was your first time?'

'French kiss?' Her body shook as she laughed. 'In standard six.'

'What's so funny?'

'I never even asked his name! It was at one of my sisters' parties. He and I smooched all evening and it was only the next morning that I realized I didn't know who he was. I was so happy to be given a French kiss at last that I didn't mind at all who gave it to me!'

I took a deep breath, mustered all my courage. It was always easier to ask such questions in the dark: 'And further?'

'Further?'

'What's the furthest you've ever gone?' My voice was so low that I could barely hear it.

'That time in the shower,' Dalena whispered. 'With Miss Lourens's brother.'

'What did you do?'

28

'We touched one another . . . He touched my tits and I touched his . . . you know . . . down there . . .'

I couldn't utter a word.

'And he became as stiff as a board.'

I didn't dare look at Dalena but I knew she was looking at me. Pulled the sheet up to my chin because the room suddenly felt cold. My body was covered in goose pimples.

'And then?' I whispered urgently, afraid that she would fall asleep.

'I had the fright of my life!' She started giggling, her teeth white in the dark again. 'I knew boys became stiff . . . but I didn't know it looked like that.'

'What . . . *does* it look like?' It was the most important question I'd ever asked in my life.

'Have you ever seen a donkey in rut?'

'You mean, his thing hung on the ground?'

'No, man, it doesn't hang! It stands up straight! It gets longer and longer like . . . like Pinocchio's nose!'

'Like Pinocchio's nose!' I whispered, amazed, and tried to imagine this odd description. Without success.

'Perhaps it also has something to do with lying,' Dalena giggled. 'A boy will say anything when he's like that: "Don't worry. I won't put it in. I know what I'm doing. You can trust me . . ."'

'Is that what Miss Lourens's brother said to you?'

'Fortunately my father caught us in time.' Dalena's sigh hung in the air for a long time, like a soap bubble before it burst. 'Otherwise I don't know . . .'

'And what does it feel like?' I kicked off the sheet again. Smelled my own sweat. Almost as strong as the fumes of Peaceful Sleep. 'I mean, if it . . . if it looks like Pinocchio's nose . . . does it feel like Pinocchio's nose, too?'

'I don't know. I've never touched Pinocchio's nose!'

She started laughing so much she had to push her face into the pillow to calm down. I giggled nervously too, frightened that a prefect or the teacher in the passage would hear us. Frightened that we wouldn't be able to continue discussing this vitally important subject.

'No, man, I mean . . . does it feel like wood?'

'Wood? Are you out of your fucking mind?'

She shook with laughter again. I was getting desperate.

'No, man,' she eventually whispered, 'it feels like meat! Like raw sausage. Raw sausage frozen hard. But of course it's not cold . . .'

'Like *warm*, frozen sausage?'

'If you can imagine something like that.'

I couldn't.

'Where is he now?' I asked to get the picture of the strangest sausage in the world out of my mind. 'Miss Lourens's brother?'

'You may well ask.'

'Didn't you see him again?'

'I told you, they all lie when they're in that condition.'

'*All of them?*'

'I've heard my sisters talk about it.' Dalena's two older sisters, both at university, had recently become my most important source of information about this irresistible subject. (Through Dalena, as I had met neither of them.) And perhaps not even a trustworthy source because, according to Dalena, neither of them had gone 'all the way'.

'They say a man can't think once his thing is hard. They say it's your own fault if you let him go too far because then you can't say no any longer. He goes quite crazy.'

'Crazy?' I swallowed heavily. I saw the shy, quiet Ben with wildly milling arms, foaming at the mouth. 'How crazy?'

'They say he'll rape you just like that.'

The room was dead quiet.

'But how can you tell . . . ?' I took a deep breath like someone preparing to swim under water. 'How far is too far?'

The silence continued. All I could hear was Dalena's regular breathing. This time she had really gone to sleep, I decided.

'I think it's when you don't want him to stop,' she eventually replied, so softly that it sounded as if she were muttering in her sleep.

'You can stay as you are,' Dalena sang while she mixed coffee liqueur and vodka in three tall glasses. *'Or you can change . . .'*

'Wrong song!' Suna laughed on the high bar-stool next to me. 'This isn't cane, it's Red Russians!'

'Black Russians,' I said and watched Dalena pouring Coke into the glasses.

'It's all the same fucking thing, man,' Dalena said in Janis Joplin's world-weary voice.

Suna was overcome with a fit of giggling. I couldn't help laughing as well. Nobody could swear like Dalena. Except, perhaps, Janis Joplin.

I could curse in my thoughts like someone who ate on the sly when no one could see her but as soon as I said a swear word out loud, I spat it out like milk that had soured. And Suna was like someone on a strict diet who enjoyed watching other people eat. I had never heard her swear but she started laughing uncontrollably every time Dalena used a rude word. And Dalena cursed like a gourmet. She rolled the words around her tongue the way my father did with good wine.

'Cheers, Mart.' She handed me a glass after adding a handful of ice to it. 'Let's drink to Heinrich's party.'

My stomach felt hollow every time I thought about the party but I knew it was too late to back out now. Suna and I were spending the weekend with Dalena because the party was being held on a neighbouring farm the following evening. Naturally, we weren't supposed to be sitting in her father's bar, but her mother had to spend a few days in hospital with some nervous complaint or other and her father was at a Broederbond affair, according to Dalena.

My father didn't think much of this I'll-scratch-your-back-if-you'll-scratch-mine Broederbond. My mother said it was only be-cause they had never asked him to become a member. I thought it was just something else he could blame her for. Her father, my Grandpa Fishpond, had supposedly been a member of the more liberal United Party. And they probably thought she was English because she dyed her hair and smoked Cameos.

'Hmmm.' Suna licked her lips. 'Where did you learn to drink this stuff?'

'Mart told me about it,' Dalena said. 'She merely looks so innocent.'

'At the seaside,' I said. 'With Nic.'

'Who is this Nic you mention so often?'

'Don't ask,' Dalena warned. 'Unless you want to spend the rest of the evening hearing all about this fabulous guy you've never met. The brownest eyes, the broadest shoulders, the best-looking legs, the most unbelievable personality, the biggest . . .'

'You're lying, I never carried on like that, Dalena!' The vodka probably also had something to do with the heat in my cheeks.

'Have you ever listened to yourself, Mart?'

'The biggest what?' Suna wanted to know.

Now it was Dalena's turn to giggle. Suna's eyes widened. My cheeks got hotter and hotter.

There were certain words even Dalena wouldn't use. When it came to sexual parts, male or female, she couldn't even mention the biological terms. Even though they sounded so chaste in our pretty biology teacher's mouth.

'*Penis!*' she'd whispered for the first time the other evening in our hostel room. 'It sounds like a new kind of headache pill!'

'And what about *vagina*?' I asked, as always braver in the dark. 'Doesn't it sound like the name of an old maid? There was an old maid named Vagina, whose looks became finer and finer . . .'

Dalena had to put her hand in front of her mouth to stop laughing.

'And testicles!' I'd giggled. 'Like something belonging to an octopus! He swings his dangerous testicles about to keep the enemy at bay!'

'And vulva could've been a car. He climbed into his new Vulva and drove away.'

'And uterus?' We were both amazed by our daring. 'Isn't there a city in Holland called Uterus?'

'Uterus and Clitoris,' Dalena had announced in a dramatic whisper. 'A Tale of Two Cities!'

'Dalena exaggerates.' I took a few quick swallows from the glass in front of me even though I knew it wasn't a cold drink. 'It was only a holiday romance.'

'That's what she tells you now!' Dalena's voice was louder than usual, even more like a boy's. 'After stuttering old Ben has won her heart.'

'He doesn't stutter, he . . .' I fell into every trap she set for me. 'He's only shy.'

'Ha!' She gathered our glasses to mix another three Black Russians, confident as a cocktail barman behind her father's counter. She was wearing a man's maroon dressing gown in a silky material. She constantly said she couldn't stand her father but she evidently couldn't resist the temptation of wearing his clothes. 'Let's drink while we can. Don't think we'll get anything more than Coke and Fanta tomorrow evening. Perhaps a couple of stealthy beers for the boys but definitely nothing for the girls! After all, nice girls don't drink!'

'Let's drink a toast to Mart and Ben!' Unlike Dalena, Suna's voice had become higher and thinner. She sounded like a six-year-old girl. It could also have been the alcohol affecting my hearing. 'To whatever may happen tomorrow night!'

'As I know old Ben, bugger all will happen,' said Dalena.

My body felt too light for the bar-stool, my feet too far off the floor. I studied the walls around me hung with dozens of framed rugby photographs. Team photos, mostly, from Springbok teams to farm-school teams with no differentiation between famous and obscure players.

'What are you going to wear?' Suna wanted to know.

'Sheesh, I don't know.' I could hardly admit that I'd struggled with this problem for over a week. 'Jeans, probably. What about you?'

'It probably doesn't matter,' Suna sighed. 'I don't have a date.'

Suna wasn't ugly. She had long, blonde hair and a great body and all; but she also had acne. Not badly, but as a result she suffered from a serious lack of self-confidence. The moment a boy looked at her she dropped her head and swallowed her tongue.

'Oh, come on, Suna!' Dalena bellowed. 'I told you I'd make you look great with my sisters' make-up. You're going to look like Cinderella at the prince's party.'

'Cinderella had a fairy godmother.' Absently Suna rubbed her pitted skin. 'You can't cast magic spells, Dalena.'

'There's nothing that foundation and blusher can't fix. There's absolutely nothing . . .'

And with this prediction my roommate fell off her high bar-stool with an earsplitting crash.

*

I sat on the balcony in front of Dalena's bedroom and looked out over her father's farm. It wasn't a toy farm like my father's. Chris van Vuuren was a real farmer, not an attorney wanting to play at being a farmer.

Over the weekend I'd realized for the first time that Dalena's father was filthy rich. You would never have guessed it if you saw her in the hostel. She wasn't one for fantastic clothes or shiny bangles or anything that showed that her people had money. I knew what my mother would say: if you were used to money you didn't have to flaunt it.

My people weren't exactly poverty-stricken, but my father's bank statement was always as unpredictable as his next scheme to make money quickly. Or to lose it quickly, which happened more often. At the moment things were going rather well with a farm and a swimming pool, but the van Vuurens' farm and swimming pool made ours seem like a suburban plot with a fishpond. The van Vuurens not only had a swimming pool big enough to hold a school gala, they also had a Jacuzzi and a sauna.

'Jacuzzi,' I said aloud to hear what this exotic word sounded like in my mouth. Almost as pretty as French. *'Je t'aime, mon amour.'*

'What?' Dalena asked behind me and I was so startled that the writing pad fell off my lap.

She stood in the French doors which opened out of her bedroom on to the balcony, yawned lazily and stretched her arms high above her head. She was wearing only the loose T-shirt in which she'd slept. *Love is . . .* I read on her breast, above a picture of two little dolls hugging one another on her stomach, with the rest of the sentence on her hips . . . *being nice to her even if she's grumpy.*

'I thought you and Suna were still asleep.'

'So you sat talking to yourself.' She blinked her eyes in the sharp morning light. 'Anyone would think you were in love.'

'Did you enjoy the party?'

'Oh, it was OK.' She dropped into the deckchair next to me, yawned again, stretched her bare legs. 'You obviously enjoyed it.'

'Where's Suna?'

'Probably still dreaming about how popular she was.'

34

She turned her head towards me, the grey-green eyes wide awake now, and smiled that impossibly wide smile. 'She was a hit, wasn't she?'

Thanks to Dalena's sisters' make-up and the low red lighting in the rondavel, Suna completely forgot about her skin problem. And once the boys saw how she could wriggle her body on the dance floor, she didn't have a breathing space for the rest of the evening.

'You didn't look so bad yourself,' I told her, my eyes on the sugar-cane fields which would soon start shimmering in the heat. 'Heinrich virtually drooled every time he looked at you.'

'Sheesh, he's as much of a used-to-nothing as all the other schoolboys. If you wear a halter top, they know you're not wearing a bra. It's enough to give them wet dreams for the rest of the term.'

I had a vague suspicion of what she meant by a wet dream, but it sounded so awful that I didn't want to believe it.

'No way do I want to bother with schoolboys any longer.' She got up and idled back to the glass doors. 'I'll leave them to you and Suna. I'm going to call someone to bring us coffee.'

In this house the whites did even less than in any other house I'd ever been in. A battalion of servants in crisp white uniforms moved as soundlessly as ghosts over the wall-to-wall carpets. As soon as you needed one, she appeared before you like Aladdin's subservient genie. You didn't even have to make the effort to rub a lamp.

It was a two-storey house which made me feel as if I were acting in a romantic movie, something about war and slaves in the American South. The balcony on which I was sitting, with its copy of Victorian wrought-iron railings smothered in purple bougainvillaea, ran right round the house. In the entrance hall, as big as a school hall's stage, there was one of those sweeping staircases I'd only seen in the movies. It was the kind on which a beautiful actress in a ballgown would appear, standing like Lot's wife for a moment before floating down like an angel.

I could see that everything around me had cost money, from the cold marble floor in the bathroom to the shaggy white rug which lay like a lazy polar bear in one of the guest rooms, but I had to admit that I didn't admire many of the objects. I couldn't help thinking of my mother and her widow's jar of axioms. People who have the most money, she liked saying, often have the least taste.

Not that my mother could've run classes in good taste. When I'd shown her an interior decorating article in *Sarie* last year in which ornaments like the three porcelain ducks against our passage wall were disparaged as the ultimate in kitsch, she'd only laughed. But a month later the ducks had gone. Only three dark marks remained, minor monuments to years of unmoving flight. My mother tried, after all, even if there were still many things in our house that would've driven *Sarie*'s interior decorator to despair.

But Dalena's mother had either never read *Sarie*, or she had enough self-confidence not to be dictated to about what she should have in her home. The walls were hung with pictures of children in ragged clothing, their eyes as large as plates with teardrops like transparent leaves clinging to their cheeks. Or stormy seascapes painted by someone who had obviously never seen the sea, with waves like blue flames topped by spumes like spoonfuls of whipped cream. At first I thought it was modern art, about which I knew nothing. But when I had another look at Dalena's mother in a family photograph, with a purple haze in her hair and her mouth in a stiff pleat, I decided that she didn't look like the kind who knew anything about modern art either.

I pulled my writing pad towards me to write to my brother. I would've liked to tell him what had happened at the party but I was scared that he would tease me. I would like to tell *someone* that I got a kiss after all, at the end of the party. And not just an ordinary kiss, mind you, Dalena.

It was while 'Nights in White Satin' was playing. We sat outside in the dark and . . . well, just sat, really. Ben wasn't chatty, exactly. Not the kind of guy who would tell everyone what he got away with with a girl, I comforted myself. Dalena, of course, would say it was because he hadn't got away with anything, yet. If only Dalena knew!

That's probably why he says so little, I thought afterwards, as speechless as he was for the first time that evening. He was saving his tongue for better uses. My mouth felt the way it did after I'd chewed too many sticky toffees. But I couldn't stop smiling.

And my roommate didn't have to know everything all the time.

Dear Child

All I have to give you today is a small newspaper report. The older I get, the larger are the gaps in my vocabulary. I had thought that the opposite would happen: that in the final analysis I would be able to say everything that could be said, if I only continued to practise.

I had imagined that to put words to paper would be like fishing. The wider the experience, the bigger the catch. Now I know this is not necessarily true. It may happen that your net becomes worn over the years, and full of holes, and that you no longer want to take the trouble to mend it because you no longer care if the small fish get away – only the really big ones are still a challenge.

There are a few things I'm trying to say, just a few, but because I'm finding it so difficult to catch the right words, all the others slip through my fingers these days. I've never been good at small talk. I was always a fiasco with a cocktail in my hand among people I didn't know well but these days I even have trouble in talking to friends. If I can still speak of friends.

That's probably why I have a growing need of these letters, to share things with you I can share with no one else, even if it's only once in a while. (Or is it because I've started writing about my adolescence that I've developed a teenage need to have some kind of a diary?)

Heimwee. That's the word I was groping for in my previous letter. *Heim* as in the German *Heimat,* wee as in *weemoed,* that indescribable longing for one knows not whom, where or what. Here is a little tale picked up in an Afrikaans newspaper about *heimwee.*

Afrikaans? Yes, now that it's no longer necessary to hang my head in shame because I come from that accursed land, I sometimes dare to walk into South Africa House on Trafalgar Square where I page through old newspapers and magazines looking for – what? Faith? Hope? Love? What I usually find is suspicion, despair and hate.

But sometimes there is something I missed in the local press. Or perhaps I've grown so used to reading between the lines in South African newspapers that I can no longer interpret the lines in British newspapers.

London – What do you do when you're in a strange country and your heart longs for your birthplace in Africa? You build yourself a mud hut in your backyard.

(A mud hut! I thought. And read on avidly.)

That's exactly what Mrs Desiree Ntolo, a refugee from Cameroon did – to the annoyance of her neighbours and the local council in Dagenham, an industrial area east of London, which has instructed her to demolish the structure within a week. Mrs Ntolo built the hut entirely on her own.

(How? I wanted to know. How do you build a mud hut?)

Using a pick and a spade she dug stones and gravel out of her garden, watered the soil and trampled out strips of mud with her feet. A council spokesman stated that the hut could not be allowed to stand since it contravenes planning regulations, but Mrs Ntolo remains defiant: 'The mud hut is in no one's way', she said. 'They must also consider my rights. If I can't go back to Cameroon, I at least want something that reminds me of it.'

(Can you guess whose side I'm on?)

Love
M.

How Will We Know Which Side to Choose?

'So South Africa is finally getting TV,' Simon grinned behind the steering wheel of Pa's new kombi. 'Any day now we'll have the idea that we're living in a civilized country!'

'Yes, I hear they're starting test broadcasts in Johannesburg next month.' I stared through the window. I was tired of seeing only green all day. It was supposed to be autumn but in this region the plants evidently took no notice of seasons. 'Here in the back of beyond we probably won't be able to get it for years."

In the Cape the trees would be losing their leaves now, the vineyards turning gold and the weather becoming a little cooler each day. Here it was always hot, hot and green. So hot and green it was enough to make you puke. We drove past a clump of the burning trees that also grew in the hostel gardens. Long, brown seed-pods hung from the branches like Christmas decorations out of season. Flamboyant, Pa had said when I'd asked him what kind of tree it was. No, I don't mean the tree's appearance, I said, I want to know what it's called. Flamboyant, Pa had said again, a flamboyant flamboyant – like a sweet sweet or a sore sore.

'What do you think of the kombi?' I asked.

My brother's upper arm bulged every time he changed gear. The muscles in his arms were as new to me as the car. That's why National Service was a good thing, Ma said. It changed boys into men. It also changed them in other ways, I had decided over the past weekend.

'What's the idea?' Simon switched on the car radio, pulled a face when he heard *Boeremusiek* and immediately switched it off. 'A kombi is a great car for a surfer. But if Pa wants to be a farmer why doesn't he buy a pick-up or a four-wheel drive?'

'You know Pa doesn't really want to be a farmer, Simon! He likes the idea of living on a farm, but surely you don't expect him to do a farmer's work, do you?'

'Well, who *is* supposed to do it?'

'Who do you think?'

'Ma?' Simon shook his head. 'She's going to leave him one day.'

I shook my head. 'I don't think so.'

My father had ostensibly bought the car for my mother – handing her the bunch of keys like an engagement ring, beaming at his own generosity – so that she could ferry bananas to the farm stalls in the district. And then occasionally he could 'borrow' it from her over a weekend, he had suggested, to transport a few friends to a rugby game in the city. Surely more practical than a pick-up?

Ma said if he'd wanted to be practical, he would've bought her a new washing machine. But my mother's favourite song was the one Shirley Bassey sang so passionately: *I love you, hate you, love you, hate you* . . . Every time Ma heard it on the radio she sang along, just as passionately, even though she was usually off-key.

'And now for something completely different.' Simon took a cassette from his jeans' pocket, smiled as if he'd produced a rabbit from a hat and pushed it into the cassette player. *'Jesus Christ, Superstar!'*

'But that's . . .' I swallowed to keep the shock out of my voice, tried to sound as worldly as my roommate. 'Isn't it banned?'

'Everything that's fun in this country is either banned or sinful.' He definitely sounded different, I decided. 'One of Pierre's pals smuggled it in from LM.'

I listened in silence to the unknown music and wondered whether this Pierre, whom I was going to meet shortly, didn't influence my brother too much. But I would never say it. I didn't want to sound like my mother.

'Not bad at all,' I mumbled when I saw Simon giving me a sideways glance.

I wasn't exactly keen to meet my brother's new friend. He sounded like the kind of guy who acted older than his age and such guys always made me stutter and stammer, like an idiot in standard three. But they had both come home for a few days, for the first time in three months, and Simon wanted to visit Pierre that afternoon. And I had to admit that I was flattered when he asked me to drive to Black River with him.

'Pierre has also seen quite a number of flicks that are banned here,' Simon said, tapping his fingers on the steering wheel in time to the music.

'Dirty movies?'

'No, man, good ones, like *Straw Dogs* . . . *Clockwork Orange* . . . *Last Tango in Paris* . . .'

'I hear it's disgusting,' I said before I could stop myself.

'What?'

'That Tango one,' I said. 'One of the guys in my class saw it in LM. He said it was too awful. There's a scene in which the man rubs butter on the girl's bottom . . .'

Simon burst out laughing.

'What?' I looked through the glass on my side so that he couldn't see me blush.

'Do you know that Pa read *Lady Chatterley's Lover* years ago?' Simon shook his head, his fingers quiet on the steering wheel. 'And all he can remember is a scene where the lovers evidently stick daisies up one another's assholes.'

'What are you trying to say?'

Simon waited until the song which was playing ended before he replied. 'Pierre says *Last Tango in Paris* is a brilliant movie.'

Pierre definitely had to be a pervert, I decided, becoming more and more uncomfortable about the meeting which lay ahead. The tarred road made a wide curve past a large blue lake and dense plantations of pine trees where sunlight threw long fingers of light through the shadows. I could easily imagine we were travelling through somewhere in another country, Canada maybe, somewhere where you were allowed to listen to *Jesus Christ, Superstar* in a car.

Pierre was tall and dark but not what I would call handsome. Too thin, I thought, too serious, with hollow cheeks and black eyes set too deeply in their sockets. That was my first impression.

His room was in the garden where he could play his music loudly without irritating his mother, he said. The walls were painted a dark blue, almost blue-black, and the curtains were drawn. You would never guess that the sun was shining outside. I sat on his bed, bored, and stared at the blue electric bulb which hung above a bookcase. If one could call such a contraption a bookcase.

The crowded shelves looked as though they'd been cobbled together by someone who knew more about literature than carpentry. I tried to read the titles of a row of tattered paperbacks in the weak light. I recognized some of the authors' names even if I hadn't read them: Tolstoy and Flaubert, Ernest Hemingway and James Joyce and Scott Fitzgerald . . . but there were a great many names I had never heard of: Durrell and Fowles and Updike . . . It was impossible for anyone of Pierre's age to have read so many books. It was simply a brag, as my Grandma Farmdam would say.

Simon and Pierre sat on the floor next to the stereo, sipping beer and discussing the Army. They had forgotten about me. And the longer I had to listen to their stupid army stories, the angrier I got. Not only with them but with myself as well. Why didn't I simply get up and go for a walk in the garden?

Ma said if you ever show a man that he's boring you, he'll never forgive you. But what would Simon and Pierre do if they had to listen to Dalena and me talking about lipstick or nail polish for an hour?

I turned my head to look at the posters on the walls. Not the ones you'd normally expect to find in a boy's room, of pop stars or pin-up girls with stars on their bare boobs cut out of magazines like *Scope*. Above the bed there was a poster of Beethoven and next to it an unknown black man with a clenched fist and next to that a soldier falling back as if he'd been shot with the word *Why?* in big black letters.

'Dark Side of the Moon' was coming out of the loudspeakers but they barely heard it. PT instructors . . . corporal . . . basic training . . . AWOL . . . to the Border . . . Swapo . . . I caught a word here and there but preferred to listen to Pink Floyd. What I found most irritating was that they said they hated the Army. How in hell could you spend so much time talking about something you hated?

'. . . between the MPLA and FNLA,' Pierre said. 'And Jonas Savimbi's Unita, of course.'

Now I paid attention because I had recently read an article in

Huisgenoot on Angola. The black people were fighting and the white people were fleeing. It frightened me.

'It sounds as if things are pretty grim,' Simon said and swallowed some of his beer. 'The Portuguese can't get away fast enough. The same thing that happened in Mozambique last year.'

It sounded as if we'd read the same article. Or maybe all South African journalists sounded the same when they wrote about the chaos ruling in the two former Portuguese colonies bordering our country. Mozambique had been declared independent the previous year, causing a flood of white refugees to stream to South Africa. Angola would gain independence in a few months' time, and once again thousands of refugees were fleeing to the last white outpost in Africa.

Our government, of course, had promised to protect its citizens from the Communist threat represented by the new rulers of both these countries.

'But I don't understand it.' Simon stared at the beer bottle in his hand. 'I thought the blacks would throw a helluva party because the white bosses had eventually gone. Isn't that what they wanted? Now it seems as if they want to murder one another.'

'That's politics, pal,' Pierre said. 'You hardly expect all of them to think alike merely because they're black?'

'No, of course not, but . . . aren't they tired of fighting? They're like a bunch of kids who've been given a cake as a present. Instead of dividing it equally, they fight over it until there's nothing left of the cake.'

'I don't think you should see independence as a gift.' Pierre smiled but only one corner of his mouth lifted. 'Or blacks as a bunch of children.'

'OK, OK, you old liberal!' my brother laughed. 'You know what I mean.'

'You must remember that the whites in Africa have always followed a policy of divide and rule. Jomo Kenyatta says the whites really pray for the blacks to keep on fighting so that the whites can remain the rulers.'

'You mean . . .' Simon absently swallowed another mouthful of beer. 'The whites leave but the divide and rule remains?'

'Something like that. But I think our government is going to do more than pray.' Pierre's slightly husky voice had developed an ominous note. 'Our guys have always been better at fighting than praying.'

Simon looked frowningly at him, his mouth open as though he wanted to ask something but didn't have the courage to do so.

'I think they're going to send in the Army,' Pierre said without looking at Simon, his black eyes on his bottle of beer.

'Into Angola?' Simon's face was a study in disbelief, his voice soaring in astonishment. 'Never!'

'Why not? The Army is already on the Border. They merely have to cross it. The soldiers, the weaponry, it's all there. Do you think they'll be able to resist the temptation?

'But . . .' Simon laughed nervously. 'How will we know which side to choose?'

'Does it matter?' Pierre shrugged his shoulders and laughed with my brother. 'Divide and rule?'

Simon whistled softly through his teeth. He no longer looked so disbelieving. I was suddenly enormously irritated. When I sighed – far more loudly than I'd intended – Pierre looked up in surprise as though he had only just realized that there was another person in the room with them.

'You're bored with our army talk.' It was a statement, not a question.

'Well . . .' I was suddenly grateful for the room's darkness because I could feel that I was blushing again. 'I'm glad I don't have to go to the Army . . .'

'What would you like to talk about?'

Was he making fun of me?

'You can always discuss books with her,' my brother said. 'She reads far more than I do.'

'But not nearly as much as *you* do,' I hastily parried and gestured towards the crowded bookshelves.

'Many of those books belong to my mother and father.' He finished the last of his beer. 'All those old-fashioned numbers. I prefer modern authors. And you?'

'No . . . I don't know . . . as long as the book reads well . . .'

Now I sounded exactly as I'd feared I would. Like an idiot in standard three. My mind changed into a car with a flat battery. I pumped the mental gas pedal up and down, as I had seen Ma doing, desperate to utter a sound. But there was nothing except a deathly silence between my ears. Pierre smiled, this time with both corners of his mouth, but the one side was still higher than the other.

'Do you feel like a flick tonight?' my brother asked, saving me from further humiliation. 'Pierre knows the owner of the café next to the Plaza. He can let us have a special home movie.'

'Special?' I asked carefully.

'Uncensored,' Pierre said.

'I don't know . . .' He couldn't possibly mean one of the dirty movies we'd discussed in the car earlier in the afternoon? 'What kind of flick?'

'Don't worry,' Pierre said. 'We won't get anything that'll make a schoolgirl blush.'

And I blushed again.

'May I invite Dalena?' I asked on the spur of the moment.

'How will she get here?' my brother asked.

'She'll manage.' Even if she had to steal her father's car and drive herself here. Dalena wouldn't let an opportunity like this slip through her fingers. She wasn't as cowardly as I was. 'She can sleep over at the farm and we can take her back tomorrow.'

'Who's Dalena?' Pierre wanted to know.

'Mart's roommate,' Simon said. 'Apparently she's a sex bomb.'

'I never said that!'

'Well, you said she's sexy.'

'Tell her she's welcome.' This time Pierre's smile was as twisted as Grandpa Fishpond's after he'd survived his first stroke. 'Tell her she's very welcome.'

'Why didn't you tell me your brother is such a dish?' Dalena wanted to know the moment I opened my eyes.

She lay on her stomach on the other bed in my room, chin in hand, as though she had been waiting for hours for me to wake up.

Immediately I closed my eyes again. The light was too bright and her voice too deep. Usually I liked Dalena's boy's voice but this

46

morning I wished she were a hi-fi so I could turn down the bass. I had gone to bed too late after drinking too much beer, trying to impress Simon and Pierre. There was a constant throbbing in my head and my hair smelled of smoke.

'Hey, you can't go back to sleep,' she whispered urgently.

'Why not?' I moaned softly with closed eyes.

'I have an important subject to discuss with you.'

I felt a pillow hitting my head. Playfully but hard enough to make me open my eyes. I knew when I'd lost.

'What is it, Dalena?'

'Tell me more about your brother.'

I threw the pillow back at her head.

'He's dangerous. He smokes and he drinks and he breaks girls' hearts by the score. What more do you want to know?'

'Sounds irresistible.' Dalena smiled her shamelessly wide smile. 'Did you like the movie?'

'I can't remember a thing about it,' she said. 'It was impossible to concentrate with your brother sitting so close to me.'

'Good morning!' My mother stuck her head round the bedroom door. 'I've brought you coffee and rusks.'

Ma was wearing her Japanese dressing gown, the one she called a kimono. One day she would see the East, she always said. (And Russia and Egypt.) She didn't bring me coffee in bed as a rule but she liked to impress my friends. She didn't wear the kimono every day, either.

'Thank you, *tannie*, that'll be delicious!' Dalena said in her sweetest voice and jumped up to take the tray with its crocheted cloth, starched stiff as cardboard, from my mother.

Ma gave a grateful smile. 'Did you have a nice evening?'

'We saw a good movie. *The Graduate*. Have you heard of it, Ma?'

'With Dustin Hoffman?' Ma seldom went to the movies these days but she greedily absorbed every bit of scandal about Hollywood stars in all her favourite magazines. 'He's so short and dull! I know I'm old-fashioned but I still like a leading man to look like a leading man!'

'Like Clark Gable or Rock Hudson,' I mumbled, my mouth full of rusk.

47

'Like Clark Gable or Rock Hudson,' Ma agreed seriously.

The moment Ma's shiny blue kimono disappeared round the door, Dalena jumped up to sit cross-legged on my bed, almost on top of me.

'Tell me honestly, Mart,' she said urgently. 'Tell me if you think I stand a chance.'

'Of what?'

I sucked the coffee out of a soaked rusk and put out my hand to switch on the radio on my bedside table. It was my first opportunity ever to tease my roommate. I had to admit it was a pleasant sensation.

'Do you think there's a chance, no matter how small . . .'

She got no further because Niel and Lovey ran yelling into the room. Niel held his arms protectively over his head while Lovey made a frustrated grab at his hair. It was only when she tickled him under his arms and he laughingly dropped his hands that we saw he had tied one of those long, old-fashioned sanitary towels on to his head, the loops hooked around his ears. I caught Dalena's eye and we tacitly agreed that we wouldn't laugh at such a childish joke.

But I had difficulty in keeping a straight face. Where had he found the thing? Ma had had that operation a long time ago and Lovey . . .

'Mart, tell Niel to grow up!' Lovey yelled when Niel grabbed her hands.

'Niel, Lovey says you must grow up!'

Dalena gave up the struggle and started laughing. Pleased, Niel turned his head towards us and with his attention diverted for a moment, Lovey jerked the sanitary towel off his head, so roughly that he seemed in danger of losing his ears. He screamed like the victim in a bad murder movie and fled, laughing.

'Men!' Breathlessly Lovey sank down on the bed opposite Dalena and me. She clutched the towel like a trophy. I still couldn't believe that my baby sister could be the owner of this strange object. 'If only they knew what it is to be a woman . . .'

I also fell into helpless laughter.

'But Lovey, that thing is miles too big for you.'

'I know,' she said, mortified. 'But Ma says I'm too young for the kind that you push in . . .'

'But doesn't Ma know about the new kind that you stick on?'

'Lovey!' Simon called from somewhere in the house. Lovey and Dalena both jerked upright.

'He said I could go with him to buy the Sunday papers,' Lovey said before disappearing. '*Ciao.*'

The sanitary towel was left lying on the bed like an ugly, stranded boat.

'This morning she's under the impression that she's in an Italian movie,' I said to Dalena.

'Why didn't he ask me to go with him?' Dalena wanted to know.

I turned up the volume on the radio and hummed 'Sorrow' along with David Bowie. Simon said his son's name was Zowie, Zowie Bowie. It would be quite fun to have a name like that, Simon said, especially in the Army. Sapper Zowie Bowie.

'He probably didn't even notice me!'

'It's quite difficult not to notice you, Dalena,' I consoled her. 'You're not exactly a shrinking violet.'

'Maybe he likes shrinking violets?'

'If you really want to know, I think he likes anything that wears a skirt. Especially after three months in the Army.'

She fell on to her back with a sigh that sounded as if it had been fished from the depths of her stomach and folded her hands behind her head.

'Listen, Dalena,' I said, my eyes on her bare legs, 'I don't want to interfere . . .'

'Then don't.'

'But I must warn you . . .' I didn't know how to say it without sounding stupid. Do it fast, I thought, as fast as possible. 'Don'tletmybrothermisuseyou.'

'What do you mean?'

Her mouth trembled as she tried to control a smile.

'You know very well what I mean.'

'I don't care what your brother does to me, Mart!' The smile spread. We were back in our usual roles, Dalena the teaser, I the teased. 'This is the first time since Miss Lourens's brother that I've had this ticklish feeling in my body.'

'Where in your body?' I asked warily.

49

But she only laughed. And I felt as if I had pushed a car to get it started, with great difficulty, only to be left behind while the occupants drove away.

London, 30 September 1992

Dear Child

John Lennon is singing 'Imagine' on the radio in my narrow London house with a front door that opens on to a pavement and a back garden smaller than a British pound note. Just imagine there's no heaven.

I hear that seventies music is becoming popular again. And the fashions keep popping up on the streets. Is *nothing* exempt from the irrational power of nostalgia?

An election is being held in Angola today which could change everything. Perhaps there will be an end to the war which has torn the country apart for so many decades. On the other hand, perhaps nothing will change. Things might even get worse. However unthinkable that might seem.

It's easy if you try, John Lennon sings. I introduced my son to him today. Why I don't know, but it was the one figure in Madame Tussaud's famous Wax Museum that caught his almost three-year-old attention. Maybe he became aware of his mother's nostalgia (back to bloody nostalgia again) as we stood in front of the four young men with their dark mop-heads, thin ties and identical jackets, tidily buttoned. Or a nostalgia emerging from the depths of the collective subconscious of an entire generation?

'And here we have John Lennon,' I said, and never got to the other three Beatles because my son stretched out his arms to grab John Lennon's legs. 'But you're not allowed to touch him.'

He was determined to touch him. I tried to pull him away but he began screaming. I looked round, saw no security guard and allowed him to touch, quickly, and with a dirty hand, John Lennon's leg.

51

It wasn't good enough. He screamed so loudly that we had to halt the excursion right there, before we could even get a proper look at Madonna or Michael Jackson. Which perhaps was also fitting, I consoled myself on the Underground on the way home. My taste in pop music never really developed beyond December 1980. On that day, when John Lennon was shot by one of his crazy admirers, I knew that the seventies had really ended. *The day the music died.*

The biggest danger in Angola, I read in the newspaper, is that Unita or the MPLA will refuse to accept the result of the election. Then the civil war and the bloodshed will continue. Until there are no civilians left to kill? Until there is no blood left to flow? *The most likely candidate for such a tactic is Unita, which has kept guerrilla operations going year after year with massive logistic and military support from Pretoria.*

Pierre was right, after all. He had the irritating habit of habitually being right. Now I wonder whether he would have been able to forecast how long South Africans would still have to wait for a free election.

Imagine it, my dear child. Just imagine it!

M.

Take the Best from the Past

It was recess and we sat on the concrete slab behind the girls' lavatories, our backs against the rough brick wall, bodies in the narrow strip of shade next to the wall, legs stretched out to brown in the sun.

'I don't want a farmer's tan,' Dalena said and took off her white socks and black school shoes.

'If a prefect sees you, you'll be in trouble again.' Suna sounded jealous as she watched Dalena wiggling her toes in the sun.

'Tell me something I don't know.' Dalena still hadn't acquired the compulsory lace-up shoes. My feet are too highly arched, she told the teachers. She had even obtained a medical certificate somewhere attesting to this peculiar foot problem. 'Any minute now they're going to forbid us to take off our jerseys when we're too hot.'

My feet were sweating in my dusty school shoes. I looked up and saw a dense cloud next to the window above my head. It was caused by the wild girls in matric taking turns to stand on a toilet bowl and blow their cigarette smoke out of a high window, ostensibly to prevent the prefects from smelling it when they walked into the cloakroom. Actually everyone in the school, from the standard sixes to the staff, knew that a few matric girls from the special class stood on a toilet bowl to smoke during recess. The problem was that no one knew how to punish them. The headmaster wanted to keep them in school until the end of the year (for the sake of the school's good name, of course) while Maggie and her wild pals were clearly doing their best to be expelled before the matric exam. As a result everyone pretended not to notice the clouds of smoke next to the lavatory windows. Even on days like this, when it seemed as if the building was burning.

53

'And what about the stupid rule that says boys and girls aren't al-lowed to speak to one another during recess!' Suna said. 'Except in that small spot where a prefect can overhear every word.'

The accepted 'case square' was precisely in the centre of the play-ground – where everyone could watch the couples who were silly enough to want to be together during recess – and it was guarded like a concentration camp by a cordon of prefects.

'You'd think they're scared the kids are going to tear off their clothes and jump one another,' Suna giggled.

'Don't underestimate the influence of pop music,' Dalena said in the sombre voice which the headmaster used in the hall every Monday morning. 'Don't imagine Black Sheep High School will escape the Communist Onslaught.'

Suna, still giggling, peered round the corner of the cloakroom wall and dug an elbow into Dalena's side. 'Hey, did you see that old Hein and his new flame are also among the lovers these days?'

'The one he hitched up with at his party?' I asked inquisitively.

'When he couldn't get Dalena,' Suna grinned. 'Jolene was the only other girl not wearing a bra.'

'But she's only in standard seven!'

'Ripe in the morning, rotten at night . . .' Suna muttered like an old woman talking to herself.

Jolene was one of those girls seemingly born with flawless adult breasts. Not even the children who were at junior school with her could recall a time when she was flat-chested. Not that her breasts were unattractively large like Laurika's. They were just big enough to upset every schoolboy's hormones whenever she arrived at a party without a bra. Which evidently happened at every party.

'She's a flirt,' Dalena said. When Suna and I both looked at her, she added quickly: 'And that's not sour grapes. I wouldn't know what to do with Heinrich Minnaar if he was handed to me on a platter!'

'What's wrong with Heinrich Minnaar?' Suna undid her shoelaces and pulled her socks down over her heels. Theoretically she was still wearing shoes and socks. 'He's not bad looking.'

'There's nothing wrong with him,' Dalena sighed. 'He's a sweet guy. I don't like sweet guys.' Suna still didn't look convinced. 'He's the kind who'll send you soppy Valentine's Day cards. I know, I got one last year. And red carnations.'

'What's wrong with Valentine's Day cards and carnations?' I wanted to know. No one had ever sent me a Valentine's Day card. Or given me any kind of flower. Except my father when my tonsils were removed, but that probably didn't count.

'It's not the cards or the flowers, Mart, it's the *soppiness*.'

Sometimes I wondered whether I would ever draw level with my roommate. She hastily tucked her feet under her school uniform when she saw a girl in a black prefect's blazer approaching but the prefect didn't even glance in our direction. Probably afraid of seeing the clouds of smoke above our heads.

'I hear you're also going to be chosen at the end of the year.' Suna gazed suspiciously at the departing black blazer. 'As a prefect, they say.'

'Says who?' Dalena virtually snorted with indignation.

'The kids, who else? After all, it's the kids who choose the prefects.'

'Yep. And Father Christmas is a fat man who comes down the chimney once a year! Do you really think the teachers will allow someone like me to be a prefect?'

'But it's –'

'Forget it. Why do you think nine out of ten prefects are the biggest shits in the school? Do you think the children have such bad taste?'

'Well, the teachers probably have a say . . .'

'The *only* say. The children's so-called choice is a joke.'

'How do you know?' I asked.

'I asked Miss Lourens,' she replied. 'But she didn't tell me anything I didn't know.'

The bell went and I listened to the scurrying around the toilet bowl below the window. If my roommate wasn't such a know-all, I thought irritably, my life might also be easier.

Dear Diary, I wrote in my imagination, *I'm bored*. The history teacher was standing with his back to the class writing a long list of dates on the blackboard. We were doing the Great Trek, as we did every year, and every year I wondered what I was going to do one day with all this information about devout Voortrekkers and bloodthirsty black barbarians.

'Take the Best from the Past, children,' old Bull's-Eye Pretorius replied when we asked him why we had to memorize all these dates, 'and Build the Future on it.'

He tended to speak his words with capital letters, especially when he referred to the Past.

How can you build a future on dead dates? That's what I would've written in my diary if I'd had one. Standing on the threshold of my sixteenth birthday, I felt an urgent need for a diary. It was the kind of thing you did when you were sixteen. But I didn't know whether I could inflict it on my grandchildren. Surely the aim of a diary was to tell your descendants something about your life? And who would want to read a boring report on boarding school life in Black River!

I could have lied, of course. Led my grandchildren to believe I had been a talented teenage poet in an attic in Paris, bothered every day by handsome men, their arms filled with carnations. And that every year my post box had been overflowing with Valentine's Day cards. But I knew it wouldn't work. I had never even been in an attic, let alone Paris. And when I recently showed Simon a poem in which I tried to emulate the young Afrikaans poet Antjie Krog, he told me not to bother. To listen to more Bob Dylan.

No, I decided, I would continue to write an imaginary diary. It was one way to survive the endless lessons about the Great Trek.

'Blood River,' Mr Pretorius murmured as though he were praying. 'Who were the Leaders when the Vow was made?'

He was really a sweet guy, as Dalena would've said, a small man with weak eyes and a soft voice. His problem was that he thought History was more important than the Future. I glanced at Dalena who was sitting diagonally opposite me. Her face was a study in concentration but I knew her well enough to know that she wasn't hearing a word he was saying. She had the ability to look as though she was listening when she was thinking about other things. I was always caught out.

'Mart?' I jerked to attention behind my desk. Mr Pretorius tapped a ruler in his chubby little hand and tried to look severe. 'Dreaming again?'

My face was scarlet with embarrassment but I knew he wouldn't punish me. I didn't do brilliantly in his tests, but still better than most of the other children in the class. No matter how you looked at it, Black River simply wasn't the kind of school that bred talented pupils like exotic blooms. It was the heat, I'd decided during the first month. You couldn't think when it was so hot. If you lived here for long enough, your mind started melting like butter in the sun. It was obvious that the headmaster and the matron had lived here for a long time.

'That's why we still celebrate the Day of the Vow.' Bull's-Eye blinked his eyes behind the thick spectacles as if he was becoming tearful. 'We celebrate the Victory of Civilization over Barbarians, of Religion over Heathens, of White over Black . . .' He remained silent for a long time while his shortsighted eyes slid slowly over the faces in front of him. 'Never forget, children,' he finally murmured, when some of us began wriggling uncomfortably, 'the Future belongs to you.'

I looked out of the long row of windows to where the country's flag was hanging limply in the heat, the colours faded from too much sun. A prefect raised it every morning after which a teacher said a prayer and shortly before the last bell it was lowered again. It wasn't that I wanted to be unpatriotic but to me it seemed like a waste of time. In this windstill area the flag never fluttered so that it could be seen properly. It just hung there, as lifeless as the children in Bull's-Eye's history class.

If I turned my head the other way, I looked straight at a collection of photographs of Boer generals with unruly beards, gaunt women and children in front of concentration camp tents and all the Prime Ministers of South Africa since 1948. Verwoerd's photograph was slightly larger than the others. Or did it just seem like it from where I was sitting?

I rubbed my fingertips over the deep grooves in the wooden surface of my desk. The messages of generations of bored school-children felt like Braille under my hands but I couldn't decipher any of it. I would've liked to know who had sat at this desk before me. I

57

would've liked to know what had happened to the girls who had scratched their names in the wooden surface, or to the boys who had stuck the gobs of petrified chewing-gum under the seat. Perhaps some had died by now? They were part of the history Bull's-Eye would never teach us because it couldn't be found in books. For all I knew some other girl might sit here one day and wonder who I had been when I, too, had become part of this unwritten history.

In front of the class the teacher's voice droned on like an electricity generator but all he managed to generate in me was an unbearable drowsiness. Diagonally opposite me Heinrich had rested his head on his arms and closed his eyes. If Bull's-Eye caught sight of him now, he would creep up to him and suddenly, with great force, hit him across the head. He would bite his lip as he did so. Unlike most of the other teachers, Mr Pretorius didn't seem to enjoy meting out physical punishment. Heinrich would get a hell of a fright, bashfully rub his hand over his dark hair and with any luck stay awake until the bell rang in fifteen minutes' time to announce the end of the school day.

I felt a small heart transfixed by an arrow under my fingers. Age had made the names in the heart unreadable. I lowered my head. It looked like . . . Manie – Marie? – and Bet – or perhaps Ben? I looked at Ben who sat in the front row of the class like a good boy. And suddenly I wanted to cry.

Dear Diary, what does it feel like to be in love? I thought I was in love with Nic but it was over so quickly that it must've been something else. I thought I was in love with Ben after he'd kissed me but when I look at him now, such a goody-goody, I don't feel a thing. Except for a little heartache that I still don't know, at nearly sixteen, what it's like to be in love.

Maybe I expected too much. I had always thought first love would be like a long deathbed – like the dirty-mouthed librarian who had died so dramatically in *Love Story* – but perhaps it was more like a common cold: something that passed within a week or two of its own accord.

'Is everything organized for the weekend?' Dalena wanted to know.

I was still gasping after hockey practice, too breathless to reply. In any case it was just about the fifteenth time she had asked. I fell back on to the grass, my eyes closed against the sun.

'You're jolly unfit, aren't you?' She sat down, cross-legged, next to me, her breathing barely affected. 'And you don't even smoke!'

'Hockey is supposed to be a winter sport!' I burst out. 'It's a threat to life to run after a ball in this heat!'

'It is winter,' she reminded me. 'Or almost winter.'

'It's absurd,' I said. 'I should never have given my name to Miss Lourens. I should've said I play chess like all the academic wrecks!'

'You can always drop out and play chess,' she reminded me. She paused meaningfully. I waited for what was coming. 'But then you'll never get to travel in the bus with the rugby players. Rugby and hockey always travel together.'

'So what?' I was coming round to her viewpoint. 'The rugby players aren't the only guys in the school.'

'All the guys who play chess have pimples and thick spectacles. And all the girls weigh three hundred pounds.'

'What a lie!' I laughed.

I sat up, still slightly breathless, and looked towards the hockey field where the younger girls were practising now. The rugby field was quite a way to the left of us but we could clearly hear the first-team players grunting as they pushed in the scrum. On the far side of the rugby field, next to a splash of purple bougainvillaea, a few standard nine boys were loudly encouraging the first team. Ben's blond hair flashed like a mirror among them.

Da Nang, Nha Trang, Qui Nhon, I heard in my head again. Since the Communists had moved over South Vietnam like a plague of locusts, I could hardly wait to read my father's newspaper over the weekends. The names of the towns and villages overrun by the Red Locusts sounded as foreign and exotic to me as 'Jacuzzi' and 'je t'aime'. Da Nang, Nha Trang, Qui Nhon, Tuy Hoa, Bien Hoa . . .

Like that counting-out rhyme of my early childhood: Eeny, meeny, miney, mo . . .

'So, is the weekend OK?'

'Which weekend?' I asked and started laughing again.

In three weeks' time Dalena was spending the weekend with us. All she really wanted to know, every time she asked such a stupid question, was whether I was dead certain that Simon would also be there.

'Now that basic training is over,' my brother wrote from Potchefstroom, 'the boys are beginning to look forward to the Border. All except Pierre who says he should never have come to the Army, he should've gone to live in another country. Some days I wonder where he gets his ideas. For instance, the other day he said out of the blue that we must stop referring to terrorists, we must remember that one man's terrorist is another man's freedom fighter. I ask you! How in hell can you think of your enemy as a freedom fighter? It makes them sound like heroes!'

In the past couple of months, I read in the newspaper, there were approximately 300 terrorist incidents in Rhodesia. Freedom fighter incidents? *During this time sixty terrorists, forty-one civilians and eleven members of the Security Forces were killed. Landmines were involved in eighty-seven incidents.* Fortunately Simon and Pierre don't have to go to Rhodesia, I thought thankfully. In South West Africa it was quieter and safer.

'My father says bougainvillaea is also called the paper flower,' I said when I saw that Dalena was also watching the standard nine boys next to the rugby field. 'And the leaves have the bright colours, not the flowers.'

'Dear Agony Aunt,' Dalena sighed, 'my roommate has a problem. She's not interested in boys, she's only interested in flowers.'

I turned my head away from the purply red paper flowers next to the rugby field and towards the hockey field where Miss Lourens was coaching the standard sixes. She had the best pair of legs in the school, the boys said. And they had more than enough opportunity to see more than enough of them because she taught Physical Training and usually wore a skirt which barely covered her bum. I wondered if Ben also . . .

'What does Ben say?' Dalena asked as if I had spoken my thoughts aloud.

'Nothing,' I said and bent my head to study my hockey stick. 'He blushes every time he looks at me . . .'

'And you blush every time you look at him. Forget it, no ways are the two of you going to get it together. You can't survive on one French kiss for the rest of the year, Mart!'

I kept my eyes on my hockey stick. Hau Bonm, Khanh Duong, Kien Cu. The names sang in my head. *Within three weeks the Communist wave coloured the map of South Vietnam. Important cities were taken almost daily, mostly without resistance.* I was overcome by the same stifling feeling I had when I was small and heard that counting-out rhyme, afraid that I wouldn't be allowed to play any longer, afraid that I would be counted out. Eeny, meeny, miney, mo . . .

'What about that pal of your brother's?'

'Which pal?'

'That Pierre guy, man. What about him?'

'What about him?'

I looked suspiciously at my roommate. Her head was working like one of those old-fashioned alarm clocks, the kind that ticked so loudly one couldn't sleep. Tick-tock-tick-tock. She had a yen for my brother and she realized that my cooperation would smooth her path. Tick-tock-tick-tock . . . And she knew how to ensure my cooperation.

'Don't act stupid, Mart.' When she was annoyed her voice always sounded just slightly higher; more like other girls' voices. 'He's a much better bet than old Ben. He's older, he's brighter, he's –'

'Uglier,' I cut her short.

'Looks aren't everything!' She almost managed to sound shocked.

'Look who's talking! When were you last in love with an ugly guy?'

'But Pierre isn't ugly!' A quick change in tactics. 'He's got an *interesting* face! Those high cheekbones! And those black eyes . . .' Her own eyes were narrowed against the bright light but I could see the flash of the yellow flecks in the grey and the green. 'He looks like . . . like a French matador or a Spanish philosopher!'

I started to laugh and folded my arms round my legs. With my head resting on my knees I listened to the groans of the rugby players and the rhythmic thwack of hockey sticks against a ball. But somewhere behind the groans and the rhythmic thwacking I still heard the counting-out rhyme: Da Nang, Nha Trang, Qui Nhon, Hau Bonm, Khanh Duong, Kien Cu . . .

61

London, 10 October 1992

My Dear Child

Now that my story has its own momentum, I can't get the decade out of my mind. Like that time with the Vietnamese place names.

If only I could erase my guilt the way Bull's-Eye erased those historical dates on his blackboard: 1652, 1838, 1948 . . .

Speaking of historical dates, I am perfectly aware of the fact that today is Paul Kruger's birthday. So you see, I'll never be able to clear my conscience. My memory is engraved with the holy days of a people I want to forget.

In the meanwhile it seems as if the worst is going to happen in Angola. Jonas Savimbi will continue to fight. Do you know what some smug Western diplomat said on TV last night? 'The trouble with movements such as Unita – which has fought a sixteen-year civil war after a long struggle against colonialism – is that they believe it is their *right* to govern the country. Savimbi hasn't fought a war for thirty years to be *vice*-president of anything.'

Thirty years of war. Almost as long as I've been alive. With no end in sight.

In South Africa, too, the blood flows incessantly. No end in sight.

'The sins of the fathers'. That verse in the Bible drove me to a frenzy of rhetorical questions during my adolescence. Why, I asked Simon, why should we even *try* to be good? Why don't we simply do as we like? If we're going to be punished for the sins of our forefathers in any case?

'And our forefathers had no shortage of sins,' Simon murmured.

He was dragging audibly on a home-made joint and unexpectedly handed it to me, one of the few times he had ever done so. I felt as grateful and as stupid as a small child allowed to draw something with her father's pen before really knowing how to hold it.

'That sounds like something Mr Maritz could've thought up!' Snorting, my mouth full of smoke, my head full of uncontrollable thoughts. 'As though there was a stupid headmaster somewhere in heaven, sucking stupid school rules out of his stupid thumb!'

Simon shrugged and slowly blew out the smoke. And then, as he usually did when he didn't know what to say, quoted Bob Dylan: '"The answer, my friend, is blowing in the wind . . ."'

At that moment they were the most profound words I had ever heard. But then they say that everything sounds different once you start smoking pot.

Love
M.

It's a Long Way to Tipperary

'Hey, listen to this bit in the newspaper.' I looked up from my patch of shadow under the umbrella to where the other four were sitting at the side of the swimming pool. 'If you smoke pot regularly you can develop breasts. That's if you're a male, of course.'

'How regularly?' Pierre asked.

'At least three times a week it says here.'

'Then we're still safe,' Pierre said to Simon without a glimmer of a smile.

'And if you're a woman?' Dalena, sitting between Simon and Pierre, asked. She was staring at her legs in the water.

'"If a woman smokes marijuana," I read from the paper, "there is a possibility of one in a hundred that her breasts will be enlarged."'

'Then it's probably worth taking the chance,' Dalena decided and kicked her legs harder. She sounded as serious as Pierre.

'I wouldn't mind you smoking dope,' my brother smiled. He leaned back on his elbows, his face turned to the sky like a golden sunflower. Both he and Dalena had the gift of lying in the sun as still as plants without any sign of discomfort. 'But there's nothing wrong with your breasts.'

In my mind's eye I saw a heavy headline on the front page of the newspaper: *Van Vuuren Blushes!*

'Well . . . I don't particularly want to look like Laurika . . .' my roommate in her shiny black swimsuit floundered, 'but I wouldn't mind being a bit bigger.'

'Who's Laurika?' Pierre asked with lively interest.

'A very forward matric girl,' Suna giggled next to him.

He actually laughed at her silly little joke. I lowered my head over the newspaper but watched them over my dark glasses.

64

Of us three girls, Dalena had the best pair of legs, but as she herself admitted, around the top she wasn't very well endowed. I couldn't complain about what went on north of my navel but I would've given anything to have smaller hips. Suna, on the other hand, was built like a shop-window mannequin: top and bottom in perfect proportion, her waist so slender she could fit into my mother's wedding dress (without the girdle which had pinched Ma so much that she looked as though she was attending a funeral in all her wedding pictures). She wore a white bikini which accented her tanned stomach, with a tiny top which became transparent every time she went into the water so that her nipples showed through the wet material like two fried mushrooms.

Just as well that she has an acne problem, I thought, otherwise she would've been an unbearable ass. And immediately I was ashamed of my thoughts.

Meanwhile Dalena had disappeared under the water with a soft splash. After a few seconds Simon sat up to see what had become of her. Only after she had completed five lengths did she burst through the surface again.

'If you smoked dope,' Simon said, 'you wouldn't have so much breath.'

'I've been ... practising ... in the bath ... for years,' Dalena gasped. 'Seeing how long ... I can keep ... my head ... under water.'

'Now why would someone want to do that?' I couldn't decide whether it was interest or sarcasm I heard in Pierre's husky voice.

'Boredom,' Dalena sighed in the pool.

Pierre was tall and slender in his trunks, and I had to admit not as shapeless as he seemed under his clothes. Sinewy, I would've said, muscular in a sinewy way. He had the darkest skin of the five of us. Probably born with a dark skin because he didn't seem anywhere near as comfortable in the sun as my brother or my roommate. His stomach hard as a brown stone smoothed by water. Actually his whole body reminded me of an elongated, water-smoothed stone, something which would easily slip out of your fingers if you tried to hold it but would also be heavier than you had expected. As if he must weigh much more than Simon even though he was a lot thinner. It was difficult to explain.

The dark, curly hairs around his navel were damp, ran downwards in a straggling path which disappeared into his trunks. I looked away quickly, at the banana trees which seemed as if they were being dragged sideways by heavy bunches of fruit. Closer to the swimming pool, near the few pawpaw trees, their trunks like slender umbrella handles, a clump of avocado trees also bore abnormally large dark-green fruit.

'It's terrible.' Dalena trod water until she reached Simon and Pierre and hung from her arms at the pool's edge between the two boys. 'I sometimes get so bored that I'd do *anything* just to make sure that I was still alive!'

'*Anything?*'

She didn't see the sharp look Pierre gave her. It seemed as if she didn't even hear him.

'That's what scares me most on earth.' She shivered as if she were suddenly cold. 'Boredom.'

My brother frowned, grabbed her by the hand and hauled her out of the pool. On the edge next to him, her body shook again as she shivered.

'Your sister is never bored,' she said absently, her arms folded across her chest. 'There's always something going on in her head. My head sometimes gets . . . just black . . . a big, black hole . . .'

Simon and Suna both looked slightly uncomfortable about this unexpected confession. But Pierre nodded slowly as if Dalena were speaking to him only.

A T-shirt with the slogan *Black is Beautiful*, I read in the newspaper, had been banned by the Publication Control Board because it was a threat to law and order. A Coloured train passenger had been set alight by two white ticket inspectors because he couldn't show them his ticket. They poured petrol over his head and set him alight with matches, I read with a growing sense of unreality, saying to him: 'You'll burn in hell like this one day, *Hotnot*.'

In Saigon there were few signs of fear while the attacking forces approached. Western inhabitants relaxed next to their swimming pools and wondered whether to have Chinese or Vietnamese food.

I folded the paper and turned on to my back. The umbrella was blue above my head, the sky even bluer above the umbrella. I should've been studying history – we were starting exams next week – but it was too hot to concentrate on the Great Trek.

'I wonder what they're going to do to him,' Suna said – and not for the first time that day – as we made sandwiches in the kitchen.

'Perhaps you should be more worried about her,' Dalena suggested.

'She's OK. She isn't in the hostel. And they say he seduced her.'

'Old Hein!' Dalena burst out laughing. 'He couldn't even seduce a dog!'

'So you think she seduced him?'

Suna looked out of the kitchen window, her hands unmoving above the tomato slices as she contemplated this exciting new possibility. I followed her gaze to a few palm-tree trunks which grew like burglar bars in front of the window and wished we could discuss something other than Heinrich and Jolene. But I had to admit I was almost as inquisitive as Suna about what had really happened.

The rumour had swept through the school on Friday morning like a fire through a suburb of thatched houses, driven by a wild gale of speculation. First we heard that a prefect had caught Hein when he was creeping out of the hostel on his way to sleep with Jolene. Shortly after, Laurika came up with the story that it was the hostel master himself who went to fetch Hein at Jolene's home early in the morning. After they had spent the night together, she added meaningfully. And barely an hour later Maggie spread the tale that the headmaster had also been present, that he *and* the hostel master had caught Hein and Jolene in bed together. 'On the job,' as Maggie put it. Jolene's divorced mother was evidently not at home and there were any number of scurrilous stories as to where she had spent the night.

'Do you think they'll be expelled?' Suna wanted to know.

'Hein will be OK. His father and the headmaster are both in the Broederbond.' Dalena wiped her brown hair out of her face with the back of her hand. The blade of the bread knife whipped through the air dangerously close to her forehead. 'I don't know about Jolene. Her father isn't a big cheese.'

'Shame,' Suna said.

'The worst that can happen to Hein is that his father will give him

67

such a beating that he'd rather become a pansy than ever touch a girl again.'

'Shame,' Suna said again but it was difficult for her not to sound excited. 'I hear his father usually beats him with the belt of his old Voortrekker uniform . . .'

Simon laughed uproariously outside on the stoep, where he and Pierre were helping my father to get the fire going while they drank beer and told dirty jokes. Since Simon's entry into the Army my father treated him more like a pal than a child, madly buddy-buddy-all-boys-together . . . In my opinion, my father was green with envy because he'd never had the opportunity to play at soldiers. He was too young for the Second World War – and now he was too old for the war on the Border.

My mother had herded us girls into the kitchen because she didn't want us to hear the dirty jokes around the fire. We were supposed to make sandwiches to barbecue over the coals later in the evening. We worked as briskly as a row of factory workers. The sooner we finished the sooner we could join the party round the fire. Dalena cut the bread and buttered each slice, Suna slapped two slices of tomato on the butter, I sprinkled grated cheese over the tomato and Dalena sprinkled salt and pepper on the cheese. (Dalena, of course, was the most energetic worker.) The only problem was that not one of us wanted to cope with the onions. All three of us were wearing a heavy layer of Suna's new aquamarine mascara and it wasn't waterproof even though it sounded as if it was meant for deep-sea divers. If the onions made our eyes water, we were going to look like we'd just gone ten rounds with Muhammad Ali. So we simply pretended to have forgotten the onions.

'But surely he'll be expelled from the *hostel*?' Despite my struggles I kept being sucked into the conversation. 'Or do you think his father can prevent that as well?'

'Man, those Broeders can manage anything.' Dalena listened to the laughter outside, her head at an angle. 'You can tell your old man isn't a Broeder. He's too jolly.'

'He can be pretty impossible at times,' I mumbled, a piece of dry bread in my mouth.

'Not a patch on *my* father,' she assured me at once. 'My mother says it's because he grew up the hard way that he's so miserable, but I think she's simply looking for an excuse for his lack of humour.'

'My father was always laughing,' Suna said thoughtfully. 'He had a gruff kind of laugh like gravel being shaken. I've never heard anyone else laugh like that . . .'

Dalena and I looked at one another but said nothing. Suna's father died when she was six. That's why she still sounded like a doting little girl whenever she spoke about him.

'My mother won't win a prize for being the friendliest woman in the district, either,' Dalena said. 'There's an American painting, I don't know whether you know it, of a man and a woman in front of a church, I think it's a church, the one holding a garden fork or something, two real old sourpusses. They always remind me of my parents. Thin and peevish. As if they're scared they won't go to heaven if they have a belly-laugh once in a while.'

'So where do you come from?' Suna laughed.

'You may well ask. My mother says they found me in the mountain and chopped off my tail. Baboon's child.'

'My mother told me that story too,' I said.

'The difference is that my mother still expects me to believe it.' Dalena sprinkled salt on a slice of tomato and popped it into her mouth. 'I think if I had to ask her about the facts of life she would rather commit suicide than admit that she and my father . . . you know . . . *did* it.'

I jumped up to switch on the radio on the windowsill so that my mother, paging through a women's magazine in the next room, couldn't overhear our conversation. I quickly changed the station from Afrikaans to LM Radio.

'And how did you find out . . . you know, where you really came from?' I asked when I slid back into my seat at the kitchen table. The music enfolded me, made me feel safe, like the darkness in the hostel room at night.

'Tcha, one of my sisters' boyfriends told me. I didn't believe him, of course I didn't. I can't imagine it to this day. I mean, if we were talking about your ma and pa, Mart, well, it's possible to picture something like that. With a little imagination. But *my* father and mother? Never!'

'I suppose it's difficult for any child to –'

'Not difficult,' Dalena cut me short. 'Impossible!'

'I know,' Suna giggled. 'Like old Maritz and his wife.'

I could just about picture the headmaster without his clothes, a large pink mountain of a man, but the picture disappeared when I reached his head. I couldn't get the shiny layer of Brylcreem out of his blond hair. Or perhaps he did it Brylcreem and all?

'Ma-art!' my mother called from the living room. 'Must you play the music so loudly?'

'Ohhh, Maa!' I called in return. 'I thought you liked Abba!'

But my mother's voice had disturbed the intimate atmosphere. Dalena's head was at an angle again to hear Simon's voice and Suna stared blindly out of the window. I stood up to turn down the radio.

'They say it wasn't Jolene's first time.' Suna sat with her elbows on the table, her chin in her hands and looked at the slowly darkening sky. 'They say she's not really –'

'Who the hell are the "they" you toss around so easily?' Dalena's voice was fiery with indignation.

'If I didn't know you better, Dalena,' I said, 'I would've sworn that you're jealous of Jolene.'

'No, it's the hypocrisy that makes me so bloody mad!' Now her voice was as flaming as the biblical burning bush. 'Everyone in the school carries on as if Hein and Jolene have committed the greatest sin since Adam and Eve in Eden! Meanwhile at least a third of the girls in standard nine and matric are no longer virgins or they can't wait to lose their virginity! Or the only reason they're still virgins is because they're too scared their pals will think they're sluts! And I don't even want to mention the boys! You know how randy the whole lot of them are!'

Suna laughed nervously. I hovered near the radio and turned up the sound louder and louder. By that time the lions in the Kruger National Park could probably have heard Abba singing 'Waterloo'. But it seemed as if my roommate's burning indignation had died down for the moment. She stared at the bread knife in her hand with a sullen mouth. I switched off the radio and walked to the opposite wall to switch on the neon light above the table. After flickering a few times it suddenly lit the kitchen as brightly as an operating theatre.

'Do you really want to go on my father's trip tomorow?' I asked in the heavy silence, in the bright light.

'If we stay here,' Suna said with a shrug, 'we'll have to swot history.'

'If Simon is going, I'm going too,' Dalena said determinedly.

My father wanted to show the surrounding area to some friends from the city, offering a kind of guided tour in his new kombi with the usual tall tales and exaggerations. He had suggested that we 'grown-up children' follow him on our own in my mother's old Cortina. The other four had agreed immediately. And I didn't want to stay at home on my own.

'You don't know my pa's trips,' I tried a final protest. 'He stops at every third tree to drink a toast to all the gold prospectors and transport drivers who were mown down by mosquitoes and flies and wild animals. After a few hours everbody is tight and then they sing the old Transvaal Republic's anthem and "It's a long way to Tipperary". And when they're really drunk, "She'll be coming round the mountain."'

'Sounds like fun,' Dalena said.

'It's disgusting,' I said. But I could see they didn't believe me.

'This is romantic country,' my father said. He was wearing a checked Andy Capp cap for the occasion. 'Romantic and wild.'

Simon and I gave one another a quick glance. The adults had formed a half-circle round my father like the followers of a soapbox preacher, serious and nodding. With the exception of my mother who stood to one side and looked as mad as hell.

'I don't think it was so romantic for all the people who died of malaria and bilharzia and other diseases,' Ma muttered as she lit a Cameo.

'Like the American Wild West.' Pa moved his cap back, wiped off a film of sweat with the back of his hand, pulled the cap over his forehead again. 'Gold prospectors from all over the world rushed here. No one asked questions about your past. You were known merely as French Bob, German George, Jolly Joe, Sailor Harry . . .'

71

Cocky Carl, I thought. That's what they would've called Pa if he'd lived then.

'That's where the trees originated.' Pa waved a hand to indicate the pines at either side of the wide tarred road. 'Planted to provide props for the mine tunnels. Today these plantations form the biggest man-made forest in the world!'

Simon and I looked at one another again and tried not to laugh. It sounded exactly like one of Pa's exaggerations but, bored on the way here, I had paged through the tour guide in Ma's Cortina and read out all kinds of useless information to the others. Among the trivia was the story about the greatest man-made forest.

'That deserves a toast!' cried Pa's noisy friend from Pretoria; the one who had had so much to say about the hills on the horizon next to the swimming pool.

'The trip has barely started,' I whispered to Dalena, 'and he already sounds tight.'

But she didn't hear me.

The Pretorian stood between his wife and two children. They looked like a cartoon of an Afrikaans family in an English newspaper. One only needed to look at their hair. The father had a neat moustache and bushy sideburns, the little boy had a crew cut, the mother's hair was teased and stiff with spray, while the little girl had two pigtails so tightly plaited she could barely blink.

The other married couple were younger and better looking with a small child on the woman's hip. The man wore white trousers and white shoes and a shirt as red as an hibiscus flower, unbuttoned to show a forest of black hair. My mother couldn't take her eyes off the forest. The woman wore red slacks and red shoes with a small white shirt unbuttoned almost as far as her husband's. My father pretended not to notice her cleavage.

'To the gold prospectors,' Pa said solemnly and lifted the glass in his hand. 'Who made this wild country a little less wild for posterity.'

'To the gold prospectors!' the Pretorian repeated Pa's words. He looked at my father the way Pa would look at a Springbok rugby player. Almost adoringly.

The women also lifted their glasses, the older woman meekly, the other one giggling, and took a careful sip or two. Ma smoked with a petulant, angry red mouth and tap-tapped her cigarette with her forefinger. If I hadn't known about her operation, I would've sworn it was the wrong time of the month for her.

Obviously she was already worried about how the lot of them were to reach home in the afternoon. Pa was too much of a cowboy to be a good driver even when he was sober. After a few drinks he imagined he was John Wayne and had to prove his manhood behind the steering wheel. And the more tactfully Ma might suggest that perhaps she should drive, the more indignantly he refused. Who had ever heard of John Wayne giving up his horse to a woman?

Where I was standing, the furthest away from my mother, I could watch everyone. Suna was staring open-mouthed at my father. Dalena was staring open-mouthed at Simon. Pierre was staring at nothing while occasionally bringing a bottle of beer to his mouth. I didn't know what he was thinking but it definitely wasn't about gold prospectors. Lovey and Niel sat in the kombi and read the comics in the Sunday papers. They had also heard Pa's peculiar history lessons to the point of boredom.

'It's going to get worse,' I said to Dalena but again she didn't hear me.

I walked back to Ma's Cortina. Betrayal, I thought, that's what it is.

'Knock it back, there's a long, long trail a-winding,' Pa called and hurriedly emptied his glass.

'You know, Mart, your father would've been a good teacher,' Suna said when we were following the kombi in Ma's car again.

'Yes, when it comes to talking rubbish he can probably hold his own against any teacher.'

'Count your blessings,' said Dalena who was sitting next to Simon in the front, her bare feet on the dashboard. She wore frayed denim shorts so skimpy that her buttocks were visible under the fringing. Her father would take the skin off those buttocks if he could see her like this. 'Let me tell you, he's an angel compared with my father.'

I decided to ignore her and started reading the Sunday paper. From the corner of my eye I saw Simon moving his left hand from the steering wheel to one of her bare buttocks. I didn't know what had happened between the two of them the previous evening but the smile that was pasted to her face this morning made me suspect the worst.

'Do you know you can land in court if you distract the driver's attention from the road?' Pierre asked Dalena.

'Or worse,' I muttered. 'We could all land in hospital.'

'Genuine,' Pierre said. 'I read in the newspaper that a Bloemfontein speed cop pulled a car off the road the other day because the driver's girlfriend had smoothed his hair. He evidently gave her the ticket.'

'Shame,' Suna said. 'It could only happen in Bloemfontein.'

'I'm not so sure,' Pierre said.

Dalena sat with her eyes closed, her feet tapping on the dashboard to the beat of the music. It was Simon's favourite, Bob Dylan, who wailed over the loudspeakers as if he had a dreadful cold. But that was simply the way he sounded.

'*Everybody must get stoned,*' Simon sang along. '*Everybody must get stoned . . .*'

'Camel, anyone?'

Pierre leaned forward between Suna and me, with the soft packet of cigarettes in his hand. Dalena took out two, one for her and one for Simon, and lit both with the same match. Suna used two matches to light one cigarette and started coughing after she had inhaled the smoke, not nearly as practised as Dalena. I regularly lit cigarettes for my brother but now it seemed as if I had to pass some or other test and tests made me nervous.

'Not for me, thanks,' I mumbled, my nose in the newspaper.

'If you read newspapers all day,' Suna said, leaning unnecessarily far across Pierre's body, 'you'll miss everything on the way.'

'Tell me if you see something I haven't seen before.' I had difficulty in keeping the irritation out of my voice.

Suna shrugged and blew a thin stream of smoke through her nostrils. She held the cigarette between two extended fingers, her little finger in the air as if she were a film star with long, red nails.

'Leave Mart alone,' Pierre said without taking his cigarette out of his mouth. 'One of us must know what's going on in the world.'

'Why?' Dalena asked, stretching her arms in a long and lazy motion above her head.

How many times was she still going to betray me today?

'It's like someone keeping cave.' One corner of Pierre's mouth moved up slowly. 'She can warn us when the time has come to be scared. Like in that game, Wolf-wolf-what's-the-time?'

'Midnight,' I said.

'OK, give us the bad news. We can take it.'

'"'The Republic of South Africa is an inextricable part of Africa,'"' I read from the newspaper, '"'and we'll simply have to find ways and means to live with Africa,' Mr Piet Koornhof, Minister of Sport and Recreation, said this week at a Republic Day celebration in Pretoria."'

'Hear, hear!' Pierre laughed.

'They'll stone you when you're trying to be so good,' Simon sang, pinching his nose between two fingers to try and sound more like Bob Dylan. *'They'll stone you just like they said they would . . .'*

I had never heard Pierre laugh so loudly. But I didn't know whether it was at the Minister of Sport and Recreation or at me with my nose stuck in a newspaper or at Simon pinching his nose to sing along with Bob Dylan. With Pierre you never knew.

London, 13 November 1992

Bonjour, mon enfant

I never did go to live in an attic in Paris. Or learn to speak French properly. Life, I read in a magazine recently, is what passes you by while you're making other plans. Yes, I still allow magazines to lead me by the nose. From Seventeen's fashion pages in my teenage years to Vanity Fair's gossipy articles now that I'm supposed to be an adult.

Oh, yes, and Vogue's beauty hints, which I started reading for the first time after my thirtieth birthday. With the kind of hopeless hope with which someone suffering from an incurable disease devours all the latest research about her condition. Old age is an incurable disease, as you'll discover one day.

Life landed me in London where I at least learned to speak a better English than I ever dreamt of in Miss Muffet's class in Black River. And where my son was born in February 1990, together with the New South Africa. Or so I thought.

The birth of the New South Africa was announced almost three years ago but the delivery is still taking place, bloody and long drawn-out. They had barely walked into the labour ward when they announced to the world that a normal, healthy baby had been born. The world is still waiting anxiously. It's beginning to seem as if the child might not make it.

I married my son's father, an attorney like my own father – come back, Freud, all is forgiven – because his firm wanted to send him overseas for a few years. Or perhaps we would've married one day in any case. But the overseas option forced two indecisive individuals to make a decision. We wanted to be together, didn't we? We wanted to get out of the country, didn't we? So, we might as well marry and leave together.

Not for ever! We didn't want to emigrate. Our friends in the Struggle would never forgive us. But to get away temporarily, for post-graduate studies or work, was Politically Correct. In our little white world the Struggle was a capital-letter issue.

'Of course we want to live in a Democratic South Africa one day!' we protested at elegant dinner tables and aesthetic barbecue fires. 'We're not running away from a Majority Government! We just don't see our way clear to coping with the uncertainty of the Interim Period.'

Call us when the revolution's over?

'Of course we're looking forward to freedom, equality and brotherhood . . . sisterhood . . . personhood?'

In the winter of 1988, the third year of the State of Emergency in the old South Africa, I was given the opportunity to go and live in another country (temporarily, of course). *I'm so ashamed I shake my head*, David Kramer sang over the slender, black hi-fi as I packed my suitcases.

By the end of that year I celebrated my first White Christmas in England with my husband. What a disappointment. The Christmas and the husband. It was probably asking too much to adapt to a marriage and a new, free country simultaneously. By the time our child was born – in the same week that Nelson Mandela was released from prison – we were no longer living together.

My husband immediately made plans to return to the New South Africa, together with thousands of refugees. As though he was one of them.

I wasn't ready to return yet. Besides, I was the mother of a child who had been born in Britain, and the wife of a husband whose an- cestors had lived in Ireland, and the author of a 'protest novel' which sold well in Britain. (Actually only a story about a group of friends in South Africa but the shrewd English publisher marketed it as protest literature.) The British would hardly kick me out.

'Divorced? No, not yet, we haven't got that far. It's quite involved, now that we're living in different countries, so we're waiting a while . . . We'll have to see what happens. I'm not unhappy here. I get homesick, of course, but I'm not *unhappy* here. And it's better for my child to grow up here. I'll probably never feel completely at home but . . . oh, well, I never felt completely at home there either.'

Is it too late to go and live in an attic in Paris?

Je t'embrasse
M.

The Star Appeared Only Once

'No, I'm not sorry the holiday is over,' Dalena said with her mouth full of cake. 'I got terribly bored on the farm. Nothing to do, no one to see.'

It was darker than usual, dark of the moon. We were devouring the chocolate cake Dalena had brought from home, flat on the linoleum floor between the two beds so that our crumbs wouldn't fall on the sheets. Quietly, so that Miss Potgieter or a prefect wouldn't hear us.

'I'm crazy about doing nothing,' I whispered. 'And I don't mind not seeing anyone.'

I ate the thick slice of cake out of my cupped hand as if I hadn't seen food for days. I remembered the horror with which I'd stared at the hostel children that first evening in the dining hall. And now, half a year later, I had become equally greedy.

'Well, occasionally I ran across someone I know at the Co-op. Like old Hein. But he's so depressed since he's not allowed to see Jolene that he's quite useless!'

Heinrich Minnaar wasn't expelled from either the school or the hostel. His father must've used his influence as Dalena had forecast. But his parents had forbidden him to have anything to do with Jolene. It was her fault, they decided, that their exemplary son had changed into a seventeen-year-old sex maniac overnight.

'It can't possibly work!' I whispered indignantly. 'That they're not supposed to see one another! They'll start imagining they're Romeo and Juliet!'

My roommate shook her head.

'No way, have no fear. In a month's time it'll all be over.'

'Do you really think so?'

'Yep. Jolene isn't the type to suffer like a martyred Juliet.' She licked the last crumbs off her hand and cut another chunk of cake. 'At the moment she's enjoying all the attention. But as soon as it blows over she'll find herself another Romeo.'

Teenage love just wasn't what it had been in Shakespeare's time, I decided. I was so swept away by our set drama that I had a great deal of it by heart. *O, she doth teach the torches to burn bright! Beauty too rich for use, for earth too dear!* My Afrikaans tongue still stumbled when I tried to say the words aloud but in my imagination I sounded like Queen Elizabeth whom I'd heard on *Radio Today*. My roommate wasn't so easily swept away. Where's the action? She wanted to know. Romeo talks so much it's no wonder he finds it such an effort to get Juliet into bed.

'I hear Maggie has invited Jolene to smoke in the toilets with her and her pals during recess! Can you believe it! A standard seven girl with –'

Dalena froze, her body tense, ready to jump into bed, cake and all. Our ears were so attuned to the almost inaudible shuffle of Miss Potgieter's slippers that she had never caught us out. Miss Potgieter was the needlework teacher who slept at the end of the passage. Or *didn't* sleep: according to rumour she floated up and down the passage all night like a bloodthirsty bird of prey, looking for victims. During the day she was a harmless old maid with fluffy blonde hair and a beaky mouth like a baby chicken, but every evening after lights-out she changed into a gigantic owl who snatched up whispering, reading, nibbling hostel mice with her claws and tore them to pieces. We waited motionless while she moved past the bedroom door. Dalena's teeth were white in the dark when the danger was past.

I cut another piece of cake. Tomorrow I would hate myself again because I had so little willpower. But no one could bake a chocolate cake like Dalena's mother – or rather, no one could bake a chocolate cake the way Dalena's mother had taught her kitchen servants to do it.

'How's your brother?' she asked out of the blue.

'I think these days you know more about my brother than I do.'

Too late I realized that it sounded like an accusation.

'Do you mind . . .' She tucked a strand of hair behind her ear, looked at the remains of the cake at her feet. 'That he and I . . .'

'Well, I don't know . . . it depends on what you . . .'

'Nothing,' she said quickly. 'We've done nothing . . . Yet.'

'Oh.' I didn't know whether to feel relieved or disappointed. 'But you must've kissed, and stuff like that.'

She shrugged her shoulders. I didn't know this shy roommate. Formerly she'd been like a treasure hunter only too eager to show everyone her prizes. Now she slammed the door in my face every time I showed any curiosity.

My brother told me even less. But he'd changed so much that I sometimes felt I was faced with a life-like wax model. Like the other evening when I found him next to the swimming pool, smoking a cigarette. Or that's what I thought until I was overwhelmed by the odour. I felt as if I was trapped in a lift with a woman who had sprayed herself with too much cheap perfume.

'What's that?' I'd asked, startled.

'What do you think?'

He looked at me and gave me a twisted smile. Like Pierre's, I thought.

'*Pot?*' My voice had been almost hoarse with shock. I'd thought they were joking about smoking pot. I might have believed that Pierre would do something like that – I could believe anything about someone who dared call his headmaster an old fart – but my brother?

'Pot, dagga, marijuana, Mary Jane, Durban Poison . . .' Simon had giggled. 'A rose by any other name would smell as sweet.'

I couldn't recall when last I'd heard my brother *giggle*. And now he sat there with a dagga zol, I thought stunned, right in front of my mother and father's bedroom window.

'What's wrong?' I'd asked when I could trust my voice again.

He simply shook his head and stared at the soggy piece of paper between his thumb and forefinger. Dragged hungrily at it, kept the smoke in his mouth with his cheeks slightly inflated and then slowly let it out. It had been a cloudless winter night, warm as a summer's evening in any other place, the sky milky with stars. The moon hung like a plump, ripe pawpaw above the highest trees.

81

'It's almost full moon,' I said. 'You're probably in your werewolf mood.'

He hadn't even smiled at my little joke.

'The Army fucks with your head,' he said eventually.

'Are you sure it isn't Pierre who's f-f-fiddling with your head?' I asked before I could stop myself.

In the bright moonlight the side of his face looked like something carved out of wood, angular planes of high forehead, thin nose and hard chin. If he weren't my brother I'd have really fancied him.

'All Pierre wants is for people to think about things. And the Army expects the opposite.' He'd sucked the last bit of smoke out of the butt, the red coal dangerously close to his lips. 'I was so sure of everything! Right and wrong, white and black, South Africa and the rest of the world. Now I wonder . . .'

He ground out the roach with the heel of his shoe using unnecessary force. I opened my mouth, then closed it again. For a while we sat motionless.

'What do you think of Dalena?' I asked.

'I wonder about her as well.'

'Why?'

'She's dangerous.'

'Dangerous?'

'More of a danger to herself than to other people. The type who dives in at the deep end – without even checking to see whether there's water in the swimming pool.' He looked up at the moon and smiled slowly. 'I like that.'

And then he started making soft little whimpering noises, his eyes still on the moon while the smile on his lips slowly disappeared.

'Let me tell you about grief and the loss of a god,' he whispered. To the moon, not to me. It had sounded like something Pierre would say.

The trunks of the pawpaw trees looked paler and thinner than usual, like the legs of old men showing under rolled-up trouser legs. I had been too scared to touch my brother.

Did other girls feel the same way about their brothers? I wondered as I lay looking at my roommate's sleeping body. Almost like . . . being in love?

Perhaps it was only because he was the first boy I'd known. From the day of my birth he'd been there. I couldn't imagine that he would ever not be there.

My earliest memory was of a Christmas Eve. I was unsure about anything that had happened before that evening, whether Ma had simply told me about it or whether I was confusing a photograph with a memory. But I remembered that particular Christmas Eve.

We had been driving home in Pa's new Opel estate car after a visit to Grandpa and Grandma Fishpond where the tree had hairy, silver decorations and doll-size candles in clip-on holders. I was five. Lovey and Niel had both been sleeping on Ma's lap. (I don't know how she bore it, but for about seven years she had to live with children who attached themselves to her body like ticks. Her seven fat years, she called them, because she was either expecting a baby or had just had one.) Simon and I squashed our noses against the back window and watched the car and the moon running a race. I hoped the moon would win but Simon said I was crazy, surely I could see the car was faster than the moon!

That's the way we had been then, that's the way we still were. It was probably the way we would always be. From his earliest years Simon had had more faith in engines than heavenly bodies. Even now I preferred a good story – even a far-fetched one – to the boring truth.

The round moon slid through the air next to the Opel, occasionally diving behind a transparent curtain of cloud before showing a shining face again. Like that game Ma endlessly played with us: *Where's he gone, where's he gone, found him!*

'*Bethlehem star, O, wondrous sight,*' Ma sang softly to one of the toddlers who had moved restlessly on her lap.

'How does the moon manage it, Pa?' Simon wanted to know. 'To fly almost as fast as a car?'

'He eats all the food on his plate every day,' Pa replied.

'Isn't the moon a woman?' I wanted to know.

'Who said so?'

'*Mamma.*'

'Oh,' Pa said. 'That figures.'

'*Li-i-ghting up the dark of night,*' Ma sang on determinedly.

'Where's the star, *Pappa*?' I asked.

'Which star?

'Bethlehem star. If it's Christmas we must be able to see the star?'

Pa stuttered, speechless for a moment, something which didn't often happen.

'No, Matta,' Ma said. 'The star appeared only once.'

'Just once?'

'Only on that first Christmas.'

'So I'll never see it?'

'Not the real star,' Pa replied quickly. 'That's why we put a star on the Christmas tree every year.'

'But it's not the real star.' I'd wanted to cry but I knew Simon would tease me if I started crying about a star. 'I'll never see the real star.'

I still wanted to cry when I thought about it.

A few months later I'd gone on a visit to my father's parents in the Orange Free State with his younger sister. We travelled by train for weeks, or so it seemed, and stayed on the farm for years. The train journey probably took a day or two, the stay on the farm was some three weeks.

On Grandpa and Grandma Farmdam's farm there was an earth dam in which a windmill with rusted iron legs stood like some strange, preening waterfowl. In Grandpa and Grandma Fishpond's suburban garden, dwarfs with scarlet cheeks and green cement feet guarded the fishpond. I didn't know why the dam and the pond had made such an impression on us. My mother said it was because everyone in this country had an obsession with water. How else? my father asked.

What I particularly remember about that holiday is that Ma made identical coats for me and my baby doll. As bright as the brightest red lipstick with collars of white fake fur which made me feel as beautiful as the picture of Delilah in the Children's Bible. I never wanted to take off the coat again. I never wanted to stop travelling. But in the end it simply became too hot, and the train stopped at a station where my grandpa and grandma were waiting. What I also remember is that I watched the kitchen cat having kittens in a cardboard box under the kitchen table. I couldn't believe it. That they came out *there*. And my father's sister hanging over the same kitchen table every morning with a white face and limp arms and vomiting outside the kitchen door one morning. I don't feel well, she kept repeating. I thought she was dying.

When Ma and Pa came to fetch us in the Opel, we took one of the small kittens home with us. He got the boring, unimaginative name of Farmcat and led a boring, unimaginative life until last year when a veterinarian mercifully killed him. Shakespeare said a rose would smell as sweet . . . but I didn't really think so. If Farmcat had had a more original name, like those cats which that English poet wrote about for instance, like Mr Mistofeles or Mungo Jerry, would his nine lives not have been more eventful?

My aunt wasn't dying after all, I heard later, but pregnant. The women on your father's side don't have easy pregnancies, Ma always said. Most women suffered but some suffered more.

I didn't know whether I wanted a child that badly.

'I thought all countries were like ours,' I said to Dalena at the back of the school bus. 'I thought everybody lived the way we do here.'

She didn't seem to be listening to me. She was reading an English paperback about a pirate abducting a noblewoman on a sailing ship. Probably full of steamy love scenes.

'I mean, white and black separate, separate schools, separate churches, separate houses . . .'

The bus had stopped in front of a café on the only tarred road of a small village. All the children had got off to empty the café on a buying spree but Dalena and I had been on a strict diet for three days. We had brought a bag of apples to chew.

Opposite the café, on the side of the bus where we were sitting, there was a one-star hotel with a corrugated iron roof which hung over the veranda like the floppy brim on an old hat. There was a bar on the veranda into which only white men were allowed – not white children or white women or black people of any age or sex – and round the corner in a dusty side street, there was a liquor store for blacks. Under a tree with bare branches and scarlet flowers sat a handful of clients, most of whose clothes were ragged beyond belief. But it wasn't their clothes which upset me on this Saturday morning. It was their faces.

Nearest to the bus sat a thin man and a girl who could've been younger than me with a crying baby on her lap. Their feet were bare and grey with dust, their eyes grey with something else, something more than liquor. But what it was I didn't know. They didn't look unhappy or rebellious or even happily drunk. Their faces were merely . . . empty.

'I was so shocked when I heard we were different from other countries! I asked my mother what "apartheid" meant, when I was about seven or eight, and she tried to explain. It must've been tough to explain that to a child . . . almost as bad as "Where do I come from?"'

Dalena frowned but didn't raise her head from her book. She didn't even want to see the café, she'd said, because then she would start thinking about chocolates and sweets. And once she started, she wouldn't be able to stop. With anything, I'd thought.

'Then she said that was why other countries didn't like us. And then it struck me! *We were different from the rest of the world.* It just didn't sound right.'

'Maybe the rest of the world is wrong and we're right,' Dalena mumbled, still not looking up.

'Oh, bullshi . . .' I shook my head. 'Surely you don't really think so?'

She dropped the book – at last – and looked at me. Yellow flecks in the grey and green of my brother's marble. By this time I recognized it as a warning, like my mother's tapping cigarette finger.

'The rest of the world isn't as different as they'd like to believe! There's inequality everywhere.'

'But there aren't laws like ours anywhere else!'

'Maybe we're simply more honest than the rest of the world.'

I looked away, through the dirty window of the bus, at the expressionless faces under the tree with the red flowers. Another of the unfamiliar trees I hadn't known when we came to live here. In the meantime I had tried to establish what this one was called, but it only added to my confusion.

'Kaffirboom,' Pa had said when I asked but Ma said, no really, the tree must have a decent name as well.

'It's a kaffirboom,' Pa said. 'It has always been a kaffirboom and it'll remain a kaffirboom.' Or did Ma want to call it a native tree? Or a bantu tree?

'Niel, bring me the dictionary,' Ma said. 'Your father is in one of his moods again.' Was it his fault, perhaps, that Ma didn't like the name of the tree? Pa had wanted to know. Was he Adam, perhaps, who had named the plants and the animals in the Garden of Eden? Ma bit her plump lower lip while she paged determinedly through the dictionary. 'Aha!' she cried triumphantly. '*Kafferboom* is translated as *kaffir tree*' – (Aha! said Pa. Shht, said Ma.) – 'or as *coral tree*. So it's a coral tree,' Ma said to me, who had almost forgotten that it was I who had started this stupid argument with my stupid question.

'No, no, no,' Pa said, and raised his eyes heavenward as in from-whence-cometh-my-help. 'There's a difference between a kaffir-boom and a coral tree. A kaffirboom is a kind of coral tree but it's not *a* coral tree.'

By this time Niel had taken the dictionary from Ma because he could see that it was one of those arguments that could last the entire evening. And Ma hadn't made a meal yet and he was hungry, as usual. 'Aha!' he called out, as triumphantly as Ma a few moments ago. 'Pa is right!' 'Ohhh!' Ma said and fiddled in her hair with her fingers as though her scalp was itching. 'Men always stick together.' 'No, hang on, Ma,' Niel said. He'd looked up the Latin names. 'A kaffirboom is *E . . . ry . . . thri . . . na caffra*,' he read aloud, 'and a coral tree is *E . . . ry . . . thrina indica*! So there is a difference,' he said, obviously relieved, and asked when we were going to eat. 'Clever boy,' Pa said.

But Ma was like those Voortrekker women who threatened to cross the Drakensberg in their bare feet. She never knew when to stop. A week later she had, so help me, taken a book about trees out of the library. '*Erythrina caffra*,' she announced crisply while dishing up, 'is a *coastal coral tree*.' I could hear with what an effort she kept the spite out of her voice. 'The *ordinary coral tree*, which grows in this area, bears the learned name of *Erythrina lysistemon*.' And she'd pronounced the strange words with such self-assurance that it sounded as if she had spent the entire day practising in front of a mirror. 'Don't argue,' she warned, before Pa could open his mouth, and pushed the book under his nose. 'Look at the photograph! Is that the tree that grows here or is it not?'

Ma always said that if you wanted to keep a man you had to pretend to know less than he did. But perhaps she and Pa had been married for so long that it had become too much trouble.

'Just look at that bunch of drunks under the tree!' Dalena said next to me. 'What would they do if you suddenly gave them equality?'

I looked away. *FNLA Forges Towards Luanda*, announced a newspaper poster in the café window. I had heard on the radio that white Angolans were leaving the country at an average of 500 per day. I heard that counting-out rhyme in my head again. Eeny, meeny, miney, mo . . .

The schoolchildren were beginning to get back on the bus with chomping mouths and plastic bags full of goodies. We were on our way back to Black River after playing hockey and rugby against another school. All our teams had lost but no one really looked upset about defeat except Mr Botha, the Afrikaans teacher who drove the bus and coached the rugby first team. We called him Mr Locomotive because he was always puffing on about the wonder of the Afrikaans language. And the miracles which the fifteen players in the rugby first team could achieve if they would only have faith.

The pride of the school, Mr Maritz called the rugby first team. I looked at the boys around me, their ungainly bodies in black tracksuits – Black River High School in large, gold letters on each back – their wet hair and their chewing mouths. And for a moment (a brief one) I almost felt sorry for the headmaster. A school had to have something to be proud of. And whichever way you looked at it, Black River didn't have much.

'If they had equality,' I muttered with my eyes on the people under the tree again, 'they probably wouldn't look the way they do now.'

Surprised, Dalena looked up from her book. 'What's your case this morning?' she asked frowningly. 'Or is it just the wrong time of the month?'

'Shame,' Suna said. 'Look at poor old Hein. I feel so sorry for him.'

Poor old Hein was sitting diagonally opposite us in the bus. He looked like a thundercloud among the smiling faces around him.

'I'd look like that too if I'd played that badly.' Dalena stared crossly at the packet of Smarties in Suna's hand. 'Even a blind guy would've been able to get that last ball across!'

'It's not his fault that the first team lost, Dalena,' I said. 'They all screwed up.'

'And he at least had an excuse for playing badly,' Suna said. She shook a handful of Smarties on to her palm and selected the brown ones, one after another.

'What excuse?'

'Oh, come on, it's obvious that this whole Jolene thing has freaked him out.'

'So, why doesn't he do something about it?'

'Why are you so hard on him, Dalena?'

'Because he's a coward! Because he's been sitting around for weeks doing nothing!'

'Shht!' I whispered worriedly. 'He'll hear you!'

When Suna had eaten all the brown Smarties, she popped the rest into her mouth in a disinterested manner. Dalena took an apple out of the plastic bag and savaged it with her teeth.

'What can he do?' Suna asked. 'He's not allowed to speak to her, he's not allowed to –'

'Who says he's not allowed to speak to her!' Dalena almost shouted. 'Why can't he speak to her? If he was really crazy about her he wouldn't pay any attention to what a bunch of grown-ups say!'

'Shht!' I warned again but they ignored me.

'It's easy for you to talk!' Suna thrust another handful of sweets into her mouth. This time she didn't even look at the colours.

'All I'm saying, Suna,' Dalena said, sighing, 'is that you must be prepared to fight for what you really want. If he wants Jolene so badly, why hasn't he got the guts to do something about it?' She was quiet for a moment. Her large mouth quivered as she fought the temptation to say something bitchy. Then she succumbed: 'Although I still don't understand what he sees in her.'

89

'Well, I feel sorry for him.' For a moment Suna stared at Hein who sat with his head leaning against the window. His eyes were closed as if he were asleep. He had heavy, dark eyebrows and long, dark eyelashes but the skin of his eyelids was so white that I could see the thin blue veins beneath. 'I hear Pine has asked Jolene to go to the rugby party with him tonight.'

'Pine?' Dalena and I asked simultaneously, stunned.

'Pine.' Suna shook her head in a measured fashion like an old woman bearing tidings of death.

'And I'm sure she agreed,' Dalena said when she had regained her breath.

'Pine is not the kind of guy one says no to,' Suna said, as if we didn't know it.

I threw a casual glance over my shoulder. As usual Pine Pienaar sat right at the back of the bus, a black bear against the light which fell through the back window; the guy with the biggest head, the broadest shoulders and the hairiest chest in the school. Evidently also the oldest guy in the school because he'd plugged grade one and was now spending a second year in standard nine.

'How can you plug grade one?' I asked crossly. 'I wonder if it's true.'

'What did I tell you, Mart?' A self-satisfied smile spread across my roommate's face. 'Jolene is not the type to play Juliet-Juliet!'

'If only poor old Hein would stop playing Romeo-Romeo,' I sighed.

'If either of you uses the phrase "poor old Hein" again,' Dalena hissed through clenched teeth, 'I'm going to beat both of you about the head with this bag of apples.'

'Shame,' Suna giggled. 'I would've liked to do something to help him, Dalena. That's all.'

'Well, why don't you do something, Suna?' Dalena's eyes had a dangerous glitter. 'Why don't you go and talk to him?'

'I can't just . . .'

'Why not? There's a seat open next to him. Or do you want me to ask him to come and sit here?'

Suna gave me a nervous look.

'Do it,' I said, to my own surprise, as though the devil in Dalena had infected me too. 'I dare you, Suna.'

Even so I was astonished when she got up and sat down in the empty seat next to Hein. Suna, who thought she had the biggest pimple problem in the Western world? Suna, who stared at her feet when a boy even glanced at her?

'Hi,' she said to Hein who had opened his eyes and was staring at her with as much amazement as I was. Her voice was high with tension. 'Would you like a Smartie?'

He frowned, making his eyebrows even heavier and shook his head. Suna giggled in embarrassment. Poor Suna, I thought, poor, poor Suna!

'Now that's what I call guts,' Dalena gasped, breathless with admiration.

'Unless you have brown ones left,' Hein said unexpectedly.

'Oh, gosh, no,' Suna giggled again and shook a handful of sweets on to her palm. 'They're my favourites. I've eaten them all.'

'Mine, too.' He looked down at her palm, coloured by the sweets, and slowly smiled. 'But if you can't get what you want, you might as well take what you can get.'

London, 16 December 1992

My Dear Child

When I was a teenager, 'Streets of London' was a heartrending song which took me away from the dull streets of Black River. Today they were a terrible reality, as reality probably always is.

My son and I took the Underground to Knightsbridge where we walked around Harrods with tearful eyes and red noses to admire the Christmas windows. It was snowing. Not the kind of snow which make sentimental suckers like me dream of a White Christmas but an unromantic, icy, urban rain immediately trampled by thousands of feet into a mud-coloured slush which turned every pavement into a deadly slippery slide, so that I had to take tiny, mincing steps while the toddler with me pulled impatiently at my hand.

My breath was white in front of my face like those thought bubbles in the comics Niel used to devour long ago: *Prince Valiant, Batman, Mad.* I stopped in front of a window, a vision of silver stars and big, golden angels, because I didn't want to think about relatives. Not shortly before Christmas when the sentimentality of the season could change even a snow-white mood into a mud-coloured mess.

My son plucked impatiently at my hand. He knew the windows were no more than hors d'œuvres. The real feast waited inside the famous building.

What can be said about Harrods' toy department in the Christmas season? That it can change even a model child into a caricature of capitalist greed? And the most exemplary mother into a potential bank robber, cat burglar, aircraft hijacker – anything to get her hands on enough money – anything to satisfy her child's unbelievable covetousness?

My child climbed on to the lap of an English Father Christmas and whispered a long list of desires into the ear of a middle-aged stranger. I looked away, ashamed of my child's shamelessness. And even more ashamed because I wanted to give him everything his heart desired.

Later, when he was staring in enchantment at a miniature city of multi-coloured Lego blocks and moving trains, I wondered whether he would remember anything about this visit. My own memory only goes back to my fifth year, to that Christmas Eve in Pa's Opel, but my life was probably so boring that there was nothing else to remember. Surely my son's life couldn't be boring? Confusing, I admit, without a father in sight and with a mother who no longer knows where she belongs. But surely not boring?

That was all that kept me here, I realized in that toy heaven this morning: the blind belief that my son would be happier here than there. If my eyes were to be opened, I might as well pack my bags.

I hope you'll have a happy Christmas, my dear child. (Choose any colour you like. Just not white.)

Love
M.

It's Still the Same War

'You must come to the chemist with me,' Dalena said as we were walking into town. 'I need something for the weekend.'

It wasn't her words but the way in which she said them that made me give her a quick look.

'What?'

'Contraceptives,' she said, her eyes on her dusty school shoes.

I stood still. Suddenly the light was so bright that I had to blink my eyes to see her. It was one of those moments that made you wish you could say something that you would remember for ever.

'Sheesh,' was all I could manage.

Dalena didn't pause. Heavily I swallowed all the objections which rose, unasked, and gave a few hasty steps to catch up with her.

'What kind of contraceptives?'

'Tch, French letters, I suppose . . . and foam.'

'*FLs? Foam?*'

I stopped again. This time Dalena stopped as well, sighing, and waited for me to pull myself together. I looked at my roommate in her grey school uniform. Behind us lay the two storeys of our hostel, painted an unimaginative yellowish-white, as ugly on the outside as it was on the inside. Fortunately somewhat hidden behind a wire fence covered in orange bougainvillaea. Further back I could see the school and the sports fields, still further away the boys' hostel, painted the same sickening colour of vomit. And above us was the merciless sun – around us a haze of heat – which burnt the whole scene into my mind for ever.

'What kind of foam?'

'You get a kind of foam which you inject if you don't want to get pregnant,' she said in her Janis Joplin voice, but the nervousness surfaced. 'It kills the sperm.' She saw that I was still staring un-comprehendingly at her. 'Like . . . an insecticide, man, like Doom.'

'But why do you need an insecticide if you can use an FL?'

'No, man, you use them together! The FL *and* the foam. To make sure.'

She started walking again, faster than before, not even looking up to see if I was following.

'Dalena, wait! I'll come with you but why . . . why must you . . . I mean, why . . . isn't it . . .?' The question which stuck in my throat like a fish bone was why didn't my brother buy his own bloody con-doms. 'It's supposed to be the boy who takes precautions,' I finally managed.

'So what?' Dalena walked faster and faster. 'Have I ever paid any attention to what girls or boys are "supposed" to do?'

'But Simon . . .' I grabbed her arm, forced her to slow her pace. 'Have you spoken to Simon about this?'

'It doesn't work that way, Mart. Only Romeo and Juliet talk about things all the time. I *know* what's going to happen this weekend.'

All that was going to happen this weekend, as far as I knew, was that Dalena and I were going to Pretoria with Simon and Pierre. She had told her parents that she was going with me to visit friends in Pretoria and I had told my parents that I was going with her to visit friends in Pretoria. What neither set of parents knew was that the friends were actually a few of Pierre's student pals who lived in a dilapidated house and that there wouldn't be a responsible adult in sight.

'But Dalena . . .'

'If we don't do it now, we'll never do it,' she said with a determin-ation which tightened her long lips.

'How can you say that!'

'It's the last time I'll see him before he goes to the Border.'

'So what? Do you think they're going to shoot his balls off on the Border? Do you think that when he comes back he won't be able to do it any more?'

I was amazed at my own indignation. And I knew, without know-ing what it was, that it was more than the mere urge to protect my roommate from her own recklessness.

'Who knows what might happen on the Border?' Dalena asked.

As if the question didn't torment me every evening before I fell asleep. In less than a month my brother would be one of the crowds of young men 'somewhere on the Border' to whom worried relatives sent soppy messages on the radio every Sunday afternoon. I'm losing my brother *and* my best friend, I thought with a lump in my throat which by this time felt far larger than a fish bone.

Wordlessly we walked on past a deserted park with a few rusted swings behind an iron fence, through an avenue of jacaranda trees to the broad main street of Black River. There were three chemists in this street but we both knew that we couldn't buy French letters in Voortrekker Road. We needed a quiet chemist in a side street where no one would recognize us, where we wouldn't run into any other schoolchildren.

'I've heard . . .' I swallowed but the lump in my throat got bigger and bigger. 'I've heard that if you're too shy to ask for it . . . you can toss a fifty cent piece into the air and then you slap your hand over it on the counter . . . with your palm . . . and then the guy behind the counter knows you want FLs.'

'And if he doesn't know?' asked Dalena. 'You'll stand there like a bloody fool while everybody else waits for you to say what you want.'

'Well . . .'

'That story is as old as the hills, Mart. Have you ever seen anyone doing such a stupid thing?'

Snubbed, I stared at the pavement and started playing Step-on-the crack, break your grandmother's back, last played when I was much younger.

'Well then, how are you going to ask for it?'

'I'm going to open my mouth and ask for a packet of condoms.' But she barely opened her mouth as she said it, her voice as tense as her lips. 'It's like buying Tampax. It's a little embarrassing, that's all.'

I couldn't even buy a packet of Tampax without blushing down to my toes — and now my roommate wanted me to buy *condoms* with her! And *foam!* I gave larger and larger steps to miss the cracks in the pavement.

'But . . . don't you have to ask for a specific brand?'

'Probably doesn't matter what the things are called. As long as they do the job.'

We had turned into a side street. She looked past me at a chemist's window behind me, avoiding my eyes. It still wasn't the right chemist, neither quiet nor small enough.

'But we're wearing our school uniforms!'

'Well, we're not allowed to come to town without our uniforms so what the hell are we supposed to do!' she snapped as though she was angry with me because she needed contraceptives.

'It won't be that bad,' she muttered after a few seconds. 'But for heaven's sake don't start giggling when you see the stuff. Just try to act normally, as though you do it every day.'

'But it's not normal for a girl in standard nine to buy FL's every day, Dalena!'

Dalena raised her eyes to the cloudless sky above us.

'The more I think about the weekend,' I snapped in turn, 'the more I think we should forget the whole idea.'

'Maybe you should stop thinking for a while,' Dalena said.

'They say that more than a quarter of a million whites are fleeing Angola,' my brother said. 'It's the biggest exodus out of Africa since the Algerian war.'

'Is anyone going to be left?' I asked, dismayed.

'Only about a fifth of the original inhabitants,' Simon said. 'They say –'

'You mean the original *white* inhabitants,' Pierre said, his voice almost as sharp as the hostel matron's. 'The whites might be fleeing, Mart, but plenty of black people are going to be left. If you regard them as *people*, of course.'

'What's got into you this evening?'

He looked down at the steak on his plate without answering me. In the flickering candlelight his face appeared even darker than usual, his eyes hidden deeper under his eyebrows and his cheeks more hollow. I looked at Simon on the opposite side of the table, behind a candle in a round-bellied bottle dripping with wax, but he shrugged helplessly.

'Could we please discuss something other than politics!' Dalena cried out angrily.

'We're not talking politics,' Pierre said and sliced his steak so forcefully that the muscles in his forearms stood out. 'We're talking about life.'

Poor Dalena. She had looked forward to the weekend so much. And here we were sitting in a noisy, smoky restaurant staring at one another like four strangers. Pierre was in an impossible mood; at one moment he would lean over his food like a morbid statue, at the next he would laugh so loudly that the people around us looked up, disturbed. And Simon, who nervously tried to fill Pierre's silences with chatter, sounded more and more as if he were reading one news report after another.

For my part, I felt more and more convinced that the weekend had been abortive from the start. And guiltier then ever because I had had to mislead my mother, because my father would have had a stroke if he knew that I was sleeping on a dirty floor in an untidy student commune, because there had been nothing I could do to stop my roommate from buying those damned contraceptives.

And even more guilty because she had to do it on her own.

'What's your case?' she'd asked after I'd fled from the chemist at the last moment. 'Do you want me to be irresponsible and take no precautions?'

'No, I want you to be respectable and not jump into bed with my brother!'

She'd given me a sharp look, opened her mouth to say something and then burst out laughing. It hadn't been a jolly laugh. And when she'd walked away, the brown paper bag with the contraceptives tucked under her arm, I wanted to cry.

It felt as if she was walking away from me for ever. But I'd had no choice. When I walked into the chemist and saw the assistant, an old lady of my grandma's age, plump and with blue-rinsed grey hair, I'd grabbed my roommate by the arm and tried to pull her through the door. When she tore herself loose, I fled without her.

How the hell could you buy *condoms*, in a grey school uniform and dusty school shoes, from someone who looked like your grandmother?

'. . . and now the last South African policemen are being withdrawn from Rhodesia,' I heard Simon saying. Another news report. He looked at Pierre. 'Never mind, I know what you want to say. What were they doing there in the first place? And why are they being withdrawn so suddenly?'

'Doesn't make me feel particularly peaceful,' was all Pierre said.

'Peace has bugger all to do with it,' Simon said, his eyes on me again. Pierre merely nodded and greedily emptied his wineglass. I had stopped counting the number of glasses he'd drunk this evening. 'The police are removed from one border and the Army is sent to another. Does that sound like peace to you?'

I looked helplessly at my brother. Would he have changed so much in the Army in any case, even without Pierre?

'It sounds like musical chairs to me,' Simon said. 'The police have dropped out but the Army carries on with the game.'

'From politics to war,' I said to Dalena. 'Do you think our conversation is making any headway this evening?'

'The women are bored,' Pierre said to Simon.

'It's got fuck all to do with boredom,' Dalena said. 'It's as depressing as listening to Leonard Cohen all evening. I can't decide between cutting my wrists with the steak knife or setting my clothes alight with the candle.'

Pierre sank forward like someone who had been shot in the stomach and laughed with such a manic expression that my brother and I also started laughing while Dalena shook her head irritably. Although, in the end, she had to join in the laughter.

Later, lying in my sleeping-bag on the dusty wooden floor of a filthy sitting room, I felt uncomfortable all over again. Dalena and Simon had appropriated the only bedroom and closed the door firmly behind them. I didn't know whether Pierre knew that the bedroom was going to be hijacked, but now he and I had to sleep here in the dust, as close to one another – or as far apart – as Dalena and I in our hostel room at night. And the room wasn't nearly as warm as our hostel room. I had become so used to Black River's endless summer that it was really unpleasant to be cold again.

A street lamp threw a dull ray of light through the uncurtained

99

windows. Pierre lay on his back, his hands behind his head as though unaware of the cold. But he had drunk so much wine during the evening that his body was probably completely numb. His breathing was peaceful, but something in his attitude – a tension in his shoulders? – made me suspect that he was still awake. I curled up more tightly, my knees nearly touching my chin, and felt a shiver like a dead finger running down my spine.

'Are you asleep?' Pierre asked.

'Hm-hmm.'

I wondered what he was thinking. Girls always wanted to know what you were thinking, I'd heard Simon complain. *A penny for your thoughts!* If it was something you wanted to share with them you would've done so without being bribed.

'What are you thinking?' Pierre asked. My jaw dropped. Careful, I warned myself, maybe he's mocking me.

'Aren't you scared?' I asked, without knowing where such a careless question had come from.

'Scared?' His eyes were still closed but I imagined I could see his mouth twisting. 'I'm always scared.'

So am I, I thought. But I didn't say so.

'I mean . . . of the Border. Of the war.'

He opened his eyes and stared at the ceiling without replying.

'I read somewhere that eighteen is the ideal age for a soldier,' he said eventually. 'You're old enough to kill but too young to be frightened of your own death.'

There were so many things I wanted to say that I didn't know where to begin.

'But I'll be nineteen next week.' He turned his head towards me. This time I could clearly see the smile. His teeth shone like candles in the dark. 'Perhaps I'm too old to be a soldier?'

'Congratulations.' I moved closer to him without thinking and stretched out my hand to touch his face. Without wondering where this daring had suddenly come from. His cheek felt as smooth and as hollow as a sand-scoured stone under my fingers. When I realized what I was doing I hurriedly withdrew my hand but he caught it like a moth in the air, folded it in his hand and released it on his cheek again. 'So you're a virgin.'

'A what?' A stunned silence next to me, followed by relieved laughter. 'Oh, the star sign.'

I felt my cheeks flushing in the darkness. When would I learn to keep my mouth shut instead of making such stupid remarks?

'What do you want to do with the rest of your life?' he suddenly asked.

'The rest of my life . . .' I mumbled, flabbergasted. My hand fell from his cheek. Most guys asked you what you wanted to do the next evening – and usually I couldn't even answer that. 'Oh, I suppose I would like to travel . . . see as many places as possible . . . read as many books as possible . . . perhaps even write a few books myself . . .'

I had never told this to any boy. I expected to hear his mocking laugh. Or at least see his cynical smile.

'I've also thought of writing a book.' There was not a hint of mockery or cynicism in his voice. 'But I don't think I'll manage it.'

'Oh, I don't know if I'll be able to do it, either,' I said quickly. 'Maybe it's just a childish dream.'

'No.' His voice was still serious. 'You'll do it. I believe you'll do it.'

It was the most beautiful thing anyone had ever said to me. *I believe you'll do it.* All at once absolutely anything seemed possible.

I shifted still closer to him. This time I knew what I was doing. Or maybe not.

'But if you can believe in me, Pierre,' I whispered, 'why can't you believe in yourself?'

He sighed and rolled over so that his face was virtually touching mine. His breath smelt of Close-Up, and underneath the toothpaste, of smoke and wine. He brought his head even closer and kissed me on the forehead. Is this what I wanted? I wondered, flustered. His lips moved lightly over my skin and rested on my eyelids. I had thought that his mouth would be as hard as the rest of his body but it felt like cool, damp cottonwool on my eyelids. No one had ever kissed me like that. As if he wanted to comfort and protect me – but about what, against what, I didn't know.

I wanted to cry but had no idea why. I felt my eyes becoming damp but he didn't take his mouth away. He put out his tongue and dried my cheeks with it, swallowing my tears as if he wanted to eat this inexplicable sadness.

And then? (As Dalena would've asked if I had to tell her.) And then we fell asleep, believe it or not. (No, I don't think there's anything *wrong* with him, Dalena.) Perhaps he'd had too much to drink, perhaps I didn't want him to do anything more, perhaps we were simply too afraid of spoiling the moment. And when I woke the next morning with his arms still around me, I closed my eyes again and pretended to roll away in my sleep.

But I'll probably always wonder if he didn't wake before I did. If he too wasn't pretending to be asleep to give me the chance to move away. Perhaps he was even more scared than I was.

For the rest of the weekend we behaved as if nothing had happened. You were right, Dalena, only Shakespeare's characters want to talk about everything all the time.

I don't like zoos, I decided that Sunday in the Pretoria Zoo where everything seemed as brown and as ugly as Simon and Pierre's army uniforms. They had put on the uniforms unwillingly because they had to hitch-hike straight to Potchefstroom later but they looked so awful in them that I wished the goodbyes had already been said. I wanted to get away from the zoo, away from this grey, dry city.

Pretoria probably wasn't an ugly city. It could even be a pretty city, especially in spring when the jacarandas broke in purple waves over the streets. But at the end of a dry winter when the yellow grass crackled underfoot and all the colours were bleached to a uniform grey by the merciless sun, Pretoria simply wasn't pretty.

It was a warm day, with an almost cloudless sky but an irritating winter wind threw dust into my eyes, made the wide legs of my jeans flap like flags around my ankles and ballooned my halter-neck smock. I felt like an old-fashioned ship with bulging sails, especially because my platform sandals were so high that it seemed as if I was treading water when I walked. But if people gave me odd looks, I comforted myself, it was because they didn't know any better. Or perhaps they were staring at Dalena, who looked more poverty stricken than the workers on her father's farm in a pinafore dress of patchwork material and a kerchief pulled down to her eyebrows.

Didn't the people of Pretoria realize that we could have walked out of the fashion pages of *Seventeen* just as we were?

'I would enjoy working with wild animals,' Dalena mused with her chin on her knees and her eyes fixed on a maned lion tearing a bloody piece of meat apart. 'But not in cages. I wonder whether I shouldn't change my father's farm into a game farm when I inherit it one day.'

Simon gave her a surprised look. 'What makes you think you're going to inherit your father's farm?'

'What else can he do? There's no son and my sisters definitely aren't the kind who want to farm. They need the bright city lights.'

'And you? You're always complaining about being bored on the farm!'

'That's because my father never allows me to do anything! When he's gone I can do as I like.' With the kerchief low on her forehead, her face seemed rounder than usual, like a watermelon with a slice cut out of it every time she smiled. 'My pals from the city can come and visit me every weekend! I could buy a plane and appoint a handsome pilot to ferry them back and forth! I could even learn to fly myself.' She winked at Simon across my and Pierre's heads. 'And I could always keep a flat in the city for dirty weekends like this one!'

'Is this a dirty weekend?' an astonished Pierre asked. 'Why didn't someone tell me?'

'Have you decided what you're going to do next year, Pierre?' Dalena asked, suddenly uncomfortable. 'If you come back from the Border.'

'*If* I come back from the Border?'

'He wants to see the world,' Simon said quickly.

'And I'm making a start by seeing the border of South West Africa,' Pierre said, his voice dripping with sarcasm. 'I suppose you have to start somewhere.'

'But I'm still trying to convince him to swot law with me,' Simon smiled. 'Don't you think he'll make a good advocate?'

Devil's advocate, I thought.

'I can't wait to see the world, either,' I said to Pierre. 'There'll be plenty of time to swot later.'

'She wants to go and live in Paris.' The way Simon said it made it sound as if I wanted to go and live on the moon. 'You can visit her there.'

'Just look for an attic with a pile of empty wine bottles and torn-up poems at the back door,' Dalena teased.

'Don't worry,' Pierre said solemnly. 'I'll find her.'

He was staring straight ahead, not meeting my eyes, but I knew he was speaking to me. My skin started tingling in exactly the same way as when I had heard him say: *I believe you'll do it.* For the first time in my life, I thought, someone was taking my dreams seriously.

'But first I have to experience the fauna and flora of the Border. Not to mention the arms and ammunitions and other attractions.' Pierre's black eyes didn't reflect the laughter of his twisted mouth. 'Perhaps I'll see Angola as well! Two countries for the price of one!'

His voice was unnecessarily loud but all three of us pretended not to have heard him.

Back on the farm, clean after a bath and in bed with a book, ready to switch off the light so that I could catch the slow bus back to the hostel before sunrise the next day, I looked up in surprise when I recognized the tring-tring-triiing of our farm line, two short rings and a long one. My mother answered. Probably one of my father's city friends who didn't realize that on the platteland no one telephoned after nine in the evening unless it was with news of some-one's death.

'Ma-aart!' Ma called, her voice annoyed. 'For you!'

'Who is it?' I asked as we passed one another in the passage.

She shrugged her shoulders. She was also in her nightgown under an old pink towelling dressing gown, its collar covered in white patches from the peroxide with which she bleached her hair.

When I heard Dalena's faint voice my first thought was that she had wrapped a cloth round the receiver so that my mother wouldn't guess who was telephoning me so late at night. Irritably I wondered what game she was playing now.

'It's Heinrich,' the faint voice said. 'He's dead.'

It wasn't a game.

'He shot himself.'

Her voice had become even more indistinct. Or was it the sudden buzzing in my ears which made it so difficult to hear her?

'No . . .'

'With one of his father's revolvers,' said the unfamiliar voice, now as faint as someone speaking from another planet. 'In the head.'

'But . . . why?' That was all I eventually managed to stutter. While other words cracked like shots in my head. *In a month's time it'll all be over. Jolene is not the type to play Juliet-Juliet. If only poor old Hein would stop playing Romeo-Romeo.* 'Why?' I repeated, not expecting a reply.

'Because he always was a bloody coward!' I could hear from her voice that she had started to cry. 'Because he never had any guts!'

'No, Dalena, don't say that!'

I closed my eyes. Saw Heinrich picking up the cocked revolver, pressing it against his soft temple, against the blue veins of his terribly white skin. At this point my mind went blank.

'Don't you think . . .' I opened my eyes when the tears started to burn behind my eyelids, 'don't you think it also takes guts to do something like that?'

'Perhaps.' She sniffed and was quiet for a long time. I could hear her wiping her cheeks impatiently. When she spoke again her voice wasn't quite so unrecognizable. 'But I think it takes more guts to go on living.'

London, 26 January 1993

My Dear Child

It's not as if I look for news about Angola every time I leaf through a newspaper. It's just that it always catches my eye like a shard of glass reflecting the sun in a rubbish heap of other news. The reports usually aren't much larger than glass shards, as if journalists are reduced to whispering when they report about that country, their voices exhausted by a war that will not end.

More than 1,000 deaths have been reported in the Angolan coastal town of Benguela as fighting between government troops and Unita rebels spread to seven major cities. A rebel spokesman said the conflict threatened to turn the country into another Somalia.

When I was a teenager, the war deserved banner headlines and front-page reports. In the meantime other battlefields have hijacked the front pages: Afghanistan, Bosnia, Cambodia, China . . . Iran, Iraq, Israel . . . Lebanon, Mozambique, Nicaragua . . . Somalia and the erstwhile Soviet Union . . . a bloody alphabet of regions where people massacre one another. A world map drawn with bodies every day. Angola heads the list, but no one is interested any longer.

An estimated one million people – one-tenth of Angola's population – could face starvation from next month if relief efforts are further hampered. 'This is far worse than during the first war,' said Mr Philippe Borel, head of the UN World Food Programme in Angola.

The country had been given its opportunity to produce its small war in the spotlight – and then made the unforgivable mistake of carrying it on for too long. 'The Forgotten War', it's called now. Next, please.

Many cities, already shattered by sixteen years of civil war and the colonial struggle before that, lie in ruins now, virtual ghost towns.

I wish you peace for the New Year, my dear child. For you and everyone else in that country and all the countries around you. Or, in any case, the hope of peace, one day, in your lifetime.

M.

OK, You've Got Me

Suna sobbed so loudly that the minister, who was surely used to such wild outbursts of emotion during funeral services, looked up worriedly from his Bible. I sank lower and lower next to her in the pew while more and more people stared at us. Grief was grief but too much was too much. Suna's whole body shook as if every sob was a landmine exploding inside her. Her hands were clenched so tightly against her mouth that they looked bloodless.

Maybe I was being unfair, maybe I would be struck by a bolt of lightning this afternoon and be thrown on top of Hein's coffin in the open grave because I didn't trust my own friend's tears, but her attitude was simply too melodramatic for me – as if she imagined herself to be the heroine in a Hollywood tear-jerker. Juliet after Romeo had taken the poison. *Blubbering and weeping, weeping and blubbering. O, she says nothing, sir, but weeps and weeps* . . .

The minister spoke more and more loudly to be heard over Suna's sobs in the stormy voice with which Afrikaans ministers are evidently born. He sounded like the sea on a tempestuous day, rushing and roaring, louder and softer.

'Therefore,' the minister bawled, bearded like an angry sea-god, and let the word hang in the air for a brief moment, 'by request of Heinrich's grief-stricken parents . . . we will read a few verses today . . . which might have been more appropriate . . . on a happier occasion.' The same heavy silence after each phrase. 'Because the death . . . of this beautiful, talented boy . . . in the prime of life . . .' – A longer, heavier silence – '. . . also means a new life . . .'

Suna's excessive behaviour had by this time infected other schoolgirls. From every part of the crowded church there were the sounds of sobbing and sniffing. Was it possible that Heinrich's suicide – over a girl! – could have changed him into a hero for a bunch of girls who previously had been barely aware of his existence?

Not that I wasn't sad. It was just that something larger than my sadness bothered me. I listened to the schoolgirls who were crying as if they were being paid to show emotion, and I looked at Heinrich's parents who sat staring as emotionless as fish at the sea-god's high throne. I listened to the message which broke like waves over the pews, and I looked at Mr Maritz who had let his shiny Brylcreemed head sink on to his broad chest. ('A dreadful blow to the school,' he had murmured in hall on Monday morning. 'A dreadful blow to the *school*.') I closed my eyes and tried to find comfort in the minister's comforting words about a new life but in my mind's eye I still saw the hostel matron constantly wiping her damp cheeks with a soggy pink tissue. (It might've been tears she was wiping away but it was probably sweat.) I couldn't understand why not one of the adults – neither one of the teachers nor Heinrich's parents or the minister – had used the word 'suicide' even once.

'"For our gifts of knowledge and of inspired messages,"' the sea-god read through his beard from the Bible, '"are only partial."' Was it my imagination or were the stormy waves showing signs of abating? '"But when that which is perfect is come, then what is partial shall disappear."'

Perhaps it was only the minister's voice which had stirred so much emotion in Suna. Now that he sounded calmer, her weeping had also become less dramatic. She was crying soundlessly now, with only a slight shiver shaking her slender body every time the voice in the pulpit was raised.

Dalena, on Suna's other side, sat with her left hand over her eyes so that I couldn't see whether she was crying or asleep.

'"What we see now is like a dim image in a mirror; then we shall see face to face. What I know now is only partial; then it will be complete –"'

I glanced at Suna who sat motionless next to me, her cheeks wet with tears, her hands defencelessly open on her lap. And suddenly it was no longer difficult to share in her grief.

*

'When were you afraid of death for the first time?' Dalena whispered, her voice urgent in the dark.

She caught me unawares, as so often before. I was certain that she was already asleep. I was lying with my eyes open, thinking about Heinrich in that deep, dark hole and feeling much more grief than I had at the funeral the day before.

'I've always been afraid of death,' I whispered. 'As far back as I can remember.'

She lay unmoving in her bed, her face invisible.

'Or perhaps not. When I was small I wasn't so scared of death. I probably accepted that I would have to die one day . . . but I was terribly scared that I would die too soon. Before I had lived properly.'

I was still scared of dying before I had lived properly. I looked at Dalena and waited for her to say something. But since Heinrich's death on Sunday she spoke far less than usual.

'I was scared of missing everything – all the things that grown-ups do.'

'Like what?' Dalena whispered, her voice as urgent as before.

'Like . . . going dancing . . . in a long evening gown.'

It was difficult to see her. The moonlight lay like a pool of water between the two beds but the rest of the room was dark.

'Or of seeing the world. I remember reading a series of books about children in other countries – wonderful, thick, blue books – I dreamed about a different country every night.'

It was quiet in the other bed. The curtains moved when a breeze as soft as a breath blew the scent of blossoms through the open window. It hung in the air for a moment like a riddle – what did a tree look like that smelled so sweet? – before the heat overcame it. Spring had come, I realized. Now the unbearably hot summer was in sight.

'I'm still scared that I'll die before I can read all the books I want to read. But at least I no longer try to bribe the Lord. When I was small I used to pray every evening: "Please, dear Jesus, keep me alive long enough and I'll become a missionary in Black Africa and convert thousands of unbelievers . . ."'

'I was afraid that I would die a virgin,' Dalena whispered unexpectedly. 'That's all.'

I held my breath. Was she finally going to tell me what had happened in Pretoria? I hadn't been able to ask, not after the news about Hein. I was afraid it would sound as if I didn't respect the dead.

'And now . . .' I still couldn't ask it. 'Are you still scared of that?' She made me wait a long time before she replied.

'It's probably not so bad to die before you've had *sex*,' she sighed eventually. She said *sex* as if it was a dirty word. And then added absently, 'Or before you've gone dancing in a long evening gown. After all, if you haven't done it, you don't know what you're missing.'

She'll tell me, I comforted myself, I simply had to be patient. Some evening or other, in this dark room, she would tell me everything.

'Who was the first person close to you who died?' she asked.

It wouldn't be this evening, I realized. The breeze blew against the curtains again. I pulled the sheet up higher over my body. Perhaps it will get cooler during the night, I thought hopefully, perhaps I won't wake up damp with perspiration again tomorrow morning.

'My great-grandfather. But I was too young to be sad. All I remember is that the funeral was quite fun. A real Boer funeral with yellow rice and raisins and enough food to feed the entire town. My great-grandmother mourned for seven years, only wore black and purple. And then she died – exactly seven years after his death – so I don't remember her in any other colour.'

She said nothing. Usually she was the one who chattered at night and I was the one who lay quietly and listened. Now I felt like a second-rate little actress who had landed in the spotlight because something had happened to the star.

'But when I was about six an old lady lived next to us in a dark house which always smelt of cooked cabbage and cat pee. I can't even remember what she looked like but I remember the day she died. I heard her servant telling our servant how cold her feet were that morning. When she made the bed and felt the old Missis' feet, she knew death was near.'

For years I touched my feet every morning when I woke. I still did it occasionally when no one could see me.

'And then my farm grandma died, about three years ago. In her sleep, just like that. She hadn't even been ill. It was a great shock to me, probably because it had never occurred to me that she was old enough to die. But when your grandma or your grandpa dies, your school pals think, oh well, it's no big deal, and you're a bit ashamed to show your grief . . .'

I was starting to enjoy our reversed roles. I wasn't doing so badly, I decided.

'But I found it awful. It was the first time I'd thought about it that way . . . first my great-grandfather and mother, then my grandpa and grandma, then my mother and father . . .' Someone walked over my grave with a heavy tread. That's what happened when you shivered for no rhyme or reason, my dead grandmother used to say. 'Then I really realized for the first time that my turn was coming too.'

She was lying too quietly.

'Dalena . . . ?' I hoisted myself onto my elbow. 'Dalena?'

She had fallen asleep. I wondered how long I had been talking to myself like a fool.

In Shakespeare's time no one evidently thought you were silly if you talked to yourself. *Romeo and Juliet* was full of monologues and soliloquies as Miss Muffet was constantly reminding us in her English class. 'And here we have another *so-lilo-quy*!' she exclaimed in ecstasy every time, as if Queen Elizabeth had unexpectedly entered the muggy classroom.

'"O, here will I set up my everlasting rest,"' I groaned and slowly sank back, my hand on my heart, the way death scenes were always played in romantic movies. '"And shake the yoke of . . . of" . . . whatever . . . "from this world-wearied flesh."' I stretched my arms languidly in the dark. '"Eyes, look your last! Arms, take your last embrace! And lips . . ."'

'What the fuck are you doing, Mart?' Dalena muttered sleepily.

Nothing was the way it had been in Shakespeare's time, I decided. These days you felt like an idiot if you were caught in a soliloquy.

'Look at her!' Suna hissed behind her hand. 'Just look at her flirting with Pine! And poor old Hein not cold in his grave!'

Dalena and I glanced covertly at one another and then looked over our shoulders to a table against the opposite wall. Where Jolene and Pine were committing the eighth deadly sin, according to Suna, by holding hands in the Portuguese café. Three weeks after Hein's death.

'What did you expect?' Dalena's attention was back on the plateful of chips in front of her. 'That she would mourn for seven years?'

'She has no shame!'

I had to take a quick swallow of my cold drink not to laugh. Suna sounded exactly like my Grandma Farmdam when she'd caught sight of a woman in a brief dress. The same words, the same shrill tone of voice.

'Come on Suna, there's no need for you to get so worked up.' I was also eating chips, the strict diet of the previous week something of the past, but I was drinking a cold drink with just one calorie to make up for the countless calories swimming on the plate in front of me like invisible germs. 'You can sit on this side of the table if you don't want to watch Jolene's shamelessness.'

But Suna remained where she was, in a purple and red dress with a halter neck, dazzling as a peacock opposite Dalena and me who looked like drab ostriches in our school uniforms. And I wondered for the umpteenth time whether Suna realized how lucky she was not having to stay in the hostel. After nine months I still envied every child in my class who could go home in the afternoon.

To walk into a kitchen, open the refrigerator and take a swallow from a milk bottle (and quickly wipe your mouth before your mother could catch you with a milk moustache), to take bread out of a bread bin and to switch on Springbok Radio to listen to the serials and *Good Advice* and *Jet Jungle* while doing your homework. To drop your school uniform on the floor and put on a bright halter-neck dress and hear your baby brother and the neighbours' boys playing cowboys and crooks in the garden. To know you need never hear another bell until you were dropped at school the following morning . . .

'I wonder what poor old Hein would've said if he –'

'If he hadn't messed with Jolene, he wouldn't be dead today,' Dalena said brusquely. 'If you want to play with fire . . .'

She should know. If playing with fire had been a school sport, my roommate would be the victrix ludorum. I looked back at Jolene and Pine again.

'They make quite a handsome couple,' I said almost deliberately. 'Both kind of tall and dark and . . .'

'. . . reckless and randy,' Dalena muttered through a mouthful of chips. 'He's about the only guy in the school with a pair of hands big enough to get a grip on her boobs.'

'Well, if someone had committed suicide because of me,' Suna said irritably, 'I would behave with more dignity.'

'Don't worry about it,' Dalena said. 'It's highly unlikely.'

'Did you hear that they've caught Patty Hearst?' I asked quickly before Suna could tell us yet again how grateful she was that 'poor old Hein' had become her friend in the last months of his life. Just a friend, she always said, no more. As if she wanted us to believe that perhaps there had been something more.

'Genuine?' Dalena raised her head with momentary interest from the plate of chips in front of her.

'Yes, here it is, in today's paper.'

Suna rolled her eyes. I was the only child in the school, as she said accusingly, who ever bought a newspaper. But the children who weren't in the hostel could presumably read their parents' newspapers – even though I couldn't imagine Suna ever being caught with her fingers in one. And the hostel children's heads were so befuddled by the bells that they had evidently lost all interest in the outside world.

'"The search for Patty Hearst,"' I read to them, '"the newspaper magnate's heiress who was abducted nineteen months ago and has since become a revolutionary, ended in San Francisco the day before yesterday when she opened her apartment door to American detectives and said: OK, you've got me."'

'All my heroes are caught by the cops,' Dalena sighed. 'Last month it was Breyten Breytenbach, now it's Patty Hearst.'

'That says something about your heroes,' Suna said pertly.

'And who in hell are your heroes? Doris Day and Pat Boone?'

I was staring at my roommate in surprise. 'I didn't know you liked Breyten's poetry?'

'I know fuck all about Breyten's poetry,' my roommate said, as I should have expected, and Suna giggled behind her hand as she always did when Dalena swore. 'I like revolutionaries that's all.'

'Well,' I said, and maintained a meaningful silence, 'that's not the only news in the paper.' Another moment of silence, kept the way the minister had on the day of Hein's funeral, to take Dalena's attention off her plate. In vain. 'They say the Army is in Angola.'

'Tcha, I don't believe it,' she said without looking up. 'It's just gossip.'

'That's what I thought at first.' But I had also thought about what Pierre had said that first day in his dark room. 'Now I'm beginning to wonder.'

Dalena wrote to my brother 'somewhere on the Border' every night but as yet we had heard nothing from him. He had, in any case, warned us before his departure that his letters would be censored. And still Dalena believed that she would know – through telepathy, intuition, Radar Love or whatever – if Simon wasn't where he was supposed to be.

'You can't believe everything you read in the newspapers, Mart.'

Dalena licked the tomato sauce off her fingers and pushed away the empty plate. I pushed my plate away as well, indescribably proud of my self-control because I had left six chips untouched.

'Exactly. The newspaper says it is "categorically denied" by the South African government. That's what makes me wonder.'

'Oh, come on,' Suna said. 'Why would the government lie to us?'

Suna's stupid question upset me so much that I ate the six remaining chips. And looked away guiltily at the Portuguese who again stood like a sweating statue behind his counter next to the fan which blew a breeze over his sad face every few seconds. Behind him hung the poster of the beach with the palm trees.

'And now LM Radio is closing next month,' I sighed. 'I'll miss the music.'

'What kind of thing do you write to him?' I asked, cross-legged on my bed in the hostel room with a clean sheet of paper on my lap.

'Oh, hang in there, *min dae*, not long to go.' Dalena lifted her pen, turned a page in her pink writing pad and started on her third page for the evening. 'You know, the usual stuff you write to a guy on the Border.'

'I don't know what the usual stuff is. I've never had to write to a guy on the Border.'

'You wrote to your brother before he went to the Border, didn't you?' Her pen moved across the pink paper, seemingly without volition. 'What's the difference? He's simply in another place now.'

'Exactly! How can I write to him if I don't know where he is! What the hell does "somewhere on the Border" mean?'

Dalena looked up frowning for a moment, her large mouth slightly open. I could see what she wanted to ask. *What's your case?* But then her hand started moving again and she looked at the paper as if curious to see what her pen was going to write. It was after study period, the half-hour before lights-out when the noise in the hostel always reached an earsplitting climax as if everyone were desperately trying to cram a whole day's conversation into the last few minutes.

'And I promised Pierre that I'd write to him as well!'

I had never written to any boy except my brother. I had never written to any other human being except my brother and my grandmothers. Oh, and to a pen friend in Paris, years ago:

Bonjour Dominique, I live in a big and beautiful country on the continent of Africa. We don't have lions in our streets or gold on our pavements, but we have many other wonderful things to behold. If you ever come to visit me, I shall give you a piece of biltong, which is raw meat, but don't worry, it has a lovely taste. Perhaps you can bring some French wine for my father, who drinks a lot . . .

If only it was that easy to write to Pierre.

'Man, just write what you do every day.' Dalena turned a page. Page four. How did she manage it? 'The things that happen every day.'

'Come off it, Dalena. Surely Pierre doesn't want to know how I brush my teeth every morning and learn *Romeo and Juliet* by heart every afternoon! Nothing ever happens in my life!'

'This isn't a classroom test, Mart!' Her deep voice rose two decibels in annoyance. 'It's just the idea that someone is thinking of him!'

'It's easy for you. You can write all kinds of sweet words to

Simon which mean bugger all! I can't write Pierre a bloody love letter!'

'Maybe he'd like a love letter.'

'Well, he won't get one from me.'

Doggedly I bent my head and started writing. *Dear Pierre*. No. Too . . . intimate. I tore out the page. *Hello Pierre*.

I looked at the bare bulb in the ceiling, at Dalena's bare brown legs below the shapeless T-shirt of my brother's in which she slept these days, at my paler legs under the absurd pink shortie pyjamas which my mother had given me the previous Christmas. As if I were six years old.

Where are you, I wanted to write. Have you had to shoot at someone yet? Has someone shot at you? Have you seen a terrorist? Or a freedom fighter? *Aren't you scared, Pierre?* That's what I wanted to write.

I live in a hot, boring town on the continent of Africa, I wrote, more for myself than for anyone else. *The sun shines virtually day and night. The vegetation is blindingly green and the people are plagued by dangerous mosquitoes and poisonous snakes and massive moths and the biggest, scariest spiders you can imagine. When I came here for the first time I was given porridge and baked tomatoes for supper. But it's not as bad as it sounds . . .*

London, 11 February 1993

My Dear Child

It's unbearable to grow old alone. And it's worse in a foreign country.

I drink too much cheap wine every evening and eat thick slices of white bread with chocolate spread while I obsessively write down my story. If I carry on like this I won't only be a lonely old woman but a drunken, fat and lonely old woman.

Today Nelson Mandela celebrates the third year of his release. And this week my son celebrated his third birthday in this foreign country. My son with the thick, dark, rumpled hair which always makes me think of seaweed, and the pouting mouth of a pin-up – and of his prickly grandmother – and a plump, white bottom which fits into my hands like two melons. Will I ever be able to love a man so unreservedly?

And then, thinking of my beloved son, I read a newspaper report which freezes my blood.

Pretoria – Five people died in incidents of unrest yesterday, including a baby who was necklaced in Evaton near Vereeniging. The baby's body was found with a man who had also been necklaced, the official police unrest report said today.

Are they burning babies now? Toddlers with plump, black bottoms? Children the age of my child?

How can I even contemplate returning to that country of grief and godless behaviour?

No.

Love
M.

More Nights in White Satin

'Now this is what I call an historic occasion!' Dalena's eyes glowed like green glass in the light cast by the bedside lamp. 'It's much more important than the opening of the stupid Language Monument!'

I had to agree with her. We lay on our stomachs on the carpet listening to the last LM Hit Parade, both deeply impressed by the importance of the occasion. The station was closing tonight after thirty-nine years.

'Almost forty years!' I whistled through my teeth in amazement. 'Almost as old as my pa!'

'Well, I don't know about your father, but mine has certainly never listened to LM. And now he'll go to his grave without ever having done so. Shame.'

She suppressed a yawn. It hadn't been easy to convince her mother that we had a vitally important reason for going to bed later than usual on this Sunday evening.

'My father isn't much of a radio listener either, except for *Squad Cars* on Friday nights. And rugby, of course. Oh, and if there's an election he always stays awake all night to listen to the results.'

I couldn't have said why because the results always remained more or less the same. But he said that he remembered the elation of the first victory every time. He was too young to vote in 1948, but he'd heard over the radio that Jan Smuts had lost his seat. It wasn't such joyful news for my mother's United Party father. That was probably why my mother still refused to stay up with my father on election nights.

I tapped my fingers on the fitted carpet to the beat of Leo Sayer singing 'Moonlighting' in a funny girl's voice. Through the filmy mosquito netting we'd hung across the open French doors, the moon licked at the sugar-cane fields with long tongues of light. On the balcony around the house several outside lights were burning and caught in each circle of light was an eddying cloud of huge moths and other insects. Beyond the mock-Victorian wrought-iron railing the too-neat garden lay in the dark, the flowers planted with military precision, the shrubs close-cropped.

But there were other insects I couldn't see – insects and spiders and larger and more dangerous animals – out there in the dark. Invisible eyes watching Dalena and me where we lay in our night-clothes on the carpet, the loose pages of the Sunday paper strewn carelessly about. I had read a report earlier in the evening about black farmworkers somewhere in Rhodesia who had murdered a white farmer and his family because he'd treated them 'like kaffirs'. And one about a landmine explosion somewhere in South West Africa. Evidently the work of well-trained terrorists.

'Shouldn't we close the curtains?' I asked hesitantly.

'No, it's too hot.'

I reached for the front page of the newspaper again. Forty thousand people had attended the official opening of the Language Monument on a granite hill outside Paarl. The monument had been erected, as our Afrikaans teacher had repeatedly reminded us this year, to celebrate the centenary of the sweetest language on earth. (That was probably why it looked like a tall white candle on a stone cake, Dalena said.) It was so hot that about fifty of the birthday guests fainted but the remaining thirty-nine thousand, nine hundred and fifty evidently suffered the heat with the famous endurance with which their forebears suffered the English concentration camps. So that they could tell their grandchildren one day that they had been there?

'Just imagine, one day we'll be able to tell our grandchildren that we listened to the last broadcast from LM Radio!'

'They won't know what LM Radio was,' said my practical room-mate. 'They won't even know what LM was. Lourenço Marques is getting a new name.'

Just as I was about to become blue, number fifteen on the Hit Parade was announced: 'Love Will Keep Us Together' by Captain and Tennille. Dalena cheered me with a broad smile as she hummed along with the radio. Shortly afterwards, when the first streaks of lightning flickered in the distance, we both sang loudly, carried away by Gloria Gaynor's version of 'How High the Moo-oo-oon', our eyes on the moon which seemed low enough to touch if you stood on tip-toe in the sugar-cane fields. By the time that Lovey's heart-throb, David Cassidy, came up with 'Get It Up For Love', the thunder was rumbling above the roof.

'Don't you think we should close the curtains now?' My voice was more urgent now. After ten months in this region I was still more afraid of thunderstorms than of murderous farmworkers and cold-blooded terrorists of whom, after all, I'd only read in newspapers.

'Dalena?'

She nodded abstractedly. She was still lying on her stomach next to me, her hands on either side of her face, her thoughts somewhere I had never been. Hastily I closed the yellow-flowered curtains, grateful that she didn't tease me because I behaved like a Cape chicken every time I landed in a Transvaal thunderstorm.

'I'm a bit worried,' she said. 'I'm overdue.'

It was so unexpected that for a moment I didn't know what she meant. Then thunder cracked like a rifle shot on the balcony and I jerked with fright. At the thunder and at her words.

'You . . . you mean . . . ?'

Would I ever, when I heard something vital, have something to say which was worth recalling? As at every other time – the day of the contraceptives, the night of Heinrich's death – I could only stutter.

'I'm sure it's not necessary to worry yet,' she said like someone trying to douse a blaze before it turned into a full-scale fire. 'I'm always irregular.'

'Irregular,' I repeated like a child learning to pray.

'Once I skipped three months . . . but the doctor said not to worry, it'll be fine when I'm older.'

'You've seen a *doctor*?' I asked, shaky with relief.

'More than a year ago.'

'Oh.'

'But as I said, it's not necessary to worry yet.' She sat up quickly, crossed her bare brown legs, tucked her brown hair behind her ears with impatient fingers. 'I've skipped a month, that's all. It's often happened before.'

'Yes but . . .' If she didn't tell me tonight, she would never tell me. Or was she busy telling me?

'It didn't matter before . . . except that it's irritating when the wrong time of the month never comes at the right time of the month.' Her lips quivered as if she wanted to smile but her eyes remained dark as if a shadow had fallen over the green glass. 'And then I was still a virgin.'

'But didn't you and Simon . . .' A wave of indignation rose in my throat like bile. 'Don't tell me you didn't use the fucking FLs!'

I was so angry that I could even swear without blushing. Dalena was the one who blushed, the one who stuttered. She touched her mouth and looked away.

'We did . . . we tried . . . but . . .'

'Did you or didn't you use the stuff?' As merciless as my attorney father when he cross-questioned a witness.

'The bloody thing burst!' she exclaimed.

'*Burst?*'

My own balloon of indignation burst with an earsplitting crack. Or maybe it was another roll of thunder. The smell of wet earth pierced the closed curtains, filling the whole room. Number six on the Hit Parade, the familiar radio voice announced, is 'Una Paloma Blanca'. An idiotic song, I'd always thought, and knew then that I would probably hate it for the rest of my life.

'But they're electronically tested. They're not supposed to *burst*!'

Dalena dropped her face into her hands and her shoulders shook. I had never seen her cry.

'You sound exactly like your brother!' Her shoulders shook. When she looked up I saw that she was laughing. I didn't know whether you were supposed to laugh about something like that. She was laughing so much that she had difficulty in speaking. 'That's . . . exactly . . . exactly what he said! When he sat there with the torn condom on his thing . . . I wish you could've seen it! And all he could say . . . all he could say was "*It's not supposed to burst!*"'

She's hysterical, I thought in panic.

'Sorry,' she said, gasped for breath and wiped the tears from her cheeks. 'I'm sorry . . . but it was so funny!' And her body shook again.

When she eventually calmed down she looked questioningly at me. The green glass was still wet but not completely clear. 'What makes you think that anything on this earth ever happens the way it's supposed to happen?'

There was an unfamilar rasp in her deep voice.

'I thought the first time would be madly romantic . . . and very painful. You know, blood on the sheets the next morning, all those things you always hear. And then everything happened so quickly . . . I was still waiting for the pain when it was all over. He wasn't even properly inside me when he came.'

I had never dreamt that I would hear it like this. I had accepted that she would tell me in the dark, in our dark hostel room. And here I was hearing it in the light, in her own yellow bedroom, in the weak light of the bedside lamp and the flickering lightning flashes through the curtains with the big yellow flowers.

'It was a bloody awful disappointment,' she sighed. 'There was hardly any blood, nothing to write home about, and he was in and out so fast, I thought he hadn't done it properly and I was still a virgin.'

There was a drumming in my head like the drumming of the rain on the balcony.

'So we tried again. It wasn't difficult to get him worked up again. He was like a cocked gun. All he needed was a finger on the trigger . . .'

She started laughing again. I didn't know why. I had never felt so excluded. Not even on the day she walked away from me with the contraceptives in the brown paper bag.

'The second time he lasted longer. I was still waiting for it to hurt. Maybe I've been on horseback too often, but there was no pain. It was very . . .' She shut her mouth and compressed her lips like a long zip in her face and stared at the carpet for a long time before looking up. 'When he pulled out, the condom was torn. Perhaps we were too excited to put it on properly. Or perhaps we moved too much. Maybe it was simply a dud.'

'But Dalena . . .' *Aren't you scared?* I wanted to ask but stopped myself in time. For a while we listened in silence to the rain and the radio. Misty's 'I'm too Much in Love' was at number three. ' "I'm too much in love" ' Dalena murmured, her eyes on the carpet, her voice a rasp which abraded my heart again. 'I like that.'

I thought of Pierre, of what had happened between us on that night in Pretoria. Not that much had happened, of course. But if either of us could have thought less and acted more easily – if we could have been a little bit more like Dalena and Simon – things might have turned out very differently. The last remnants of my self-righteous indignation evaporated.

We sat motionless for a long time until the last number one on the last LM Hit Parade was announced with a roll of drums and a blare of trumpets: 'El Bimbo' by the Bimbo Jets!

Almost as bad as the one about the white dove.

The radio voice, which had become as familiar to me as my own family's voices, informed us that early the following morning the old station in Lourenço Marques would be replaced by a new one in Johannesburg. The new station would be known as Radio Five. 'Goodnight,' the voice said for the last time, 'to you and to you and to you . . . and may God bless you . . . always.'

'Don't worry.' I said eventually. 'You don't have to worry yet.'

White roses bloomed like miracles in Dalena's hands. She folded pieces of crêpe paper – as adroitly as a magician pulling silk scarves from his fingertips – and as I watched, they changed into roses which looked so real that I had to stop myself from smelling them.

Unexpectedly we had emerged as the champions in this flower-folding game, even though we were both struggling to concentrate on it. Or perhaps exactly because we were incapable of concentrating properly. We worked as fast as two machines – I cut the paper, she folded it, I twisted a thin piece of wire around the end to form a stem – while the other girls sweatily tried to produce the perfect paper rose for the matric farewell. 'As though there was a bloody cup to be won!' Dalena had exclaimed an hour ago, the last time she'd opened her mouth.

She didn't look at her fingers – as if they were no part of her – but stared at a spot on the wall of our hostel dining hall while the pile of paper flowers in front of her rose higher and higher. I had tried to talk about the thing that was bothering her. But she either changed the subject or pretended not to have heard me. And as usual I didn't have the courage to say what I wanted to say in broad daylight.

We were sitting on the bare floor of the dining hall which was becoming unrecognizable before our eyes, decorated with tall cathedral candles, white crêpe-paper roses and mirrors draped in white sheets. The theme for this matric farewell was my suggestion, written anonymously on a piece of paper as all the standard nines were asked to do: Nights in White Satin. In honour of my first (and only) unforgettable kiss from Ben. And in memory of Hein at whose party it had happened. *Nights in white satin, never reaching the end* . . .

'It's quite funny to see boys in the dining hall, isn't it?' Dalena gave no indication that she had heard me. 'That just shows you how deprived we are. Or is it depraved?'

'Both,' she said without a smile.

While the girls folded paper flowers and laid the tables, the boys did the jobs that they regarded as masculine enough, like posing on ladders to give the girls an opportunity of admiring their bums. Ben stood on one of the tallest ladders, as self-assured as a tightrope walker. I became dizzy just looking at him. What was the next line again? *Letters I've written, never meaning to send?*

'I miss old Hein,' I sighed.

Not a word from Dalena.

'I'm glad I'm not in matric now,' I tried again. 'Not that I'd mind finishing with school! But I don't have a clue which guy I would've invited to the farewell.'

Suna was with a group of girls in the centre of the floor, giggling as they judged the boys' bodies. Pine had been awarded the highest marks so far but I didn't agree. He was too muscle-bound, too heavy about the shoulders for my taste, not tall enough. I preferred a slender, taller type of body, more like . . .

'Or what I would've worn!' I said before I started wondering again why we heard so little from Simon and Pierre. And why the letters we did get all sounded like impersonal newspaper reports. Luckily I didn't have to worry about a breathtaking outfit now. We standard nine waitresses were all expected to wear shiny white dresses designed by Miss Potgieter, as unimaginative as only a needlework teacher's designs could be. My mother had to make mine last week which resulted in a major mess.

Ma was the kind who pricked her finger when sewing on a button. By two o'clock on Sunday morning, an empty packet of Cameos and an overflowing ashtray next to Grandma Fishpond's old sewing machine, one swear word had erupted from her mouth. 'Who the shit does Miss Potgieter think she is? Coco Chanel?'

When I'd tried on the finished product the next morning, I wondered whether I shouldn't fall ill just before the farewell. The hem was too high above my ankles, too short for a long dress and too long for a short dress, the seams were too tight and askew across my breast. 'It flattens my tits,' I moaned. 'Look, I can't even breathe properly!' 'Never mind,' Ma had comforted me, 'it'll look better by candlelight.'

When I took it off I saw that she had left a cigarette scorch on the shiny material which would cover my bum. 'Never mind,' Ma consoled me again, 'everything always looks better by candlelight.'

'What do you hear from Simon?' I asked Dalena without expecting an answer.

'I had a letter the day before yesterday,' Dalena replied without looking at me, placing another flower on the pile.

'Why didn't you tell me!' I cut the paper resolutely. It seemed as if I had to squeeze everything out of her these days. 'What does he say?'

'Tcha, what he can say that won't be censored? It sounds as if they lie in the sun all day baking their balls.'

'Is that all?'

'Hmmm.'

'When are you going to tell him?' I asked, too annoyed to consider what I was saying.

'What?' But she looked at me as if she knew what I meant.

'That you're overdue.' Now I was the one who looked away.

'Are you out of your fucking mind!' Her voice cracked like a pubescent boy's. 'What can he do about it! Except worry!'

'What can you do about it? Except worry?'

'It's not necessary to worry yet,' she murmured while another perfect paper rose flowered under her fingers.

It had begun to sound like an incantation. *It's-not-necessary-to-worry-yet*. Or a counting out rhyme. Eeny, meeny, miney, mo. Da Nang, Nha Trang, Qui Nhon . . .

Someone had organized it so that Ben and I served at the same table. (Dalena widened her marble eyes like taws when I asked her about it.) Luckily we had been so busy all evening serving food and taking away empty plates that there had been no opportunity to start a conversation. He did mumble, blushing, that I looked pretty in my shiny outfit. (My mother was right. *Anything* looked better by candlelight, even this badly fitting satin dress with the black hole on the bum which made me feel like a branded ox.) And I mumbled, blushing, that he didn't look too bad, either.

The standard nine boys' outfits had also been designed by the Coco Chanel of Black River. White shirts in the same shiny material as the girls' dresses – with wide sleeves and large pointed collars – and black trousers. Most of the boys simply wore the trousers of their Sunday suits but Ben had bought a new pair of pants, low on the hips and tight across the bum with wide Oxford legs from which a pair of platform shoes of black patent leather protruded like the wet snouts of two dogs. He looked taller and older and more attractive than I'd ever seen him look.

I caught my own eye in one of the mirrors we'd borrowed from a shop selling glass in town. I looked like an angel on a Christmas card, I decided (not without admiration), with a head of blonde curls created by the electric curlers of Suna's mother, sky-blue eyelids courtesy of Dalena's sisters' make-up and a beautiful hydrangea-pink mouth coloured with my own new lipstick. Actually, I had to admit, all the girls looked like angels. Probably because the candle-light reflected the shiny white outfits over and over again in the mirrors, changing everything around us into a silvery-white glitter as if we were standing in the middle of the Milky Way.

I was proud of what we'd achieved with the dull dining hall, I realized with surprise. It was the first time anything had happened in this school to make me feel proud. It had to be the alcohol affecting me.

Of course we weren't allowed to serve alcohol, but someone had spiked the standard nines' fruit punch in the kitchen with something much stronger than fruit – again Dalena merely widened her eyes when I wanted to know more – with the result that the waiters and waitresses were, by that time, in various stages of inebriation, from faintly giggly to dangerously unsteady on their feet. It was the exemplary ones, especially, who had never drunk alcohol before – and so didn't have the faintest idea why the fruit punch was so delicious that evening – who had dropped a few plates by then.

The poor matrics, I'd remarked. It must be terrible to watch a crowd of standard nines getting more and more sloshed while you sipped cold drinks. It wasn't necessary in the least to feel sorry for them, Dalena assured me, the whole crowd would go on to an all-night party after the official farewell where there would be enough liquor to keep a dozen elephants drunk for three days. Black River wasn't a school exactly rich in tradition, but one of the few traditions which was kept was that matric pupils were not supposed to remember their matric farewell.

When Mr Maritz tapped a glass calling for silence, I hurried to the kitchen with a last pile of dirty plates and quickly swallowed another glass of punch. Back against the wall of the dining hall, Ben suddenly stood too close to me, his smell so sharp in my nostrils that I wanted to sneeze. The overpowering smell of Jade East blended with something like mint near his mouth – and whatever it was that made the fruit punch so delicious.

'I'm very grateful tonight,' the headmaster began his notorious speech which evidently remained unchanged year after year, 'that this school still produces the kind of pupil of whom parents and teachers can be proud.'

Ben's hand rubbed against mine and my whole body went rigid. Even my jaws went rigid. A half-chewed Beechie lay like a pebble in my mouth.

'Afrikaner boys and girls who haven't succumbed to the Communist onslaught of seditious music and liquor and drugs, who haven't lost their Christian National identity . . .'

Ben's fingers slid teasingly slowly over mine. Was he too shy to grasp my hand firmly, I wondered nervously. Or was this what they meant by foreplay?

'I'm very grateful tonight,' the headmaster said but his voice sounded more worried than grateful as one of the standard nine boys rushed out of the hall, his hand over his mouth, 'that our school still produces the kind of boy who is eager to fight on the Border, the kind of boy who is willing to lay down his life for his country . . .'

The candlelight threw eerie shadows over Mr Maritz's face. The enlarged pores on his nose made me think of a photograph of the surface of the moon which I'd seen in a *National Geographic* in my father's study. If the dining hall had changed into the Milky Way, then surely the headmaster could look like the moon? I felt laughter rising in my throat but swallowed it with the Beechie.

And the hostel matron was beaming like the sun, I thought in amazement, her round face shiny with pride and a heavy gold chain shimmering around her neck. A gold medal was pillowed on her gigantic breasts like a child's head. I swallowed and swallowed but realized that I wouldn't be able to contain my laughter much longer.

'I'm very grateful tonight that our school still produces the kind of girl who is eager to fulfil her modest role as wife and mother, the kind of girl who is submissive and chaste . . .'

To hell with foreplay, I decided, grabbed Ben's hand and clutched it almost convulsively but it didn't help. I began giggling so uncontrollably that the headmaster was quiet for a brief, very brief moment, but long enough for the exemplary Ben to jerk his hand back in terror, as if I'd burnt him with a cigarette. At that moment I realized he was not like Pierre at all. He would never be anything like Pierre.

And for the second time that evening I unexpectedly saw my reflection in a mirror – but this time I only saw a slightly drunken angel in the middle of a home-made Milky Way. And suddenly I was so sad, I wanted to weep.

London, 21 March 1993

My Dear Child

According to my mother, who still reads *The Stars Foretell* in the newspaper each morning, every human being is inextricably bound to one of the elements. Some, like me, drift through life like aquatic animals because they always want to be somewhere else. (According to my mother and the stars, that is.)

Sometimes you swim against the current, my mother wrote in a recent letter, *simply to be otherwise. Your father thinks that's why you left the country, to conquer a brave new world. But I think you simply chose the line of least resistance, drifting with the current as usual.* (I know, Ma, I've always maintained that I'm a coward.) *That's why I believe you'll always be able to keep your head above water, Mart. That's what makes you a survivor.*

A survivor? Like my mother? And the Voortrekker women who bashed barefoot across the Drakensberg? Sometimes it's easier to carry on with something – a difficult choice, a difficult route, even a difficult life – than to turn back half-way and acknowledge that you were wrong.

And Simon always lived with his head in the clouds, according to Ma. Even if later those clouds were no more than marijuana smoke. (According to me, that is.) But was it the stars which determined that he would contain such a large, empty space that he would become as weightless as a cloud?

Or that Dalena would burn her fingers in her own fire?

Which brings me to Pierre again. Who still bars my path like a rock whenever I want to make the easy choice, every time I want to drift with the current. Then I come up against his inflexibility, then he forces me to ask the questions he would've asked.

I'll always remain grateful to you for that, Pierre. You hid in that room where it was always night, our own Orpheus in his underworld, and used your tongue like a lyre to seduce us. You taught us to question.

But you probably know what happened to Orpheus. He was torn to pieces – *and all the king's horses and all the king's men couldn't put Humpty together again.* It's my son's favourite nursery rhyme. Presumably because it ends with total destruction.

We went to the play park in Kensington Gardens today. It was supposed to be a beautiful spring day but as usual the London weather had refused to listen to the previous evening's TV forecast. I wanted to get away from the merciless sun of Black River but after another wet, cold, dark winter in a strange land I feel like a mermaid imprisoned in an underwater cave. Now I yearn for a sun which will make the heavens burst into flames, a fire to cleanse my conscience.

No, I haven't forgotten the date. When the police shot sixty-nine people in Sharpeville that day, I was even younger than my son. Just as innocent, just as guilty.

Love
M.

No Point in Upsetting People Unnecessarily

'"Angola was declared independent by the Portuguese yesterday!"' I read the front page report as if I were announcing a Springbok Radio serial. *The Game Ranger! The White Veil! The Secret of Nantes!* '"In the midst of large-scale chaos!"'

I lowered the newspaper which I had borrowed from Bull's-Eye and waited for a reaction. Dalena was fiddling with the buckle of her school shoe as though she hadn't even heard me. Suna frowned, at least, but it might simply have been because the sun was in her eyes.

'"According to sources the MPLA has bombarded Luanda's water pipeline with mortars and put it out of action,"' I read on, less dramatically.

'My,' was Suna's only reaction.

And Dalena was as quiet as she had become during the past month.

It was recess but we weren't sitting against the the lavatory wall. In summer we preferred a shady spot, like most of the other children in the playground. It was a case of first come first served, like the twelve slices of bread in the dining hall. Today we had been quick enough to park ourselves under the overhanging roof of some temporary classrooms.

'I wonder what it means,' I said. 'For us.'

Dalena gave me a fed-up-to-the-back-teeth look.

'You're obsessed with Angola,' she had accused me from her bed a few evenings ago.

'But it's our neighbouring country! What happens there –'

'It's the Porra's problem,' she informed me with an impatient click of her tongue. 'We've got enough troubles of our own.'

'Who's to say it's not our problem as well? Who's to say poor Simon and Pierre aren't in Angola by now?'

'Are you going to start that again?' she'd sighed.

'But the English newspapers say –'

'What do the English newspapers know?'

My roommate's obtuseness made me so mad that I put the pillow over my head.

'"'The hellish danger of Communism,'"' I quoted from another front page report, '"'with the chaos and disorder it carries in its wake, has reached South Africa's doorstep. It must be stopped, not only for the sake of Southern Africa but for the sake of the Free World,' Mr P. W. Botha, Minister of Defence, said last night."'

I looked towards the square where the country's flag was hanging limply in the sun as usual. In the distance a few boys were listlessly kicking a soccer ball. A prefect with brightly polished shoes tripped over Suna's outstretched legs and shook her head angrily as she walked away.

'That comes of walking with your nose in the air,' Suna mumbled and stuck out her tongue at the straight back in the prefect's blazer.

'Don't you see?' I said to Dalena.

'What?' She looked pale with a thin layer of sweat gleaming above her large mouth.

'He says the Communists must be stopped. What do you think that means?'

Dalena didn't reply.

'"Minister Botha warned that South Africa must be prepared to spend more than R1,000 million per annum on its military safety. As long as the world remains in the state it is, he said, South Africa has to pay the price . . ."'

Dalena's fingers flew to her mouth. Her face was paper white with a yellowish cast.

'What's wrong?'

'I feel sick,' she mumbled and with her hand held like a mask over her mouth, she jumped up and ran off.

'Shit,' I said, so startled that I didn't even realize I was swearing.

'What's wrong?' Suna asked, too surprised to giggle, as Dalena disappeared round the corner in the direction of the lavatories.

I also felt sick. This was the way it always happened in books. The heroine fainted or became nauseous and then you knew she was expecting a baby. It was fear that was making me feel sick, I realized, fear which clutched at my insides with a dirty hand and sharp nails.

'What's going on?' Suna asked again.

'Something she ate upset her.'

I could barely recognize my own voice. Suna gave me a suspicious look. Or was it my imagination?

'I think it's the samoosas we bought in town yesterday,' I painted myself into a corner. 'So I'll probably be sick as well.'

'Well, never mind,' Suna said consolingly. 'It can't be that bad. Perhaps you'll miss Miss Muffet's test on Shakespeare.'

'But I like . . .'

My voice faded into silence. I was the only child in the class who liked Shakespeare, Dalena had said only last week. Commiseratingly, as though I had an incurable disease.

It's not necessary to worry about it yet, I said to myself. But I knew it was no longer true.

I had invited Dalena to spend the weekend with me. The time had come to discuss the whole thing. If she continued to behave like a mule, I would have to force her in the right direction.

But what was the right direction, I wondered, when we were lying next to the swimming pool. How do you force someone to talk about something happening in her own body? Let alone what was going on in her head.

We were lying in the shade because the sun felt too dangerous even for my roommate that day. On our stomachs, I with a book, she with her eyes closed. But I couldn't concentrate on the book. Her body in the black swimsuit hadn't changed, I decided, had even got a little thinner. She didn't eat as greedily as she used to.

'What are you staring at?'

I was startled when I saw the green of her eyes showing through her lashes. Her face was turned to me, her cheek on the towel.

'We've got to talk, Dalena,' I said quickly, before she could intimidate me with one of her looks again.

'Must we?'

'Yes.' Nervously, because she didn't pretend not to have heard me as she usually did. 'How long since : . . ?' My voice stopped but now I had to ask what had to be asked: 'How long are you overdue?'

'More than two months. But I'm still hoping I'm not really pregnant.' Her eyes were closed again, I saw, squeezed shut. 'Maybe it's just a false alarm, because I feel guilty, because I worry . . . I've heard it can happen – a sort of hysterical condition.'

'You're not the hysterical type, Dalena,' I said as gently as I could. She turned her head away. I stared across her sweaty body to the banana trees quivering in the steaming heat. When she spoke again her voice sounded as if it was coming from far away, further than the hills where the furthest banana trees and the wilder, more luxuriant vegetation fused into a blue haze.

'No, I suppose not.'

'What are you going to do?'

'Do?' She looked at me again, her eyes questioning. Or pleading?

'When are you going to tell Simon?'

'Simon doesn't have to know, Mart!' Her voice was so hoarse that it frightened me. 'No matter what happens. He doesn't have to know.'

'But . . .'

'You must promise me you won't tell him.'

'But Dalena . . .'

'*Promise me, Mart!*'

'But Dalena, you can't –'

'I can do as I like!' This time her own voice frightened her. She looked away at the swimming pool. 'Sorry. I didn't mean to shout at you. It's just that . . .'

I shook my head, at a loss.

'What *can* you do, Dalena?'

'I don't know.' She stared at the swimming pool as if seeking an answer in the water. 'But I'll come up with something.'

'You mean . . .'

Now I had to keep my eyes on the water as well. But I couldn't say it, even though I wasn't looking at her. I was staring at a frangipani flower floating on the water.

'I can't have a baby now, can I?' Her voice had become as pleading as her eyes. 'I can't get married now, Mart! And I can't rear a baby on my own.'

'What about . . .' I blinked my eyes against the glittering reflection of the sun on the water. 'Adoption?'

'My father will throw me out of the house if I tell him. And my mother will have another nervous breakdown and land in hospital. That's her way. That's how she controls us all.'

'Your sisters? Couldn't they help you?'

'What do they know?' A grimace of contempt. 'Blooming Holy Virgins! With a whore for a youngest sister.'

'You're not –'

'No. They don't have to know. Rather that they never know.'

She pushed her hair behind her ears with that impatient gesture which had become a nervous habit recently. Like Miss Muffet who was always scratching her scalp with a long pink fingernail, slowly while we were doing boring grammar, faster and faster when she became excited about literature. 'Attention, class, we are reaching a climax!' She made Shakespeare sound like sex, Dalena had said long ago, when she still said things like that. When she hadn't minded if her hair hung in her face occasionally.

'Have you tried to work out precisely how far gone you are?'

'I don't know how. And I don't want to think about it.'

'Well, if you want to do something, you'll have to do it soon, otherwise . . .'

Otherwise what? What did I know about such things?

Unexpectedly she jumped up and dived into the swimming pool. Her body barely made a splash in the water as if she had become as light as the drifting frangipani flower. When she burst through the surface again, after three lengths underwater, I had taken a decision.

'My mother has this thick medical book, about sex and birth and stuff like that. She hides it in my father's study so that Niel and Lovey can't read it.' Dalena hung on to the edge of the pool, her wet hair clinging to her head, and stared into my eyes. 'Of course she doesn't know they can recite the juicy bits in their sleep by now.' Not even the trace of a smile on her face. 'I'll fetch it this evening, then you can read all about it, everything you want to know.'

'All I want to know, Mart, is what I must do to stop being pregnant. And I'm sure your mother's book won't be able to help me with that.'

I didn't know whether she had heard how sharply I drew in my breath because she had disappeared under the water again.

'Just listen to this!' Ma said, a section of the Sunday paper open on her lap. '"The Minister of Foreign Affairs was questioned in London about South Africa's 'alleged involvement' in Angola."' Ma cleared her throat portentously. '"In reply to the question about how many South Africans were fighting in Angola, the Minister said: 'I wish to reiterate that there are no South African troops in Angola.' The audience of some 250 laughed . . ."'

Ma was quiet, waiting for my father to respond.

'Did you hear that, Carl?'

'Hmmm,' Pa said without looking up from his section of the paper.

They sat in two armchairs on either side of a low, wobbly table. On the table, which Simon had made in woodwork class years ago, stood two glasses of white wine on either side of an abalone shell piled high with cigarette butts. Niel and Lovey were lying on the carpet studying the comics in the paper as though they had to write a test on them the following day. I was reading *Catch-22*, which Pierre had lent me some three months ago, but as at the swimming pool the previous day, I was having difficulty in concentrating on the story. My thoughts kept wandering to Dalena, who was somewhere in the house staring at a thick medical book as if she also had to study for a test – the first one in her life she would prefer to fail.

'Do you still want to tell me the Army isn't in Angola?' Ma's voice was looking for trouble. 'Listen to this: "Another questioner said that if South Africa had nothing to hide, as the Minister stated, why were South African newspapers forbidden to report even on accounts in overseas papers of the alleged South African involvement in Angola. The Minister said the situation in Angola was confused and the news reports were unreliable. Under these circumstances there was no point in upsetting people unnecessarily. The audience laughed again."'

Pa looked at Ma over his reading glasses, his eyebrows two angry question marks.

'What are you trying to say, Marlene?'

'They're lying to us, Carl. That's what I'm saying. The government is deceiving us!'

Pa's jaw dropped at the acrimony in Ma's voice. Then he evidently realized that he looked foolish and closed his mouth with a snap as if he had taken a bite at something invisible in the air. 'Well, if they're doing that, they'll have a very good reason.'

'I'm hungry, Ma,' Niel whined. 'When are we going to eat?'

'When I've finished reading the paper and finished my drink,' Ma said, her voice still rancorous, and lit a cigarette.

She was wearing a small, red, buttoned shirt in a stretch fabric over a Cross Your Heart bra which made her fairly large breasts look like two cones, and a floral skirt which hung down to her ankles. Pa was wearing pale blue shorts with knee-high pale blue socks and white shoes. That was what they called casual wear for a Sunday – a little more elegant than casual wear on any other day.

In the kitchen Maria was softly singing something in her own language while she opened the two taps in the sink. She was 'on duty' over the weekend, as Ma put it. Actually she was nearly always on duty.

'But Ma . . .'

'Drop it, Niel,' Pa warned from behind the newspaper. 'Think about all the children who have nothing to eat today.'

Niel lifted two fingers and made a rude gesture at Pa's newspaper. Lovey clapped a hand over her mouth, her eyes wide. Every time she moved her head, she shimmered like an angel in a school concert. Last night, on her way to her first official evening party, she had strewn handfuls of gold sequins on her hair. She wanted to look like Gary Glitter, I assumed, not like an angel.

Last night, with the help of Ma's medical book, Dalena and I had worked out that she could be thirteen or fourteen weeks pregnant.

'"The development of a fertilized egg into a human being is one of the greatest wonders of the world,"' I'd read aloud. '"Each one of the thousands of people born every day, starts life in a fraction of a second when a sperm no larger than a fiftieth of a millimetre, penetrates an egg the size of a pinpoint."'' She lay on the other bed in my room with her back towards me but I knew she was listening. '''Of the some 500 million sperm which start the race towards the egg, great numbers are simply lost, while some are attacked by the woman's immune system and others die of exhaustion. Only about 200 are strong enough to reach the goal where the leader fertilizes the egg."'

'The victor ludorum!' she'd sighed. 'Is it really necessary to make sex sound like an obstacle race?'

Pa looked up from his newspaper. 'Boy, but this Breyten Breyten-bach can make the language sing!' he whistled through his teeth. 'Communist or no,' he added absently. 'Have you seen what he said in court before being sentenced, Mart?'

'Not yet, Pa.'

'Well then, listen to this. You're always saying you want to write one day.'

'''"In my heart, my lord, the motive for my actions was always love of my country."''' Pa gave full value to each word but especially the last five. '''"It might be paradoxical . . ."''' Do you know what paradoxical means?'

I nodded quickly, not wanting to listen to one of Pa's long explanations now.

'''". . . but for me the issue was the continued existence of our nation, an existence with justice as Van Wyk Louw formulated it, the content and quality of our civilization . . ."'''

Pa looked up to see whether I was still attending. I nodded again and he read on eagerly. Somewhere over his voice, I heard Maria singing in the kitchen again. It sounded like a lullaby, or perhaps something she had learned in her church. Pa didn't think much of Breyten Breytenbach's politics but as an attorney, as someone trained to appreciate the spoken word, he was entranced by the peroration.

But nothing – not even the charmed words of a poet or a black woman's sweet singing voice – could hold my attention that morn-ing. I stared at the bald patch on my father's head which was usually hidden under one of his absurd bits of headgear. Behind him, above the bar counter, hung a Spanish bullfight poster. His own name shone among the bullfighters' exotic names, as out of place as a piece of local sausage in a bowl of paella: Carl Vermaak. He'd had it printed in Spain years ago, the only time he'd been overseas.

Ma liked calling this room a family room. No one needed a lounge these days, she said. All those chairs standing around so stiffly simply for the minister's seat to warm them once a year! No, a family room was far less trouble. It didn't need to be kept so tidy. And if, eventually, we were able to receive television in this area, the family room would immediately become a TV room, Ma had already decided. Then we could have supper on trays while we watched TV. Far less trouble.

She wasn't lazy, Ma liked saying, she merely believed in the conservation of her own energy.

At the moment, the future TV room consisted of Pa's 'bar corner' (which had taken up far more than a corner and threatened to spread to the rest of the room like some monstrous creeper), a few old armchairs with different covers (mementoes of various lounge suites from various periods in our lives), dozens of photographs of us four children which Ma had hung so haphazardly on the walls that it seemed as if she'd been drunk and wearing a blindfold when doing so, and a whole lot of delicious monsters in plastic pots. (As if the world outside wasn't green enough.) Ma might not have been able to write a book about interior decoration but she could get anything to grow in a pot. If she planted a feather, my father liked to say, a chicken would come up.

' " 'My lord, allow me to end by quoting from a poem,' " ' Pa was still reading enthusiastically, ' " 'wonderful, flaming words which were ignited ages ago but will always remain burning because they come from the depths of a human being's experience and compassion – and therefore they belong to all of us . . .' " '

Outside, behind the open glass sliding door, the sky was an unnatural blue like a picture which a child had coloured too brightly. Next to the veranda a bunch of poinsettias hung from a tree like scandalous red underwear on a circular drying line. Further back were the bare trunks of pawpaw trees, the bare branches and the blush-pink flowers of frangipani trees and the banana plantations shamelessly exposed to the sun. This was a wild, lascivious world, I realized again that morning.

'"'When I was a child, I spoke as a child, I understood as a child, I thought as a child,"'' Pa read with a beaming face as if he himself had conjured up the words in a packed court. '"'When I became a man, I put away childish things . . .'"'

My mind drifted back to the previous evening. '"At twelve weeks the foetus is about seven and a half centimetres long and weighs between twenty and thirty grams,"' I'd read as Dalena lay on her back and stared at the ceiling. '"It has started to look like a real baby although the head is still comparatively large in proportion to the little body. The fingers and toes are already —"'

'How big is seven and a half centimetres?' Her voice was morose, her eyes still on the ceiling.

'About as big as my ring finger?' I'd guessed.

She raised her hand and stared absently at her fingers.

'"The fingers and toes are already formed but still webbed. The baby can kick, bend its arms and open and close its hands —"'

'It's not a *baby*.' Dalena had turned her back to me again. 'It's no bigger than an insect!'

'Do you want me to read some more?'

'Not now.' She gave an exaggerated, not quite convincing yawn.

I looked at the hump of her back. Her breathing became regular almost immediately like someone falling asleep under an anaesthetic. Not very convincing, either.

"Night,' I mumbled. 'I'll leave the book in the bedside cabinet so you can read it tomorrow . . . If you want to.'

And then I sat and stared at a drawing of a woman who was three months pregnant, her stomach cut in half lengthwise, the foetus exhibited like a toy in a shop window. It did look rather like an insect, I thought. A largish insect in a small plastic bag filled with water . . .

'"'Meanwhile these three remain: faith, hope, and love.'"' By this time Pa was completely carried away by his own performance. Lovey was enjoying the unexpected concert while the sun played with the gold sequins in her hair. Niel listened impatiently, unsure whether it would be impolite to read Prince Valiant's cartoon adventures while Pa sounded as if he was conducting a prayer meeting. Even Ma listened, her head on one side behind the screen of cigarette smoke which she slowly exhaled through her nose. ' " 'And the greatest of these is love.' " '

Pa lowered the newspaper, virtually breathless, and shook his head. 'Wonderful, flaming words,' he murmured, his mouth full of unwilling admiration. 'Bloody clever to quote the Bible, hey?'

London, 27 April 1993

Dearest Child

When I think about Jan van Riebeeck – which fortunately doesn't happen very often – I see him as a clumsy, over-eager schoolboy holding a tray of orange segments next to a rugby field. The kind who would love to be on the field but isn't good enough to be chosen for the team and is therefore asked to take refreshments to the tired players. Half-time oranges.

Not really a worthy task for the 'founder of a nation', would you say? And yet that's what Jan van Riebeeck had to do, according to the history books of my youth, when he landed at the Cape of Storms and Good Hope on 6 April 1652. He was asked to found a victualling station for tired sailors on the ships of the Dutch East India Company and I've always had this image of him holding a tray of oranges, standing knee-deep in the water, as it were, half-way between West and East.

He wasn't asked to 'found' a country. (In any case, how does one found a country? Like a company?) He wasn't asked to 'plant' a colony, like a tree, or a time bomb to be set off by the sheer weight of numbers, in some distant future. No one expected him to build a nation. What tools are required for that, anyway, except suitable sexual ones?

And what, I'm wondering tonight, as incessant questions flower on paper, what would Jan van Riebeeck have said if he could have seen his victualling station in April 1993? A horse of another colour – a bloody horse staggering above an abyss – its mouth wrenched by politicians despairingly clutching the reins. That's the picture we're getting *here*, in any case, in newspaper reports which give me sweaty nightmares while my little boy, sleeping next to me, apparently also gallops through bloody dream landscapes on wild ponies. The difference is that he does it with a smile.

South Africa's political leaders will meet tomorrow for a final push to avert the chaos that has threatened to engulf the country since the assassination of South African Communist Party leader, Chris Hani. They will have to nail down an agreement that will set the country on the road to majority rule within six weeks.

President F. W. de Klerk said this week that it would be the most crucial and decisive period in South Africa's history.

'We dare not allow a handful of violent people to turn the country into a Yugoslavia,' Mr de Klerk told Parliament.

Sleep well, my child, while you still can.

Love
M.

Everything Is Under Control

Everything in the doctor's waiting room looked old and dilapidated. The orange plastic chairs, the magazines with curled-up covers, the green carpet which in some places was as bald as the lawn in a public park. Even the Christmas cards on the reception desk looked as if they had been received ages ago, to be displayed just before Christmas each year.

On the dirty-white wall opposite me hung two framed prints of Cape Dutch gabled houses and a poster of a chimpanzee on a lavatory. He wore a shirt and tie and trousers pulled down over his hairy legs. His sad brown eyes reminded me of the Portuguese café owner in Black River. *The heart is a lonely hunter.*

I picked up the previous day's newspaper from the magazine table because I was too ashamed to look at the other people in the waiting room. (Surely they must all be aware of what Dalena was at this very moment asking the doctor behind the closed door of his consulting room.) I paged through the newspaper, determined to find something on which I could concentrate, even if it was only a photograph. But each picture changed into Dalena's face, Dalena looking at me as she'd never looked at me before. *Just suppose . . .*

I had known her for almost a year. I knew every expression on her face, from that impossibly wide smile when she was excited to the yellowy-green sheen in her eyes when she was irritated, but I had seen her scared only twice. That day, next to the swimming pool, when she had told us about the way things sometimes turned dark, I hadn't understood what she was talking about. Last week in our hostel room, I'd known what she meant.

'It's time you saw a doctor,' I'd decided when it eventually penetrated that my brave roommate didn't have the courage to do it on her own. 'I'll go to Pretoria with you next week.'

She looked up from the letter she was writing. Her eyes brimmed with so much gratitude that I looked away guiltily.

'Would you?'

What else could I do? I knew she would refuse to see a doctor in Black River or any neighbouring town. And I couldn't run away again.

'Yes. I've already told my mother that I want to go and buy Christmas presents as soon as the holiday starts.'

'Christmas presents?'

'Well, if you can think of a better excuse . . . We can go by train and stay over with those pals of Pierre's. I'll phone them tomorrow.'

'You've got it all worked out, haven't you?'

Her smile opened like a fan. But in the past month her eyes had always been more grey than green, as if the marbles had been smudged by a sweaty hand.

Below our bedroom window I could smell the shrub that had made me want to cry that first evening in the hostel. Moonflowers, Pa had said, because they spray their scent on the moon at night. Beware of an attorney with the soul of a poet, Ma always warned, but Pa thought that a poet with the soul of an attorney would be even more dangerous.

Just suppose, I wondered, just suppose . . .

And then she asked it.

'Just suppose . . .' It sounded as if she were forcing the words through barbed wire in her throat. 'Just suppose I'm pregnant?'

I looked so dismayed that she burst out laughing and quickly, in a high, bright voice, started speaking about something else.

The Directorate of Publications had released the latest list of un-desirable publications, I read in the newspaper in the waiting room. The list included the following books: *Manual do Guerrilheiro Urbano* by Marighella; *Group Sex* by Dean McCoy; *Some Thoughts on Chairman Mao* by Thuso Mofokeng; *Gay News*, Nos 97 and 80 . . . While I read and re-read the titles, the door of the doctor's consulting room opened, slowly and creakily as in a horror movie. Dalena stood there looking at me. Expressionless.

I couldn't get out of the waiting room fast enough. I dropped the open newspaper on the orange chair and rushed after her without giving the other patients a glance. In the lift she stared intently at the flashing red lights above the door, as if we were two strangers who happened to be caught in this confined space, while I waited for her to say something. It was only when we were outside and walking in the direction of Paul Kruger's statue on Church Square that I could bear it no longer: 'What did the doctor say, Dalena?'

'I've conceived.' The strange word in her mouth startled me more than its meaning. No one except our pretty biology teacher ever used words like 'conception' and 'menstruation' and all the rest. 'About fifteen weeks gone.'

'What now?'

'Don't worry. I'll come up with something.' She walked as if she were scared of missing an important appointment. It wasn't easy because the pavements were so crowded that she had to push people out of her way to pass them.

'Have you discussed it with anyone?'

'What?'

'What you want to do?'

'No.'

'Well . . . don't you want to speak to me about it?'

'No.'

'Dalena!' I grabbed her arm, breathless, startled to feel the bones under my fingers. I hadn't realized how thin she'd become. 'Hang on a minute. What's the big hurry?'

She stopped so suddenly that a man with an Afro hairstyle which surrounded his head like a black cloud bumped into her and muttered a curse. What had happened to the spirit of Christmas, I wondered, dismayed.

'The shops close in an hour.' I could hear that she was also breathless. 'We still have to buy Christmas presents.'

Speechlessly I stared at her.

'That was the excuse for coming to Pretoria.' She gripped my elbow as if I were blind and guided me firmly on. 'We can't go home empty-handed!'

I stumbled along, speechless and blind, but unfortunately not deaf. Bits of Christmas songs swirled out of every open shop door like driftwood: *Oh, what fun it is to ride on a one-horse . . ., Rudolph with your nose so bright, won't you guide my . . ., I'm dreaming of a white Christmas . . .*

I lay stretched out on my back while the sun stroked my body like a soft, warm hand. Not that any hand had ever touched my body in that way – low over my stomach, high over my thighs, even between my legs. It felt as if I were naked, as if I were slowly submerging my lower body into a lukewarm bath.

Just imagine lying naked on a beach and not caring if other holidaymakers stared at you! I sometimes dreamt that I was the only naked person in a crowd but it was the kind of dream I always had to struggle out of, sweating, as if out of a deep, dark hole, until I eventually woke up, endlessly relieved. I didn't know why it didn't feel like a nightmare today, but I suspected it had something to do with the inexplicable attraction I felt towards Pierre.

I resisted the temptation to touch the top of my new bikini to make sure that I wasn't really nude. The sand enfolded me like a soft mattress with comfortable hollows for my bottom and my shoulder blades. The murmur of the sea deafened all other sounds as if I had two huge shells pressed to my ears. I should have turned on to my stomach to ensure an even tan. But I felt too lazy to move a muscle.

Dear Dalena, I wrote in my imagination (as I did every day at the seaside), *You won't recognize me when you see me after the holiday! I'm browner than Pierre!* (OK, perhaps not as brown as that, but browner than I'd ever been in my life.) The previous year I hadn't picked up much of a tan because I was so in love with Nic that all I wanted to do was sit in his kombi and watch him surfing. Now there was another girl decorating his kombi. Which didn't bother me at all.

What did bother me was that I never really saw him surfing. Surfers in their black wetsuits all look alike once they're in the water. All you can really see from the beach is a collection of black flecks against the waves. You don't have a clue as to which fleck you're supposed to admire.

Of course I never told Nic this.

His new girl probably wouldn't, either. She looked like Goldie

Hawn, all blonde curls and cute smiles. *I don't know whether it's sour grapes, Dalena, but when I listen to Nic now, he sounds so . . . I don't want to be nasty but I could swear he's had too many blows on the head from his own surfboard. I can't help wondering what Pierre would have to say about him.*

I sat up when a sea breeze lifted the big straw hat off my face. She'd said she would come up with something, I kept assuring myself. She'd also said that she would write to me. And I had heard nothing from her. *Just suppose . . .*

The evening before I'd accompanied her to the doctor, I was eventually brave enough, or desperate enough, to call the thing by its name.

'How are you going to do it, Dalena?' I'd whispered louder than usual because it was hissing with rain.

'How am I going to do what?'

'How are you going to get rid of the baby?'

'It's not a baby,' she'd whispered. 'It's a foetus. *If* there's anything at all.'

A flash of lightning lit the hostel room for a moment. She lay in a small bundle on her bed. Like a foetus, I thought.

'Well . . . what are you going to do . . . *if* there is something?'

'I've heard you can go to Swaziland. Or Lesotho.'

'For an *abortion*?' When I had eventually managed to say it, the rumble of thunder made my voice inaudible. I didn't know whether I felt disappointed or relieved. 'But how will you get there? How will you find out . . . ?'

'Don't worry, Mart,' she'd whispered. 'Just enjoy your holiday.'

Dear Dalena, I wrote later, in the house by the sea, *It's Christmas Eve and I yearn to see my brother. And Pierre, oddly enough.*

In fact, I couldn't stop thinking of Pierre, but I wasn't ready to tell this to my roommate. She would jump to the conclusion that I was in love with him, while I was becoming convinced it was something else. Something more, I would have said, but she wouldn't have understood what I meant. I wasn't even sure what I meant myself.

To think they'll be in the bush tomorrow, chewing dog biscuits while our Christmas table will be groaning with turkey and cold meats and twenty different salads and side dishes!

Do you know I haven't wanted to read a single newspaper during this holiday? I've only wanted to lie in the sun and forget about the world. But it's impossible to miss the posters in the cafés! Have you seen how many South African soldiers are being killed 'In the operational area'? Have you noticed that's what they call it these days? No longer 'on the Border'. It makes me wonder.

I lowered my pen and listened to my family's voices in the living room, the younger children noisy with excitement, the adults more sober and subdued. How could I ask what I had to ask on paper? Suppose the letter fell into the wrong hands? (*Is there any news from Swaziland? What is the weather like in Lesotho? Do you still have that tummy problem – or are you better?*) What my roommate was planning this time was more than just another naughty prank to be kept secret from her parents. It was something no one must ever know about, it was . . .

'*Illegal*,' I said aloud as if it were a French word I was trying to pronounce for the first time.

It felt as if I had burnt my tongue on the sound. Could they send her to prison for it? Did my silence make me an accomplice?

'Ma-art!' my father called, his voice unnecessarily loud. His brag ass voice, as Mother would say when the family was out of earshot.

It was almost eleven o'clock. Almost time for my father to slip away, unnoticed, to put on a creased plastic coat, a torn plastic hat on his head (even sillier than the caps he usually wore), and a false white beard which hooked over his ears with elastic. To play a perspiring Father Christmas as he did every year, for all the cousins who were still stupid enough to believe in a Father Christmas who looked as if he'd wrapped himself in a red shower curtain. After which Grandpa Farmdam would read from the Bible, as he did every year, and pray for almost as long as the headmaster did. And then we would all sing 'Silent Night', as we did every year, while Ma wept without restraint. When Ma heard 'Silent Night' or the 'Wedding March' or the national anthem she always became tearful.

'It's because of all those who are still with us,' she had tried to explain to me, sniffing, one Christmas, 'but might not be with us in a year's time.'

'So you're doing some crying for those who still have to die, Ma?' Niel asked, frowning.

'I suppose you could put it like that,' Ma had replied, her mascara smudged black under her dark eyes, which she dabbed with a crumpled tissue extracted from beneath her bra strap.

Niel had stared at her with the same dark eyes and suddenly called out: '*In anticipation!*'

'What's that mean?' Lovey had wanted to know, almost as inquisitive as I was about unfamiliar words.

'Like in "thanking you in anticipation" at the bottom of a letter,' Niel had said, his eyes still on Ma's wet face. 'If Ma starts crying now about all the people who still have to die, she won't have to cry so much once they're dead.'

'I suppose you could put it like that,' Ma had sniffed. But she hadn't explained what her problem was with the 'Wedding March' or the national anthem.

'Ma-art!' Pa called again. 'Come and read us a bit of French!'

I decided to ignore him. It was one of his party tricks to take out a bottle of French wine and to ask me to read the label even if no one understood a word. Even if I didn't understand any of it.

A few years ago I'd acquired a set of cassettes to teach myself French (*in anticipation*, I'd thought, of the attic in Paris) but never advanced any further than a few simple sentences: *Je m'appelle Mart Vermaak*. Which sounded so absurd that I'd decided to give myself a new name should I ever land in Paris. Martine Verlaine was my favourite: *Je m'appelle Martine Verlaine*.

But all Pa really wanted was for me to impress a few people with my mock French accent. It was hardly difficult, as everyone who came to visit us knew even less French than I did. All I had to do was to purse my lips and to keep my voice breathy. Pa thought all French girls sounded as if they were having sex all the time.

I long for you as well, I wrote to my roommate. *You may think I'm an idiot but I've been wanting to cry all evening. Not like my mother about everyone who might not be with us next Christmas, but about everyone I'm missing right now . . .*

'Mart isn't wearing a hat,' Niel said when Pa lifted his glass for a toast to the Christmas meal.

This was after Grandpa Farmdam had prayed for almost five

minutes. It was supposed to be a brief grace but Grandpa Farmdam had no notion of brief prayers. He had started by asking a blessing for every single dish, from the turkey and the cold meats, the bean salad and the beetroot to Ma's famous trifle into which she put so much sweet wine that even the children were slightly tiddly when they got up from the table. And then he prayed for those in authority, for each and every cabinet minister, for all the ministers of the church and headmasters and Defence Force officers in the country, and for every young soldier far away from his family . . . And just as we thought he'd finished, he added that he might as well ask our Heavenly Father to help us chase the Communists in Angola into the sea.

'Put on your hat, Mart,' Pa said and lowered his glass.

'Sheesh, Pa, it looks so silly!'

'We're all looking silly,' Pa said, as if that was a reason.

I stared at the stupid paper hat in front of me while everyone at table stared expectantly at me – Ma and Pa and Grandpa Farmdam, Pa's sister and brother-in-law, Ma's sister and brother-in-law, Niel and Lovey and six other children between the ages of three and thirteen – each one wearing a ridiculous paper hat. As if the whole family worked for a circus, I though rebelliously. Where had the tradition originated that we had to look like clowns while we ate our Christmas meal? With a sigh I stuck the blue and red paper hat on my head and lifted my glass of sweet sparkling wine.

'I want to propose a toast to Simon.' Pa was wearing a purple and yellow paper hat, torn on one side because his head was so big. 'And to all the other soldiers who have to be somewhere on the Border today.'

'In the operational area,' I muttered but only Ma heard me. And she was biting her lip so hard not to cry that she couldn't utter a word. A green and orange paper hat perched precariously high on her new, uncombed hairstyle. She had left her can of hairspray at home and decided to let her natural curls go their own way in the damp sea air. The result was a wild tangle which made her look easily ten years younger, but she kept touching her head in an uncomfortable way. She was afraid, she'd confessed that morning, kneeling in front of the stove, that perhaps she looked a little too *wild* for her age.

Meanwhile Pa's toast, like Grandpa's grace, had got out of hand. He was making a speech about all the dangers besetting our country, but if we stood together, like the Voortrekkers of old, we would overcome, like the Voortrekkers of old. I gave Ma a quick glance because I knew what she thought about the so-called banding together of the Voortrekkers. The Afrikaners had always been a contrary bunch, Ma said, with more wilfulness than wisdom. But her bottom lip had whitened from being bitten.

Niel held the glass of sparkling wine in front of his nose as if it were a rose he wanted to smell. Exactly like Pa, I realized. And every time Pa said something amusing – not exactly screamingly funny – Niel and he laughed with their heads thrown back at exactly the same angle. Occasionally you looked at those close to you as if your eyes were spotlights, lighting them blindingly. I had always thought Simon was Pa's son because he looked like Pa. I had never noticed that Niel was really the one who spoke Pa's body language.

Lovey's paper hat, purple and red and much too big, had sunk so far down on her forehead that she had difficulty in seeing her food. The smaller children wore triangular cardboard hats with elastic under the chin but Lovey refused to be reckoned among the smaller ones any longer. She was counting the days to the end of the holidays when she could go to high school with Niel and me.

'Only two more weeks,' she sighed. I sighed as well because I didn't want to be reminded of school, especially not on Christmas Day. 'Then Simon comes home, doesn't he, Ma?'

The turkey turned bitter in my mouth.

'Then Simon comes home . . .' Ma rubbed the soft blue-white skin under her eyes.

'I don't understand the Army!' I burst out, the piece of bitter turkey still in my mouth. 'Why couldn't they send the boys home two weeks earlier!'

'The Army knows what it's doing, Mart,' Pa warned, his voice quiet and reasonable, as if he were speaking to a difficult client.

'But Simon said that previously they . . .'

'Previously things were different.'

'But surely the terrorists won't attack them on Christmas Day!'

'I don't think the terrorists will pay any attention to Christmas Day.' Pa's face flushed slightly and his voice sounded less reasonable. 'Not forgetting the Cubans.'

'Tcha, our Army can send those terrorists to glory just like that!' Niel's knife swished through the air to illustrate his point. 'That's what our cadet teacher says. And he was on the Border himself!'

'Yes, we'll show them they musn't tangle with a Boer.' Pa lifted his glass as if he wanted to propose another toast. 'As the English discovered at the turn of the century.'

There is no need to panic, the Prime Minister had said in his Christmas message last night. *Everything is under control in the country and on its borders.* Which made me wonder again.

'Will the war be over soon, Pa?' Niel asked.

'Heavens, yes!' Pa said. 'The Communists don't have a snowball's hope.'

'I hope it's not too soon,' Niel said, his dark eyes yearning. 'I want to go to the Border too . . .'

Ma opened her mouth as if she wanted to say something, but only emitted an almost inaudible sigh.

London, 15 May 1993

Dearest Child

They're still calling it the chicken run, I note in the newspaper. Some people even speak about rats leaving a sinking ship.

And this brave mouse is thinking of swimming back to the sinking ship?

For many of those who have opted to leave South Africa at this troubled time and start a new life elsewhere, the act of emigrating is a psychological necessity – the only effective relief from what they perceive to be an unbreakable cycle of political violence, rising crime and personal physical danger.

Or do I want to struggle against the current again, simply to be otherwise, as my mother said? As self-willed as my father? As melodramatic as my sister? As full of false self-confidence as my younger brother?

Everyone knows someone who is thinking of leaving . . .

Or because all the questions we ask are eventually blown in the wind, as Simon would say? No matter where you live.

Love
M.

A Dim Image in a Mirror

It was the worst month of my life. Later, the year would obviously leave a bitter aftertaste in the mouths of everyone in the country but for me, personally, 1976 tasted of trouble from the very first month. The holiday was over, I realized when I opened my eyes. The light was different here, whiter and warmer than when you woke at the sea. The smell was different too, sweet and humid instead of salt, too sweet and too humid, like fruit rotting in the sun. And the sounds were different. Or the lack of sound. At the sea I had become so used to the murmur of the breakers in the background like the almost inaudible background hiss on a long-playing record that after a while I barely heard it. Now I wondered why I hadn't appreciated it more. All I could hear that morning was the threatening silence in which another unbearably hot day was being hatched. Even the birds were quiet as if it was too much trouble to sing, as if they wanted to conserve their energy for the heatwave which would engulf them later in the day. The holiday is over, I said to myself, before my eyes closed again.

I was back in my own bedroom, in my own bed with the red-patterned quilt under my own poster of James Dean in *Rebel Without a Cause*. I had never seen the movie, it was before my time, but Ma always said it could've been my motto in life. Next to me was the bed where Dalena sometimes slept below a poster of Marilyn Monroe in a wide-skirted white dress billowing in an updraught.

Well, you had to put something on the walls and I wanted to be different. Suna's bedroom looked like most other girls', with pictures of couples walking hand in hand on a silver beach or embracing as the sun sank in a golden glow behind them. As usual, Dalena was different without even trying, with only two posters on her walls – one of a galloping, sweating thoroughbred, and one of a singing, sweating Janis Joplin – and a large framed photograph of my brother next to her bed.

I put out my hand and with my eyes still closed switched on the radio between the two beds. Eventually, I supposed, I would get used to Radio Five, but it simply wasn't LM.

On the following day I had to go back to the hostel but the idea didn't upset me that morning. Actually I felt quite excited – because I'd be seeing Dalena again and because of our new room. When we were allowed to choose a new room at the end of the previous year we didn't scramble like all the other girls for one with the best view of the boys' hostel or – second prize – as near to the bathroom as possible. All we wanted was to get as far away from a bell as possible. We borrowed the needlework teacher's tape measure and carefully measured the distance between each door and the two bells in the passage, and in the end chose a room which no one else was interested in, one at the back of the hostel.

'*Bad company till the day I die*,' I sang along with the radio. Ma was listening to another station in the kitchen, to a woman's serious voice, probably *Monitor*, the Afrikaans news programme. Lovey was packing her suitcase for the hostel (for about the twelfth time since our return on the previous day) while Niel delivered a running and wholly unwanted commentary. 'You won't need that ... just remember initiation ... rather too little than too much ... it's not that bad ... never enough food ...' He sounded like Gerhard Viviers in the broadcast box at a rugby match.

And at the weekend Simon was coming home!

I had tried to phone Dalena the previous evening, uneasy because I hadn't heard from her once during the holiday, but I got no reply. We wouldn't be able to talk on the phone in any case, I'd consoled myself. Not on this stupid farm line where someone was always eavesdropping.

I kicked down the sheet. I had forgotten how quickly the temperature rose here, with the sun like an oven set to high from early morning. Outside the kombi had stopped – probably Pa who had gone to buy the papers. These days the back door screeched like a cricket when it was opened. Pa had promised to do something about it months ago.

'But you don't know what girls want!' Lovey exclaimed, her voice shrill with irritation.

'But I know what they need!' Niel replied and I wondered why the words sounded so familiar. 'In the hostel they . . .'

But I was no longer listening to my brother's unwanted advice because my father's lowered voice in the kitchen – and my mother's deathly silence – made me sit up slowly. Or was it Ma making that strange noise? Like a puppy whimpering.

I switched off the radio with an arm that moved as slowly as if I had changed into a weightless astronaut. Something had happened, I realized, something was wrong. I wanted to squeeze my eyes shut and pull the red-patterned quilt over my head but I couldn't move. I could only wait with my hand frozen on the radio while somewhere that puppy kept on whimpering.

Until I eventually heard someone say: 'I'll tell Mart.'

It had to be Pa, but there was something wrong with his voice.

'Mart?' Pa stood in the door with a newspaper in his hand, his face golden brown and unshaven after the holiday, his eyes as stunned as a lost child's. 'I've got bad news for you, Matta.'

'Simon?'

He shook his head and came to sit on my bed. Of course it couldn't be Simon, I thought in a moment of terrible relief. If something had happened to Simon, Pa wouldn't have read the news in the paper.

'It's Pierre.' An icy wind blew through my gut. 'He was shot on the Border.' An icy gale wild enough to blow me off the bed. 'Fatally.'

Pa unfolded the newspaper with clumsy hands as if he didn't trust his voice to say more. On the front page, among the young faces of a few other soldiers, Sapper Pierre Malan smiled his crooked smile in a small black and white photograph for the last time, slightly out of focus like all the other front page pictures of dead soldiers I had looked at during the holiday. As if seeing them through a dirty window. Or like a dim image in a mirror. *Through a glass darkly.*

There are moments in life so unbearable that one immediately ejects them from memory, before they have the opportunity to leave traces in the mind.

I remember very little of the next few minutes. I know that my body started to shake, that I beat myself with my fists so that my father had to hold my arms to calm me. But that was purely the external reaction, hysterical, perhaps even melodramatic. What happened in my head and my heart I would probably never know.

And that was just the start, the first week of the first month of a new year.

When I walked into my room in the hostel on the following morning, one of the younger girls was waiting for me, awed by my new status as a matric pupil. It seemed as if she could barely refrain from curtseying. Matron wished to see me urgently, she said humbly, eyes on the floor. Please.

'Close the door, Mart,' Mrs Retief said in a not unfriendly tone when I walked into her office. Or as friendly as you could sound if you had a butcher's saw for a voice. 'You and I must have a serious talk.'

She looked very small behind her empty desk even though she sat on two plump cushions. She was a short little woman, shorter than some of the standard sixes, with tiny feet which always reminded me of the pictures on Chinese porcelain plates. Which only made her large breasts look even larger. Black hair fastened in a neat bun low in her neck and a nose that could slice bread, as sharp as her voice. And yet something about her face, perhaps the lively black eyes, made me suspect that she had been a pretty girl many years ago.

'It's about your roommate.' She indicated a chair next to me as if she could see how weak my knees had suddenly become. 'Dalena van Vuuren.'

As if I didn't know my roommate's name. I sank down on the chair and waited for whatever was coming.

'She's not coming back to school.' I could hear what she was saying but couldn't comprehend it. 'Her parents have sent her away as a result of . . . um . . . circumstances.' It was as if my mind, after the news of the previous day, couldn't assimilate another shock. As if there had been a short circuit caused by an electrical overload.

Everything darkened. 'You obviously know about the . . . er . . . the tragic occurrence?'

Tragic occurrence?

'Mart?' The voice penetrated the darkness in my mind. 'Mart, are you listening?'

I had always thought it would be very romantic to faint if you heard bad news, like the heroine in a story book, but at that moment I knew that it would never happen to me. I would only feel as sick as I felt now, my face cold and clammy, my hands so shaky that I couldn't use them at all.

'What . . . what tragic occurrence?'

'The unfortunate *condition* your roommate is in.'

I could only stare beseechingly at the matron. Had something happened to Dalena? Had the . . . operation gone wrong?

By this time Mrs Retief was close to tears. Not about what had happened to Dalena, I would realize later, but because of my shocked refusal to understand what she found impossible to say.

'Her pregnancy,' she mumbled as indistinctly as possible.

'Oh, that.'

'Yes, that.' She leaned forward, folded her fat little hands on the desk, obviously relieved that we finally knew what we were talking about. 'Evidently you told no one else?'

Slowly I shook my head. I'd thought that it was all over. I'd thought . . .

'I'm glad to hear it. I'm sure you'll understand, Mart, that it's the kind of . . . rumour which is better not repeated. For the sake of the school and the hostel's reputation, obviously, but also for the sake of Dalena's future. Her parents have asked that we merely say that they've sent her to a good school in the Cape, if anyone wants to know where she is, because they were dissatisfied with her marks last year. And with her relationship with your brother. Do you understand?'

I looked away. Outside, behind the wire mesh in front of the window, the clouds were blue-black, the colour of bruises. The unmistakable smell of a threatening thunderstorm surrounded us. When I looked at the matron again, behind her empty desk in her bare office, I felt an inexplicable pity for her. Exactly above her head hung the only wall decoration in the room, a framed square of black velvet embroidered in pink curly letters: *What is a Home without a Mother*. Without a question mark.

A rhetorical question, as Mr Locomotive would say in our Afrikaans class.

'We don't expect you to lie.' Her fat little hands were raised in a warding off gesture. 'Let's regard it as — as a rescue attempt. A small white lie to save your roommate's reputation?'

I nodded. Mrs Retief sighed in relief, then bent as far forward as her excessive breasts would allow. 'I'm sorry about the tragic death of your friend on the Border, Mart. If there's anything I can do . . .'

'Where is Dalena?'

Her black eyes flickered like a car's emergency lights.

'I want to know where they've sent her!' I realized that I sounded rude but I was helpless against the tide of rebellion which surged up in me. 'Surely I have the right to write to her?'

'I'm sor —'

'I'll tell no one, Mrs Retief.' Trying to hide the rebellion behind a few placatory words. 'I promise. I just want to write to her. *Please?*'

She coughed uncomfortably. 'I'm afraid I can't help you, Mart. Her parents didn't tell me.'

I didn't believe her. If she could expect me to lie about Dalena . . .

'If there's nothing else?'

I got up and walked to the door.

'If you need something to help you to sleep . . .'

I looked back questioningly, the door handle cold in my hand.

'A pill?' A sigh drifted slowly across the endless distance between us. 'I know it's not much consolation now, Mart, but believe me, one day it'll help to remember that your friend died a hero's death.'

I heard my own laughter and saw the startled look she gave me. The bitterness tasted like medicine in my mouth.

'He . . . he sacrificed his life for his country.' The matron's fat little hands fluttered in front of her as she searched for a conviction to hold on to, but she could find no comfort on that empty desk. 'So that we can all live in safety . . . so that we don't —'

'He didn't have a choice, did he? No one asked him whether he wanted to be a dead hero!'

I fled out of the bare office. My lips were compressed to keep the bitterness in, and the sudden salt taste of tears out.

I knew they would be waiting for me, a quiet group on the lawn in front of the hostel, bewildered by death. Pa perspiring in a black suit, Ma uncomfortable in her black dress and high-heeled shoes, Niel more serious than usual in his grey striped school blazer, Lovey obviously proud of her new uniform in spite of the sombre occasion. A study in black and grey, slightly faded in the bright sunlight like an old-fashioned, over-exposed family photograph.

Completely out of place in these colourful surroundings – behind them the bougainvillaea spilling orange-red over the fence, closer to them the flamboyant flamboyants and at their feet on the grass a few frangipani flowers, as bright a pink as icing sugar to which too much cochineal had been added.

What I hadn't expected was to see Simon with them. With them and yet apart, as watchful as a wild animal which didn't want to come too close to humans. Simon, and yet not Simon, an alien young man with a rigid face. For the first time he looked like a soldier in his uniform, not like a boy who had borrowed adult clothes in which to play war games.

Of course I'd known he would be at the memorial service. I'd only forgotten it temporarily, possibly because during the past week my mind had become as heavy as a sponge unable to absorb another drop of water. I had known that he had finished his National Service. I had known that he and Pierre would be coming home together over the weekend.

The Homecoming. For months it had played in my head like some fantastic movie. I had looked at every scene from different angles, listened to the words of every actor over and over again. Mart Vermaak – producer, director, scriptwriter and star – with Simon Vermaak, Pierre Malan and Dalena van Vuuren in the other leading roles, the rest of the family playing minor parts. Ma preparing the fatted calf, Pa proposing one long-winded toast after another, Niel hanging on Simon and Pierre's every word while they told war stories, Lovey inquisitively asking Dalena: 'Is Simon your boyfriend or what?'

162

But now, after Pierre's death and Dalena's disappearance, nothing was left of the movie. I wasn't ready to see my brother yet, I thought desperately. Not here. Not now.

I walked over to him and hugged him, his body harder than before under my hands. When I looked at his face I saw that his grey eyes had become just as hard.

'Where's Dalena?' Simon asked when we got into Pa's kombi and caught me so unawares that I stumbled over the adjustable seat. 'I'd have thought she wanted to come too.'

But his voice sounded disinterested, I realized, as if it were simply a polite enquiry.

'We've got ample room,' Ma said, eager to please Simon.

'She's ill,' I said, more for Ma's benefit than Simon's, without looking at either of them, my eyes on the hostel, which didn't look as ugly as usual through the kombi's dusty windows. 'She hasn't been at school all week.'

'What's the matter?' Ma turned in her seat next to Pa and looked across Niel and Lovey's heads at Simon and me in the last row of seats.

'I don't know, perhaps she's just . . . maybe it has something to do with Pierre.'

We drove through the best part of town to the church. Deserted streets in the shadow of jacaranda trees, gardens with rolling lawns spilling on to quiet pavements, swimming pools glittering behind fences. This was where Pierre grew up. This was where he hid in his midnight-blue bedroom when the glitter of swimming pools became too blinding. Simon was also staring through the dirty window of the kombi but his face remained a hard, expressionless mask.

Later, I decided, later I would tell the obligatory lie about the 'good school in the Cape'. For the present, all I had to do was to survive the memorial service.

The church was one of those modern face-brick buildings full of hideous wood and shining glass. The ugliest kind of church imaginable, I'd always thought, so modern that you were actually astonished to hear an old-fashioned church bell ringing in the asymmetrical tower. As if you had expected some or other electronic apparatus imitating the tolling of bells.

Inside, the light fell so glaringly through the great glass windows that I constantly had to blink to see the young, modern minister – with long sideburns and hair curling wildly over his collar – in the pulpit. The pulpit was as modern as the minister and as asymmetrical as the church tower.

All round me sat middle-aged men in brown uniforms, medals pinned to their chests, and women in grand black outfits. The mayors of three towns, wearing heavy chains of office winking in the bright light, were present, as well as a few members of parliament and, so it was said, a cabinet minister and a deputy minister of something or other. Not Defence. The previous year, when the police were still fighting in Rhodesia, the Minister of Police had made a speech at every funeral of a policeman who had been killed by terrorists. All those newspaper reports. *We will not give up the fight against terrorism and Communism. Our enemies must know that every single person we lose on the Border binds us more closely to our country, South Africa.* But now that the Army was fighting in South West Africa and Angola, apparently so many soldiers were dying that the Minister of Defence could no longer attend every funeral.

I had the same feeling of unreality I'd had during Heinrich Minnaar's funeral the previous year. I didn't want to cry in front of all these strangers who hadn't known Pierre. I refused to cry during this absurd performance, a memorial service with full military honours, I ask you! Soldiers in the front of the church next to the coffin! As if death were a concert.

What would Pierre have had to say about this, I thought despairingly. Wherever he might be.

He hadn't believed in a heaven – or had he? We had never discussed it. There were so many things we had never discussed.

He had evidently told his parents that he didn't want to lie in a grave one day, wasting a piece of soil that could be put to better use. So they had arranged a cremation instead of the ritual funeral with which Border heroes were generally honoured. But he hadn't thought to tell them that he didn't want a cremation with full military honours. He could hardly have covered every possibility.

I didn't know where he was now. But the feeling grew that he was watching this unsought hero worship with his twisted smile. These mayors and members of parliament and other VIPs who had come to say goodbye to him, these sniffing old ladies who hadn't known him at all, this minister who couldn't even pronounce his name correctly.

I had to close my eyes to ward off the tears. But then I heard his bitter laugh above the modern minister's modern words of comfort, and I couldn't help smiling with him.

That evening, in my own bed, I cried until my heart felt empty and light.

I had been crying every evening for a week, but until then it was more about Dalena than Pierre, my tear-filled eyes on her empty bed in our dark hostel room. It seemed as if she was the one who had died. Pierre's death seemed unreal – a soldier killed on the Border! – just another of those shocking reports that appeared in the newspapers so regularly these days.

But tonight, after I had seen the dark coffin in the ugly church, I knew that Pierre was dead. Tonight I cried because I would never see his black eyes again, never hear his husky voice or smell his smoky breath, never touch his long body again. Tonight I thought of that night I had spent with him in Pretoria and I cried because of what had happened, and I cried even more because of what had not happened.

I lay alone in my bed, drenched in sweat and tears, and I longed for Pierre's hard, living body as I had never longed for anything in my life before.

Whereas my roommate miraculously arose from the dead. When we came home from the memorial service, an envelope with unfamiliar handwriting and a Cape postmark was lying on my bed. I opened it with a feeling of premonition and read the letter with its more familiar handwriting with growing joy.

Yes, OK, OK, Dalena wrote, *I know it is a dim idea to send a letter to your house. I'm not that stupid yet (even though it feels as if my mind is shrinking as fast as my stomach is growing), but if I'd sent it to the hostel, it would probably never have reached you. My mother doesn't want me to have any contact with anyone in Black River (obviously shit scared that the neighbours will find out that her daughter has disgraced the family) and especially not with the sister of my so-called partner in crime. It wouldn't surprise me at all if old Boobs Retief was bribed to check on your post. I know my mother. She'll sink to any depth to protect her own respectability.*

So I asked the girl in the room next door to write the address on the envelope so that your brother doesn't perhaps recognize the handwriting. It's like the Army here, we're all in the same shit (or with buns in the same oven), so we have to help one another. 'Here' is a 'Home for Unmarried Mothers' as you must have figured out by now – even though my respectable family would rather commit suicide than admit it to anyone in the Lowveld. It's in the Cape where you come from, close to the mountain and the sea you were always carrying on about and which means fuck all to me. It's quite funny, isn't it? You were dragged to Black River from the Cape and I from Black River to the Cape and now neither of us is where we want to be.

If only we could exchange places! Not that I want you to be pregnant, hey. All I have to say about that, is that it's vastly overrated.

Naturally I would have preferred to be banned to Pretoria or Johannesburg but my father doesn't think that's far enough into the outer darkness to punish me properly. My mother also wants me as far from home as possible, but for her it's more about pride than punishment. Her greatest fear is that someone we know might see me in my 'condition'. Can you imagine how the neighbours would gossip about stuck-up old Tossie van Vuuren's daughter who has become a 'fallen woman'. All the way.

The next sentence had been heavily crossed out with black lines but I still managed to decipher it. *I didn't want to send an address because I'm afraid that your brother . . .* She had given me a box number and asked me to write to her there. And asked whether I couldn't get a box number in Black River where she could write to.

Earlier that evening, while we were eating cold chicken in the kitchen, Ma was in a state because Simon had locked himself in his room after the memorial service.

'Shouldn't we go and speak to him?' she'd asked Pa with pleading eyes.

'Leave him alone,' Pa said. 'He has the right to be alone.'

'But he's been alone for hours!'

She pushed her plate away, virtually untouched, and lit a cigarette. On any other evening she would've waited until everyone had finished eating. In the bright light above the kitchen table I could see the wrinkles around her petulant mouth as she sucked audibly on the cigarette.

'He probably needs it,' Pa said in that restful and reasonable attorney's voice, his eyes on the chicken piece in his hand. 'On the Border there was no door he could lock behind him.'

My mother shook her head and fiddled with her hair as she always did when she didn't know what to say. Her hair-do was still stiff with lacquer after the service that afternoon, the uncombed curls now only a pleasant holiday memory. She stared blankly at the kitchen window. Somewhere in the dark, behind the palm trees, the farm-workers' noisy Friday night party had already begun. Maria stood in front of the sink, her back turned towards us like a broad shield. But in the way she held her head, I could see she was also listening to the party noises.

'I wish I could do something for him,' Lovey sighed like an interpreter who had to spell out Ma's dumb needs for us, and picked listlessly at the food with her fork.

When she'd walked into the church this afternoon, I remembered with a wrench of the heart, her skin was as brown as Pierre's. Now, under the remorseless kitchen light, her face had an unhealthy greyish sheen, the colour of the new school dress which she still refused to take off. There was no need for her to act in a movie tonight. Reality was bad enough.

Niel looked anxiously from Ma to Pa but ate as greedily as ever. If he'd heard at table that an atom bomb was about to explode within minutes, he would probably have cleared his plate before seeking shelter.

'I know you want to help him, Marlene.' Pa had gnawed the chicken piece down to the bone, without Niel's enthusiasm but dutifully, like a child who had to earn his pudding. 'But he's not still a little boy who can cry on your lap. He's got to cope with this in his own way.'

'But what's he *doing* in his room!' Ma had stubbed the cigarette as if killing an unpleasant thought. 'Just suppose . . .'

And then she got up hastily and started carrying the plates to the sink. Maria had looked up in surprise, momentarily caught unawares by this unexpected help, before letting the usual black curtain down over her face.

I must ask you please not to tell your brother anything for a little while longer, Dalena's letter continued. *I'm busy writing him a letter but it's the most difficult thing I've ever had to do. I've probably torn up and thrown away an entire notepad! But nothing he can say or do will change anything, Mart. I must have the baby adopted. I must try to get on with my life.*

I lay listening to the dark because I knew I wasn't the only one in the house having trouble falling asleep. But all I could hear was a cricket screeching in the passage and the croaking of frogs near the swimming pool. And further away, the slightly drunken voices of the farmworkers, and still further away, somewhere in the hills, the primitive beat-beat-beat of drums sending unintelligible messages through the dark night.

Dearest Child

Congratulations on your seventeenth birthday. I say it with love but also (even if I'm reluctant to admit it) with a feeling of envy because your life still lies ahead of you like an empty book whereas mine has been filled half-way. Maybe more than half-way, perhaps it's nearly at an end, how can I know? And this is a book in which nothing is ever erased.

Listen to me! I sound like an aunt who wants to read you a lesson for life! May the gods protect you, even if they can do nothing else for you, against adults who want to read you lessons for life. My own past was full of them, teachers, church ministers, fathers of the nation *et al.*, and I still have difficulty in digging a tunnel through all the trash under which they buried me. I constantly have to stop myself doing the same thing to my son.

At the moment he's playing in our cramped British backyard, as shamelessly naked as a small barbarian, with a zebra skin I brought from Africa draped round his shoulders. He's pretending to be a roaring zebra. While I have to bite my lip, like my mother, not to tell him that zebras aren't supposed to roar.

It's one of those muggy London summer days which makes the backyard feel even smaller than usual, like a submarine in which the oxygen is running low. Actually on such days the whole city feels like a submarine with too little oxygen for too many people. The sun is different from the sun under which I grew up, not as white and angry, more like a naughty boy slowly dripping golden syrup on a crowd of crawling ants. A syrupy, sticky heat which drives office workers to the nearest park during their lunch hour so that they can get rid of their clothes.

Yes, that's what the British do when the sun shines. On a day like today the parks are full of men who have loosened ties and peeled off shirts to reveal thin pink bodies and hairy arms, and women who step out of tights and roll up blouses so that the sun can shine on blue-veined legs and soft stomach-fat. It took me years to get used to such a shameless trait in such a sober nation!

Where I grew up decent people only took off their clothes at the sea or next to a swimming pool. They definitely didn't bare their bodies in front of strangers over lunch time picnics in the nearest park. But today, after five long English winters, I was ready at last to behave like the people around me. I sat in a park with my skirt pulled up to my panties, tucked my shirt into my bra and felt the sun licking my legs and my stomach with a sticky tongue. And wondered if it meant that I was finally starting to feel at home in this strange land.

'Have you ever seen a real live zebra, Mummy?' my son asked.

'Herds of them,' I replied. 'Hundreds of them.'

'Lots and lots of real, live zebras?' Amazement, jealousy and admiration succeeded one another like shadows on his face. 'In Africa?'

'In Africa,' I replied, 'near a banana farm which belonged to your Afrikaner grandfather.'

'What did they sound like, these hundreds of zebras?' he anxiously wanted to know.

What now? I wondered.

'Like this?' And he gave a bloodcurdling roar, his head thrown back and his eyes closed in concentration. 'Or like this?'

The second roar was softer but more long-drawn than the first.

'Like that,' I lied. 'Exactly like that.'

Sometimes his enthusiasm reminds me so much of his father that I want to cry.

Of course I loved his father – at some stage. (It was hardly difficult. He was attractive and intelligent and good-natured with a smooth, witty tongue and a musical way of speaking which he inherited from his Irish ancestors.) But he was too much of a lightweight to love as unreservedly as I love my son. He was such a lightweight that I wanted to fasten him to my wrist like a balloon to stop him from being blown away by every new caprice and fancy in his life.

And what caprices and fancies he had! Threatened bird species and medieval church music and the way political prisoners were mal-treated world-wide and homeopathic medicine and Mediterranean food and many, many more, too many to recall. He indulged these caprices with as little discrimination as Dalena's cantankerous father had displayed when hanging the rugby pictures in his pub years ago.

We're not talking about life-long passions. We're talking about whirlwinds of enthusiasm which briefly disturbed everything – one after another, *ad nauseam* – and caused so much dust eventually that we were unable to see one another.

And I knew the fault was mine. I was attracted to this man from the start because he reminded me of my father and my elder brother. He had the makings of my father's impractical and un-bridled passions but also that emptiness which I suspected in my brother long before I could put it into words, an emptiness that could never be filled by any passion – or any human being.

Sometimes I think it was Pierre who spoilt all other men for me. Because he was so deceptively heavy, with his slender body, that I weighed every one up against him ever after, and found them all too light.

Today you're venturing upon your eighteenth year, my dearest child. No longer a 'child', are you? And in a week's time I will have spent a year writing a story about a handful of 'children' which you might read one day without realizing that it has anything to do with you.

If my father had been here he would have proposed a toast im-mediately. All I can do, this evening, is to click a glass against a mirror. To your birthday, to my story, to your future, to my past, to both our stories.

Love
M.

The Key Questions Remain

'Simon?' I pressed the receiver tightly against my ear, the only way in which I could bring my brother closer. 'Simon!'

'I had a letter from Dalena yesterday.'

He said it the way you might say: 'It was a nice day yesterday.' And yet there was an almost undetectable quiver in his voice when he mentioned her name.

'Is that why you're phoning?' I asked carefully.

Behind me a few girls were waiting in a semi-circle to use the telephone, like vultures round a wounded animal, mercilessly watching for the smallest sign of weakness. It wasn't as if they were hoping for someone to get bad news over the phone but no one would be sorry if it happened. An unpleasant call was always shorter than a pleasant one. Nature is cruel, as Miss Ferguson regularly reminded us in biology class.

'Yes,' Simon said. 'I have to speak to you.'

I shifted closer to the wall, curved my shoulders to broaden my back, dropped my head even lower over the receiver. 'Not on the telephone,' I whispered.

It was impossible to have a private conversation on a hostel telephone while a bunch of vultures moved restlessly behind you making impatient noises. And if you were connected to a farm line full of bored eavesdroppers, you might as well blazon the secrets of your heart on the front page of the local newspaper.

'Of course not. Can you meet me in town tomorrow? Not at the hostel,' he added before I could reply. 'I don't want Niel and Lovey to see me.'

'Sure,' I said at once, eager to see him even though I knew it wasn't going to be easy to speak about Dalena. 'It's our free afternoon so all the hostel kids will hang around the café next to the Plaza, probably Niel and Lovey as well . . .'

'Can't you meet me at the hotel?'

'Are you mad! If I had go anywhere near the hotel in my school uniform, I'll be expelled the next day!'

'Oh, come on, we're not going to get drunk in the bar! Can't we have coffee in the lounge like respectable people?'

It was wonderful to hear his voice again. In the past month he'd withdrawn completely from the world. Lay in his room all day or drove around aimlessly in my mother's car or sat on the veranda staring at the banana trees. Only spoke if we asked him a question and then his answer was usually something like: 'What's the point?' Ma was so desperate that she wanted to send him to a psychologist. When she cautiously suggested this to him, he merely shrugged his shoulders and asked what the point would be. It was wonderful to hear him saying something else.

'It doesn't work that way, Simon,' I tried to explain. 'Our headmaster doesn't believe there's such a thing as a respectable pupil. He believes that any pupil walking into a hotel will immediately lose all self-control and wind up paralytic.' Simon whistled sympathetically. 'The worst of it is, the schoolchildren are so repressed in Black River that it's probably true.'

'How can you bear it?' A rhetorical question, not so, Mr Locomotive? 'Well, where else?'

'What about the park near the hostel? Do you know where it is?'

'Yes, Pierre always . . .' He hesitated for a moment. His voice had sounded the way it did when he mentioned Dalena's name. 'He always said that's where Black River's dirty old men pick up little boys. He got his first indecent proposal there.'

'Yes, it's not exactly a glamorous park.' *Send your daughter to Black Sheep High School,* someone had written in pencil on the wall next to the telephone. *We maintain a proud tradition of juvenile delinquency.*

'But then Black River isn't exactly a glamorous place.'

'OK, can you be there at three o'clock?'

'Three o'clock,' I agreed, my voice suddenly breathy with nervousness.

I had never been in the park before. Only looked through the railings when walking past. Never seen dirty old men, I had to admit, only black women who spoke loudly and unintelligibly to one another while white toddlers played at their feet.

That afternoon only Simon and I were there.

'I knew it was an awful park,' I said apologetically, my eyes on the rusted slide and the broken swings, 'but I didn't know it was this bad.'

'So she didn't send you an address either?' Simon wanted to know again.

'No. I told you I know no more than you do.'

'I can't believe that you kept it from me . . .'

He didn't sound as angry as he had been half an hour ago, but I found the despondency in his voice almost worse than his anger. We sat on the grass, in the shadow of a large tree which had shed clusters of yellow flowers, in the middle of the deserted, neglected park. One day, I promised myself, I would still learn the names of all the unfamiliar trees in this strange region. The grass was overgrown, the shrubs around us almost jungly in their luxuriance. In this area plants didn't need the interference of humans to flourish.

'I'm sorry, Simon,' I said for the umpteenth time. 'I had no choice. I promised her . . .'

The more I said it, the feebler the excuse sounded.

'I know,' he said impatiently. 'I'm not angry with *you*.' He rubbed his hand through his hair which was growing almost as wildly as the plants in the park now that he was no longer in the Army. 'I'm not angry with her either. I'm mad as hell at myself. Do you understand? I'm so angry because I was so stupid! Because I never thought that anything like this could've happened! There were a helluva lot of things to worry about on the Border but this was the one thing . . .'

I glanced covertly at him. His face, which was tanned a month ago, had developed an unhealthy yellowish colour. His black T-shirt hung loosely on his body. It was obvious that he had lost a lot of weight.

'And suppose you had known?' I said softly. 'Say you'd found out one way or another . . . what could you have done, Simon?'

He raised his eyebrows but didn't look at me, said nothing.

'You were on the Border. You couldn't possibly have come home for a weekend! What could you have done – except worry about that as well!'

I picked a blade of grass and stuck it in my mouth. It had a sharp and bitter taste. He only stared at his black jeans. These days he almost always wore black.

'Dalena knew you weren't at a picnic, Simon. Every time we opened a newspaper there was a report about a soldier who'd been shot. What the hell could she have written to you? "Oh, by the way, I'm expecting a baby but don't worry, I'll get rid of it?"'

He shook his head, took a packet of cigarettes out of his jeans pocket and lit one. For more than a minute we sat next to one another without speaking while he dragged on the cigarette and I chewed the blade of grass.

'And even if you were here,' I said at last, my eyes on an elderly woman who had just appeared under the flamboyants at the park gate, 'even if you weren't on the Border, you wouldn't have been able to do anything. I mean, surely you wouldn't have got married?' He looked sharply at me, frowning, then as sharply turned his head away again. 'Neither of you wants to get married now. You could have helped her perhaps . . . with an abortion . . . but I think she deliberately waited until it was too late before telling her father.'

'OK.' He killed the cigarette in the grass with more force than was necessary. 'But now that I know, I want to do something. I can't simply . . . I have go to Stellenbosch next weekend. I can visit her, surely?'

'So you've decided to go to university?' I asked, surprised.

Last weekend it hadn't seemed as if he still wanted to study. Last weekend it seemed as if he was going to spend the rest of his life lying on his bed and wondering what the point would be . . . Pa tried to talk to him, Ma tried to talk to him, even I tried.

Pa told him about the wonderful world of the law which was waiting for him, like a secret door which would swing open if he possessed the legal password. The *legal* password, Pa had repeated in case Simon hadn't caught the pun. Simon hadn't even smiled, only asked what the point would be. Ma tried to seduce him with tales of drum majorettes and sock dances and carnival floats and all the other things she regarded as 'student fun'. He'd opened his mouth as if he wanted to say something, then merely shook his head. I'd reminded him, out of desperation, that it would be one way of getting out of the house and smoking as much pot as he wanted to. Maybe that did the trick. At least he didn't repeat the question which by that time the entire family feared like a dangerous disease.

'Can you believe it? But I don't know whether I still want to study law. Pa has always taken it for granted . . . and I've always gone along with it to please him.' Now he was also looking at the grey-haired woman walking slowly through the park without seeing us in the shadow. She was wearing a long, white dress in a soft material and held a parasol over her head, with a cane in her other hand. She looked like a ghost from my grandmother's photo album, an aged guardian angel in the heat which shimmered about her. 'But I want to trace Dalena.'

'And if you trace her?'

'I don't know, there must be something I can do. Even if it's only to be her friend?'

The grey-haired woman looked around briefly before she unexpectedly sat down on one of the crooked swings. She swung slowly and gracefully, her face still in the shadow of her parasol while I stared at her in amazement. And then, just as unexpectedly, she got off the swing, adjusted her soft white dress and went on her dignified way. I turned to Simon to see whether he'd seen it too, but he was dejectedly scratching in the grass with a twig.

'Do you think she's interested in your friendship?' I asked cautiously.

'Of course not!' He laughed, but it was the kind of laugh that had belonged to Pierre before, so bitter that it twisted his mouth. 'She made that quite clear in her letter. But if she has the right to make her own decision about this thing, then I have the right to stand by her no matter what she decides!'

His voice was accusing, his head ducked down between his shoulder blades, something he'd done since childhood when he was in one of his rebellious moods. As if he wanted to scrum on his own against the whole world. But he no longer looked like a rugby player,

I decided, more like a thin, black crow with his shoulder blades jutting out like wings on his back.

'I don't know whether it'll work, Simon. Dalena has always been the all-or-nothing type . . . you know her, after all. If she doesn't want your child, she won't want your friendship, either.'

'I can try to talk her round,' he said obstinately. 'She doesn't know anyone else in the Cape. She's going to need a friend.'

I followed the grey-haired woman with my eyes. Was I going mad or had I seen her a few minutes earlier swinging like a child? She looked like a supernatural apparition again, almost transparently white and floating against a tangerine pride of De Kaap shrub. Suddenly everything seemed unreal, not only the woman on the swing but Pierre's death, Dalena's disappearance, this whole strange conversation with a brother who had become a stranger, in a neglected, deserted park.

'I hope you find her, Simon,' I said eventually.

When we got up to walk back I could no longer contain the question. 'How did Pierre die?'

He shrugged his shoulders and quickly walked ahead of me. 'Mortar attack.'

'I know that, but how? Where were you? Were you in Angola?' I spat out the blade of grass and hurried to catch up with him. 'Were you led into an ambush? Was it during the day or at night? I know he wasn't killed outright but . . .'

His mouth was tightly compressed, his eyes on his tackies.

'How long did it take, Simon?' I begged. 'Before he died?'

'Long enough to . . .' He lit another cigarette and drew the smoke in sharply. 'Long enough.'

'Don't you want to talk about it?'

He walked in silence to the park gate, then stood and looked at me. The two flamboyants on either side of the gate framed him in bloody red. The heat of the sun was so fierce that I felt dizzy.

'I'll tell you one day,' he said. 'One day . . .'

The expression on his face was wholly unfamiliar to me.

He and I walked through the barred gate together. On the pavement I had to shield my eyes with my hand against the sharp light. 'Have you heard that the Army is being withdrawn from Angola?'

Slowly he shook his head and mumbled: 'If I could only work out what the point of it all was . . .'

'"The key questions about South Africa's involvement in Angola remain unanswered,"' Ma read from the English newspaper.

Pa gave her an edgy look, lifted the Afrikaans newspaper and read aloud: '"South Africa will continue to protect its interests where necessary and won't allow the chaos and disorder reigning in Angola to spill over into areas for which it is responsible."'

'"The general public has nevertheless concluded that the whole exercise was an error of political judgement,"' Ma read on as if she hadn't heard him.

Simon and I looked at one another where we sat on either side of them on the veranda. Lovey and one of her new high school pals lay a little below us next to the swimming pool. For the past half-hour Niel had been executing a breathtaking diving performance to try and impress them with somersaults, back-flips and jack-knives, but their only reaction was to give giggly screams every time he splashed them.

'"Unfortunately the details of the military operations in Angola must still be kept from the public. The time for the 'whole story' has not arrived,"' Pa read, unruffled.

'"Never again must South Africa be kept in the dark so shamefully!"' Ma ended, firmly folded the paper and looked challengingly at Pa.

Her eyes were hidden behind her Jackie Onassis dark glasses but her whole attitude was one big warning: *Don't push me.* And over the years Pa had learned to respect that warning. He lowered the newspaper on to his bare chest and lay back, smiling, in his deck chair. *Real men love rugby*, the cloth hat pulled down over his eyes announced.

'*How many roads must a man walk down,*' Bob Dylan moaned over the stereo, '*before you can call him a man?*'

Ma pulled a face as if a presumptuous stranger had pinched her bottom, irritated and yet amused as well. Simon smiled because he knew she wouldn't complain about his music today. He was leaving for university tomorrow.

Pa wanted to have a barbecue this evening to celebrate the start of Simon's 'carefree student days'. He was so excited I could have sworn that he was getting the chance to be reckless and randy again. Ma was sad, of course, that her favourite was leaving home, but also grateful that he wasn't going to spend the year lying on his bed and wondering what the point of it all was.

'Oh my, the good, old Stellenbosch,' Pa sighed and swallowed beer from an enormous mug. 'When I think about all those pretty girls in their short dresses . . . hey, ho potato, bend or I'll bite you!'

'Haven't you noticed that the mini is out of fashion, Pa?' I asked.

'And not a day too soon,' Ma said. 'That was one style which was only meant for girls under twenty.'

'It's the one style I'll miss,' Pa sighed, pushed back the cloth hat and looked out over the farm as if he had planted every banana tree with his own hands.

'*Yes, and how many times can a man turn his head,*' Bob Dylan droned on, '*pretending he just doesn't see?*'

Lovey ran up the steps in a bikini as red (and about as small) as the poinsettia flowers next to the veranda.

'Would you bring me a cold drink as well, Bobby?' her new friend called from the swimming pool.

'*Bobby?*' Simon asked.

Lovey gave him an annoyed glance over her new, droopy dark glasses and disappeared into the house, hips swinging. I didn't know which movie she was playing in today but the swinging hips in the minute bikini made her look like a younger edition of a Bond girl.

'When I think about rugby at Coetzenburg . . .' Pa cosseted his nostalgia with another couple of swallows from the beer mug. 'And the Old Main Building . . . and the oak trees in autumn . . .'

Niel had ended his diving performance the moment Lovey had disappeared and put his towel down next to her friend.

'Do you like Bob Dylan, Linda?' I heard him ask confidentially but his voice left him in the lurch and soared on *Linda*.

'I don't know,' Linda replied disinterestedly. 'Who's Bob Dylan?'

Simon's jaw dropped, exaggeratedly stunned, and we both started laughing.

'*At Coetzenburg flows a lovely stream,*' Pa started singing the old

Varsity rugby song with swinging shoulders and a swinging beer mug, like Mario Lanza in *The Student Prince*. *'Hey, hey, hey ho!'*

Ma watched him over the edge of her dark glasses and shook her head. The fire hadn't even been lit and he was already half seas over.

'My brother came back from the Border last month, you know.' Niel was still trying to sound confidential but it was pretty difficult with a voice which jumped up and down like an unbroken horse. 'I think he still has a thousand yard stare . . .'

Simon had turned his head away. It seemed as if he was studying the scarlet splashes of the poinsettias against the cloudless blue sky.

'What's a thousand yard stare?' the lovely Linda wanted to know. Still not burning with interest.

'It's when . . . your head's not quite right. It happens to a lot of guys on the Border. Especially if your best pal is blown up in front of your eyes.'

'Is that what happened to your brother?' For the first time she sounded impressed with something Niel had said.

'Have you finished packing, Simon?' Ma asked hurriedly.

'If you ask me once more, Ma . . .'

'Sorry,' she laughed but her fingers pecked at her hair like hungry birds again.

'Anyone would think you can't wait to get rid of me.'

'Sorry,' Ma said again, her voice suddenly thin and high.

I looked at her in surprise but she got up and fled to the kitchen.

'What do you hear from Dalena?' Ma asked while we were making sandwiches in the kitchen.

'She writes occasionally.' I started peeling off the outer layers of an onion, keeping my voice casual. 'Why?'

'I just wondered,' Ma said just as casual, her eyes on the grater and the piece of cheese in her hands.

She suspected something. She knew something was wrong. I had told the obligatory story about the good school in the Cape, but as she always said, she was no ostrich with her head in the sand. She might not know the difference between an ostrich and a turkey, as *Pa* always said, but he was grateful that she wasn't a magistrate. She would have caught him out every time he tried to lie in court.

'Do *your* parents argue all the time?' I'd asked Dalena one weekend.

'Never!' she'd laughed. 'They barely speak to one another!'

I had looked enviously at her. We were sitting in the back of the kombi. In front Ma and Pa were arguing about the name of a film they'd seen some twenty years ago.

'*Woman of the Year*,' Ma persisted. 'With Katharine Hepburn and Spencer Tracy.'

'No, I never saw that,' Pa said, shaking his head. 'You must've seen it with one of your other boyfriends.'

'Of course you did! You bought me a box of chocolates!'

'Probably that number with the ears that stuck out, the guy who worked on the railways. What was his name again?'

'It was the only time you bought me chocolates without my hinting until I was blue in the face.'

'Just think, if you'd married him your children would've stood next to a railway line with snotty noses.'

'*Woman of the Year*.'

'And waved at the trains!'

'Do you think it's normal to carry on like that?' I wanted to know from Dalena.

'I wouldn't know,' she said. 'But if my parents have a normal marriage, I don't want to be normal.'

'But they're always so polite to one another.'

'Precisely. "Could you please pass me the salt, Mother?" "Do you think it's going to rain tomorrow, Father?" I'm sure they've never seen one another in the nude!'

I'd given a quick glance to the front but my mother and father were so caught up in their argument that nothing could have diverted their attention.

'I'll tell you why I remember it so well!' Ma exclaimed. 'When you gave me the chocolates, you said I was not only the woman of the year but the woman of your life!'

'*Me?*' Pa stared at her in such astonishment he almost hit an oncoming car. 'Did I say that?'

In the kitchen, Ma sighed, her eyes on the palm trees in front of the kitchen window. 'Poor Simon. It can't be easy to lose your best friend and your girl in one month.'

'Tcha, you know what Simon's like, Ma.' The tears veiled my eyes as they always did when I worked with onions. 'He'll be OK . . . with all those pretty girls in Stellenbosch.'

'I hope so.' Ma placed a slice of tomato on each slice of bread and strewed over the grated cheese. 'But Dalena was . . . special, wasn't she?'

Everything became so hazy that I had difficulty in slicing the onion.

'And he won't easily find a friend like Pierre again.'

'No,' I sniffed, 'friends like that don't grow on trees.'

I tried to laugh but when a tear fell on the kitchen table like a fat raindrop, I dropped my head on my arms, in among the sandwiches, and felt my shoulders shaking. And when my mother came and stood next to me, pressing my head against her stomach, I cried the way I'd cried when I was small.

'I miss him, Ma!' I sobbed with my face pressed against my mother's soft stomach, a pillow which smelled of smoke and baby powder and perspiration and bread. 'I don't know why . . . I didn't even know him that well . . . but I miss him!'

'Never mind, Matta,' Ma murmured and awkwardly rubbed my head, as she'd done when I was small. 'Never mind, never mind . . .'

London, 4 July 1993

Dearest Child

Now I have to accept that I'll never 'find' you. Of course it was never anything more than a dream to carry me through sleepless nights. But of all the losses we have to endure, lost dreams are perhaps the most unbearable.

My mother sent me a small news item which answered a few questions which perhaps would've been better left unanswered. No, I'm not going to quote it to you, not yet. Over the years I've acquired the writer's habit of making notes of anything that happens to me before processing it — so that I *can* process it — but there are still some things which touch me so deeply that I have to absorb them first.

The report was wrapped in a letter which contained some good news as well. (Now I feel like an indifferent master of ceremonies who tries to amuse wedding guests with a feeble joke: *First the bad news* . . .). The good news, and it's not a joke, is that the first democratic election in South Africa will probably take place on 27 April next year. (Not that my mother necessarily sees it as good news.)

Of course I'd already read it in the English newspapers but it was as unreal as news reports will probably always seem to me. I needed my mother's words to make it true for me.

Oh my, Mart, my mother wrote, *I don't know whether I feel hopeful or despairing about the long road still lying ahead of us in this country. You know I was never an ardent admirer of old white men who expected young white men to sacrifice their lives for their country and the nation, but now that I'm an old white lady myself, I'm getting more and more scared of young black men who want to drive me and my kind out of the country with slogans like 'One Settler*

One Bullet'. But I'd rather die of fear before showing them that they scare me! I was born here, damn it, all my ancestors are buried here, where do they want me to flee to! But then, it's not young black men who are going to rule the country after 27 April next year. My biggest nightmare is that the old white bosses will simply be replaced by old black bosses and that young men of all colours will continue to kill one another. Your father says I'm becoming a feminist in my old age.

It's only just occurred to me: if the election takes place towards the end of April, you'll be too young by about six weeks to vote. It almost seems unfair!

    Love
    M.

A Wonderful Freedom That Will Be!

'"What did he still have to fight for? It was folly!"' My voice sounded too loud in my ears. Don't get carried away, Mart, I admonished myself. It's only a story. '"In any case it was all folly . . ."'

'*Folly?*' asked one of my classmates in imitation of an old woman's heavy voice.

I glanced up briefly from my book. Mr Botha was leaning against the edge of his desk in front of the classroom, his long, thin legs stretched out. Absently he rubbed one long, thin hand over his hair which became thinner and more transparent day by day. (As if he hoped that the bald spots would sprout a new growth if he only continued to rub.) He stared at the floor but every time he looked up, his eyes shone.

'"Yes, it was folly!"' I used the phoney voice which I usually reserved for reading the French labels on Pa's wine bottles. Not that I was trying to sound as if I was having sex while reading *Mother Hanna*. A more serious kind of phoney voice. '"They were discarded on the veld – to no purpose!"'

Mr Botha, more generally known as Mr Locomotive, had decided to give every child in the class an opportunity to read a section from the Afrikaans drama in our set books, the idea being that we would choose the best actors to perform *Mother Hanna* later in the year for the rest of the class. With costumes and make-up and all? an excited Suna had wanted to know. With costumes and make-up and all, Mr Locomotive had confirmed.

'But you don't have to wear make-up,' he'd immediately added when he saw the boys' faces. 'And you don't have to learn the words by heart. You can act with the book in your hand.'

Otherwise some of the boys would have deliberately read so

badly that they couldn't be chosen to take part in the production. Mr Locomotive had been steaming along for so many years, through classrooms and across sports fields, that he had learned to drag even the most unwilling wagons along with him.

'"You all think you can win your freedom by dying for it, Ma,"' I read further in amazement. '"But what will we do with it if we're all dead? What a wonderful freedom that will be! Wonderful! Wonderful!"'

The words sounded so familiar. Maybe all wars were similar? Maybe I should forget about writing poems and become an actress?

'Thank you, Mart.'

I lowered the book, completely breathless. Was it my imagination or was I hearing rousing applause? It was my imagination. But Mr Botha was giving me a pleased smile.

'Now, who hasn't had a chance to read Maria?'

Here and there a girl put up her hand. Then a surreptitious giggling and guffawing because Pine's muscular arm hung in the air like a large exclamation mark. Mr Botha tried to ignore him but Pine started snapping his fingers.

'Yes, *Miss* Pienaarr' When Mr Locomotive started rolling his r's, you didn't bug him. It was his way of building up steam before hitting you with a load of sarcasm. He folded his arms across his chest and looked at Pine the way a show judge would look at a prize bull. 'Do you want to be an actrress as well?'

'Sir, Miss Muf –, I mean Miss Meyer says that in the old days girls' roles were played by boys. You know, sir, like in Shakespeare's time?'

Pine was tilted back at a dangerous angle, his chair balanced on only two legs, his eyes challenging and as black as the hair on his arms and legs. Not worried in the least by the way the teacher was regarding him. Mr Locomotive was coaching the rugby first team again this year and Pine Pienaar knew he was the best player in the school, now that the previous year's matric boys had all been swallowed by the Defence Force.

'Can't we have a chance to read Maria as well? Perhaps one of us can do it better than Mart?'

I quickly lowered my eyes to my book, my cheeks flaming with indignation. He was looking for it, I decided. Since the beginning of the year he'd been looking for it.

'We're not busy with a pantomime, Pienaarr,' Mr Locomotive said. 'Perhaps we can perform *Cinderella* later this year and you can play one of the ugly sisters.'

One of the other girls started reading Maria's role. Now the drama didn't sound so great any more, I decided. I held my hands like blinkers on either side of my face, my elbows on the desk so that it seemed as if I was following the words on the page but all I could see was Pine Pienaar's body. It wasn't a boy's body any longer. It was almost a man's, big, muscular and hairy. My stomach lurched the way it did when a lift descended too quickly.

'Death is the main theme in this drama,' Mr Botha reminded us. 'Please note how often the word "death" – and other words pertaining to death – are present.'

If Dalena were here, I thought longingly, she would almost certainly have asked him why all our set books were so obsessed with death, from *Romeo and Juliet* the previous year to *Mother Hanna* this year. In history class we learned about dead heroes and in biology class we looked at dead animals. Mathematics was virtually the only subject that had nothing to do with death – but it was so difficult that you had to work yourself to death to understand any of it. No wonder suicide had become so popular with schoolchildren throughout the country.

It was almost the end of the first term but I still missed my roommate every day, as much as the day the matron had summoned me to her bare office. If only I'd hugged her just once, I sometimes thought in my dark bed, just once put my arms round her and felt her body against mine, perhaps I wouldn't long for her as much. Of course she would've asked me whether I'd lost my marbles. But I should have done it, I thought. Or would that have made the longing even worse?

'Do you know something?' I said to Suna the following day in the café next to the Plaza, 'I couldn't understand why you cried so much at Hein's funeral last year.'

She looked up in surprise from her plate of chips. She was wearing a striped T-shirt and the new narrow-legged jeans which fitted so tightly across her bum that she had to lie on her back to close the zip. Evidently it was the best way to get into the new jeans. Which sounded absurd, I would've said if asked, but so far no one had asked, and I was probably just jealous because I had to sit opposite her in an ugly school uniform.

'I thought you were exaggerating. I mean, you didn't know him that well . . .' She blinked her eyes like someone in the dark unexpectedly caught in the light of a torch. 'But now I think I understand. Perhaps you were just friends . . . but there was a possibility that you could've become more than friends, wasn't there?'

Suna looked down at her plate. She rubbed her fingers over the pitted skin on her cheek and with the other hand dragged a chip back and forth, back and forth through a dollop of tomato sauce.

'I don't know . . .' she said eventually.

'It's the way I feel about Pierre,' I tried to explain. Suna squirmed uncomfortably on her chair. Didn't she understand what I was saying or were the tight jeans pinching her? 'If I think about him now – not that I think about him all day long – I wonder what might have happened. Maybe nothing! Maybe he would have remained my brother's pal, no more than that, but maybe . . .' Then it was my turn to stare uncomfortably at my milkshake while wondering what on earth had possessed me to start this stupid conversation.

Until Suna said thoughtfully: 'And now the possibility is lost for ever?'

I nodded my head eagerly. Sometimes I thought Suna was as thick as two bricks but on a day like today I wondered whether she didn't just pretend to be a dumb blonde. Marilyn Monroe was apparently also far brighter than she seemed.

'I always thought people cried about things that were gone, you know, things you'd lost, people who were gone . . . but now I wonder whether you don't feel even worse about the things you've never had – about lost opportunities.'

'I wasn't crying about Hein,' she mumbled with her eyes on her plate. 'I was crying about my father. About Hein as well, of course, but mostly about my father.'

'But he's been dead for such a long time . . .'

'My mother says you never stop crying about someone you loved.

At every funeral . . . and Hein's funeral was worse because my father died in the same way.'

'The same way?'

She kept her eyes on her plate while her fingers incessantly rubbed the rough facial skin.

'He gassed himself in his car.'

I was so stunned that I could only stare at her. 'I didn't know . . .'

'No one knows,' she said quickly. 'You're the first person I've ever told.'

When she eventually looked up I wondered why I'd never realized how blue her eyes were.

'Why?' I asked bewildered.

She shrugged her shoulders. The smear of tomato sauce on her upper lip looked like lipstick, carelessly applied.

'Why does anyone commit suicide? My mother says he suffered from depression . . .'

'No, I mean why . . . did you tell me?'

'Because you told me about Dalena.'

If I'd spoken then, I would have burst into tears. After Simon had left for Stellenbosch, I felt that I would go mad if I couldn't speak about Dalena to someone, so I told Suna. By this time it had become a weekly ritual for me to read to her from Dalena's letters, usually in the café next to the Plaza.

'What's the latest, anyway?' Suna wanted to know.

I put my hand into my shirt pocket, under the grey dress, and took out the letter. Carefully opened the pink paper and gravely cleared my throat so that I could get my voice under control.

' "Hello! I never thought I'd miss all you old turds in Black River but I'm so homesick I even long for Mr Maritz's endless prayers!" '

Suna clapped her hand over her mouth to stifle the giggle in her throat. I looked up from my letter and for the first time saw a new film poster at an angle behind her head, a massive shark with a girl as small as a doll drifting on the surface of the water: *Jaws*. At the front of the café, closer to the sad Portuguese owner, sat Lovey and her new friend, Linda (who didn't know who Bob Dylan was) with Niel and one of his standard seven pals. A year ago Niel would rather have written a hundred English essays than speak to his younger sister in public. But since the lovely Linda had appeared on the scene, his hormones were in as much of a state as his elder brother's had been the previous year.

'"I've decided to do my matric through the post,"' I continued, '"like all those weird people in all those weird piccies in the magazines we used to laugh at so much. I don't know whether I'll do it through the Achiever College or Mr Management's School but I can see my mother choking on her tea and cake when she sees her daughter's face among all the other drop-outs and weirdos in the magazines. Good school in the Cape, ha ha!

'"But let me tell you about the latest arrival in our House of Sin in the Cape. I know I live on a farm, but this one is a *real* farm girl! Barely fourteen and not exactly bright. To be honest as stupid as a sheep. I mean, she must know where lambs and other small animals come from, on a farm you can hardly avoid it, but I swear she doesn't have a clue why her own stomach is getting bigger and bigger. They say it was her uncle or even her father who put the bun in her oven. Interbreeding. That's probably why her lift doesn't go all the way to the top floor. But there are so many stories about the girls here . . ."'

'Her *father*?' Suna said with stunned blue eyes.

Above the table where a few matric boys had come to sit, hung another new poster: *The Rocky Horror Picture Show*.

'Weird,' Simon had called it when he'd phoned from Stellenbosch recently. Men in women's clothes and make-up. He was crazy about it.

'"The girl in the room next door is going to pop any day now. (I wonder why everyone talks about 'pop'. As if the baby will shoot out like a champagne cork. If only it was that easy.) Anyway, I have to help her bath every evening because she can't reach her feet any more. I'll spare you the gruesome details but I promise you she's a sorry sight in the nude. The skin over her stomach is stretched as thin as an over-inflated balloon and looks as if it'll burst if you press too hard . . ."'

'Shame. She doesn't say anything about her own stomach, does she?' Suna said.

I shook my head. The more her own body distended, I thought sadly, the less she said about it. As if she were merely an incidental visitor in that peculiar boarding house, an outsider who felt compelled to amuse us with funny stories about the funny inmates.

By the twenty-eighth week, I'd read the previous weekend in my mother's medical book, *the baby is a little longer than thirty-eight centimetres and weighs approximately nine hundred grams. Its whole body is covered with vernix, a cheese-like substance which protects its skin against the fluid in the uterus.* 'Cheese-like?' It was like Antarctica, I thought, the world in which my best friend found herself. If you had never seen a snowflake, it was almost impossible to imagine a frozen, blindingly white continent.

'What's vernix, Ma?' I went to ask casually.

'*Vernix?*' Ma was sitting in an armchair, her legs folded under her and looked up from the women's magazine on her lap. 'Are you doing a crossword?'

'No, I read it somewhere. It has something to do with babies, doesn't it?'

'Oh, *vernix*! Yes, when a baby's born it has a waxy, white layer over its skin, rather like cream that hasn't been rubbed in properly.' Was there suspicion in my mother's eyes? I looked away and heard her paging through her magazine. 'Otherwise all new-born babies would look like crumpled laundry.'

'They look like crumpled laundry in any case.'

'Wait until you have your own baby,' Ma smiled. 'You'll soon change your tune.'

'Ma, do you think it's abnormal for someone not to want to have a baby?'

'At your age?' The expression in her dark eyes was impossible to read. 'No, Matta, you're far too young. There's lots of time for such things.'

Poor Dalena, I thought. Poor, poor Dalena . . .

'Look who's here,' Suna warned.

When I looked up Pine Pienaar was edging his way past our table. I looked down immediately but not before I'd seen the way he smiled, as if he knew something I hadn't even considered. His white T-shirt strained across his back, I saw as he walked away, and his faded jeans were patched on his bottom. When he shifted in next to the other matric boys at the corner table, he muttered something which made them laugh and peer at us over their shoulders. Pine didn't peer – it wasn't his style – but stared unashamedly at me as he lit a cigarette.

'What's his case?' I asked with a glowing face.

'Can't you see?'

'He's been looking for trouble for weeks.'

'It's not trouble he's after,' Suna said, her voice suddenly as sophisticated as Dalena's. 'It's your body.'

'But what . . . what about . . .' Stuttering. 'Jolene?'

'Overs kedovers.'

'Over?'

'They broke off the other day. By this time the whole school knows Dracula has scented fresh blood.' Suna leaned over the table and said confidentially: 'Except the poor victim who spends her days with her nose in a newspaper.'

By now it wasn't just my face that was glowing. My whole body was blazing under my school uniform.

It was recess and we were leaning against the outside of the lavatory wall, but it wasn't the same as the previous year. And not just because Dalena had disappeared. The cloud of smoke above our heads had also gone. Jolene and a few other girls sometimes hid behind a lavatory door for a surreptitious cigarette but they weren't as brave – or as stupid – as Maggie and her pals had been. Nothing was the same as the previous year, I thought, depressed.

The headmaster had decided to fight the cigarette devil with a new weapon. It was not only impermissible for schoolchildren to smoke, he had announced dramatically in hall one Monday morning, it was also *unhealthy*. Modern research had indicated that the habit constituted a serious danger to health! It was probably the Communists' doing that it had become so popular among the defenceless Western youth! So that we could all become smoking, drinking zombies, the living dead, interested in nothing more than pop music and pornography.

After this shocking revelation about the latest Communist ploy, the staff and prefects were taking stronger action against pupils who were caught with cigarettes.

'Have you noticed that Jolene has a new love in her life?' Suna asked, an expression between horror and envy on her face.

I looked at the case square where Jolene was whispering something into the ear of a standard nine boy. He looked shocked for a moment before a slow blush, like a wine stain on a white tablecloth, spread over his face.

'And I swear she's telling him dirty jokes! Under the noses of the prefects!' Suna shook her head and looked at one of our classmates who walked back and forth in the case square like a soldier on guard duty, her black prefect's blazer so big that her fingers were barely visible below the sleeves. 'Old Marinda is going to start goose-stepping any minute now.'

'I don't understand it,' I sighed. 'She was quite nice last year . . .'

'People change when they become prefects,' Suna sighed in sympathy.

'Do you think Dalena would have changed?'

'If she'd become a prefect?'

I nodded and looked at my legs which were showing angry red marks from the sun.

'Do you remember what she said last year?' Suna looked at her legs, too, as golden brown as boiled condensed milk, shaved as smooth as silk. 'That they wouldn't allow her to become one? Well, she was right.'

'How do you know?'

'My mother spoke to Miss Ferguson.'

Here we go again, I thought: *You know, Victoria Ferguson?*

'You know, Victoria Ferguson?'

As if there was any other Miss Ferguson in the school. Suna's mother had recently started playing bridge with the biology teacher but the way in which Suna carried on it was as if they were building a bridge together. As if no one except Suna's mother, Victoria Ferguson and (perhaps) Albert Einstein had ever been clever enough to understand such a complicated game. I preferred not to tell her that Dalena had christened the biology teacher Clitoria Ferguson last year.

'Well, she says that last year Dalena's name headed the list of those chosen by the children. And old Maritz crossed it out.'

'Genuine?'

'Yep. He evidently made a long speech in the staff room. Said it was the teachers' duty to protect the pupils against their own irresponsibility.'

'But then the so-called election is a joke!'

'Exactly.' Suna looked like one of those toy dogs in the back of car windows, constantly nodding their heads. 'Just as Dalena said.'

'But what's the point of it all?' I sounded just like my brother, I thought fearfully. 'Then he's simply wasting everybody's time, isn't he?'

'My mother always says a woman must let a man believe that he's the boss – even if everyone knows who the boss really is.'

'Hmm. My mother is of the same school.'

'Well, that's probably what old Maritz does.' The bell rang to announce the end of recess. Thankfully I drew my legs up out of the sun. Suna's golden legs remained on the ground next to me for a few seconds longer. 'He lets us think we have a say over our lives but we all know who has the last word.'

'I know where she is,' Simon wrote from Stellenbosch. 'I tried telephoning a few times without saying who I was but she evidently refuses to take any calls. So I drove to the place and sat in the street in front of the entrance for an entire day, hiding behind a newspaper like a stupid detective in a stupid movie. Just as I was about to give up, when it was starting to get dark, I saw her in the garden. It was a helluva shock. The big stomach, I mean.

'I got out of the car to go and speak to her but the moment she saw me, she turned round and walked away. Just like that, without even looking surprised, as if it was a scene in a play which she'd rehearsed for weeks! I stood at the gate like a fool and called to her. She could hear me, I'm certain she could hear me, but she simply walked through the front door and disappeared. The name of the place is the Daisy Home. Can you believe it?'

*

'I'm going to visit her,' I announced. 'I'm going to the Cape during the holiday.'

Suna had started to get up but now she sank back on her heels against the wall. I didn't know which of us was the more surprised by the unexpected announcement.

'It was Simon's suggestion. Of course he's hoping that I'll be able to convince her to see him. He says he'll get the money to pay for my flight ticket. Students always seem to have more money than anyone else. I'll just have to think up a story for my parents . . .'

Around us hundreds of children were walking back to class. All we could see, where we were still sitting against the wall, was a forest of moving legs. Boys' legs in long, grey socks, girls' legs in short, white socks.

'I suppose I can say Dalena sent the ticket, but I'm scared my mother might decide to phone her mother . . .'

'I don't think you have to worry about that,' Suna said absently. 'Her mother will probably just say yes and hope your mother doesn't ask too many questions. Otherwise she'll have to admit that she lied about the good school in the Cape.'

'I hope so . . .'

The legs around us were getting fewer. Reluctantly we got up and idled to our history class where we had at least progressed from the brave Voortrekkers' struggle against the cunning Zulus to the brave Boers' struggle against the wily British. If you could call it progress.

'And Dalena?' Suna asked before we walked into the classroom. 'Does she know you're going to see her?'

'Not yet.' I didn't know why my voice suddenly sounded so anxious. 'But Simon is sure she won't refuse to see me.'

'Come, you two old *tannies!*' *Tannies!* Suna rolled her eyes. It was the soldier prefect in the big blazer who had come up behind us. 'Stop babbling. Recess is over.'

'PS,' Simon wrote. 'I hid behind the newspaper for a whole day and all I can remember is one sentence: *The last South African troops will probably be withdrawn from Angola at the end of the month, closing the chapter of South Africa's involvement in Angola.* Can you fucking believe it?'

195

London, 29 August 1993

Dearest Child

It's so difficult to cling to hope. To me it seems like snow. Every time I think now I've got hold of it, it melts between my fingers.

More South Africans have died violently since 1990 than the total number of GIs sacrificed by the US in nearly ten years of war in Vietnam's killing fields.

When I read reports like this, all my faith in the election which is to be held next year evaporates.

In less than three and a half years in South Africa, 52,800 people have died violently. Commonly they were shot, but stones have been dropped to crush skulls, and assegais and knobkerries wielded in tribal vendettas. People have also been knifed in shebeens, bludgeoned to death or flung off trains.

And what then of love? Does the word still exist in that country?

When I started writing this story more than a year ago, I hoped that things would become clearer along the way. But the more I progress, the more hazy everything becomes. Or is it just that bloody nostalgia we drape over everything like mosquito netting? Because we're not brave enough to tackle the past without protection? I believed that my past would help me to predict my future – to make a decision about my and my son's future – but the more I pick at the past, the looser all the seams of my life feel. The more difficult it becomes to make any decision – about anything at all.

I hoped and believed that one day, when I was old enough, I would be able to look back at the past and forward into the future with a clear and fearless eye. But now I wonder whether I'll ever be old enough to see clearly and fearlessly.

The worst is yet to come, they say. That's what Dalena said years ago, when she was about as old as you are now. I'm afraid that all that's left to offer you, is love.

Love
M.

They Say the Worst Is Yet to Come

'Pa wasn't exactly overjoyed when he heard that you'd taken yourself out of residence,' I said cautiously, before he could become annoyed with me again.

'I can imagine.'

He was lying on the carpet, smoking, his back against a low pine bed, his head against the foam rubber mattress. The bed hadn't been made and the ugly orange floral pattern on the mattress showed under the crumpled sheets. The curtains next to the bed were twice as long as the window and lay on the floor in heavy, dark-green folds. They looked like old stage curtains stolen out of a church hall somewhere.

Looking at my brother now, he seemed a likely person to steal curtains from a church hall. He stared at the ceiling, but I doubted whether he could see it through the marijuana smoke which floated like wisps of fog about his head. He started laughing slowly, like a record revolving at the wrong speed. That was what he did these days when he became stoned.

'Was it really that bad, Simon?'

He stopped laughing and raised his head to look at me. His pupils were so large that his grey eyes seemed black. His hair was much longer and darker than when I'd seen him last. Or perhaps it just seemed darker because he hadn't washed or combed it in days. The golden-brown stubble around his mouth reminded me of an arid lawn. And yet he was still a dish, I decided unwillingly, even if it was a rather dirty, neglected dish these days.

'I know Pa thinks I'm not man enough to take a little initiation . . .'

'Well . . . he said it was tradition . . . stuff like that.'

'Fuck tradition.' He pinched the joint between three fingers and sucked hard at it. Inhaled the smoke as eagerly as I'd inhaled the smell of the sea the previous day. 'Not very long ago it was tradition to hang people in public!' When he exhaled the smoke, very slowly, his mouth pouted like my mother's. I was noticing things this evening that I had never noticed before, like that first weekend in Black River after he had started his National Service. But that weekend he had seemed harder and stronger and older than before – and now he looked softer and weaker and younger. 'I was fucked around by the Army for a whole year, Mart. I refuse to be treated like a mentally retarded child for another year!'

We sat in opposite corners in a room as cramped as a built-in cupboard. If I'd wanted to stretch my legs I'd have virtually had to put my feet in his lap. But my brother preferred living in a cupboard to going back to a university residence. What my enraged father would say if he could see this hole, I didn't want to think about.

'What's he up to!' Pa had exploded and thrown Simon's letter towards Ma. 'I thought the Army had made a man of him! Now he's behaving like a pansy!'

'Pa . . .' Ma tried to placate him.

'Yes, never mind, I know you'll come up for him! He's never made a mistake in his mother's eyes!'

'Pa, don't . . .'

'Can't you see that's where it all started, Marlene? You can't coddle a boy like that! It's what I've always said. Now look what's happened! He undergoes initiation – like thousands of first years before him – and he can't take it! He runs away! It won't surprise me in the least if I have to hear –'

'Carl!' Suddenly my mother's voice was so sharp that my father's words died away from sheer fright. 'It has nothing to do with coddling. You know that as well as I do. It was the Army that muddled that child's head! Write a letter to the Minister of Defence if you want to bawl out someone!'

I hadn't told Simon about this outburst. There were enough things for him to worry about that evening. I paged through an old newspaper while he stared at the ceiling again. The defence budget was double that of two years ago, I read in one of the reports. I wondered what he would have to say about that.

'Listen to this,' I said to take his attention away from the ceiling. 'Here's a story with the headline 'Stewed Brits? – More people enter London restaurants than those who come out, according to a survey taken by the London City Council about British eating habits. Officials who meticulously monitored the attendance at twelve restaurants, either couldn't count or discovered a strange British phenomenon . . ."'

He barely smiled. It was as if anything I said this evening remained hanging in the dagga smoke above our heads, as if nothing really got through to him.

'So?' He killed the roach in the empty beer can next to him. 'What's your plan of action?'

'Action?'

'How are you going to get hold of Dalena?'

'Well, I phoned the home and left a message for her that I was in Stellenbosch. Now I'll just have to wait until she phones back.'

If she phones back, I thought.

'When did you phone?'

'Just after I arrived . . . the day before yesterday.'

'The day before yesterday!' It became ominously quiet in the room. Like in the hostel, in the study hall, where your own breathing sounded too loud. Somewhere behind a closed door someone was listening to Radio Five. 'Perhaps she didn't get the message?'

'I phoned again yesterday. And this morning as well. I've now spoken to three different girls and they all promised they'd tell her.'

He chewed his thumbnail and stared at his bare feet below his frayed jeans. When he was small my mother had rubbed castor oil or something on his fingertips to stop him chewing his nails. He hadn't done it for years.

'And if she doesn't phone?'

The question hung in the air as heavy as the marijuana smoke in the quiet room.

'I know her,' I lied. 'Don't worry. She'll phone.'

Later that night we fled out of the small room, as relieved as prisoners escaping from a cell, but when we walked through the deserted streets the feeling of relief disappeared like the puffs of our breath in the icy air. I had wanted to get away from the church hall curtains for a while, the stupefying smoke, the unmade bed and the uncomfortable silence between us. But the cold and the darkness and the mist in which oak trees appeared one after another like ghosts made me feel even more depressed. We walked into a student bar – as empty as the streets – and ordered two glasses of wine.

'A student town without students is like a toyshop without toys,' Simon mumbled. 'All those who haven't gone home for the holidays, are watching *Rich Man, Poor Man* tonight.'

The barman poured the wine without taking his eyes off a TV screen on which a thug with a black eyepatch grinned like an old-fashioned pirate.

'Is this the series everyone is so mad about?' I swallowed the wine like water, suddenly in a hurry to reach Simon's cramped room again. 'I don't know when we'll ever be able to get television on the farm.' I was afraid that Dalena might call while we were out. But I didn't want to tell Simon that, because I was even more scared that she wouldn't phone when we were there. I gave an exaggerated yawn and rubbed my eyes as if I had trouble in keeping them open. 'It must be the sea air that makes me so sleepy. I think it's time to go to bed.'

Not until after eleven o'clock the following evening, after another long day of anxious waiting, did the telephone in the passage ring. I had just dozed off in the borrowed room opposite Simon's and burst through the door in my striped flannel pyjamas. Simon stood next to the telephone and looked uncertainly at me. All he was wearing were the shorts in which he slept. I could see the gooseflesh on his bare torso.

'You answer it!' he whispered nervously.

I was gasping for breath, I realized when I picked up the receiver. 'Hello?'

'You're just like that bloody woman in the Bible!'

I immediately recognized the deep voice. The relief hit my knees like a hammer. I had to hold on to the wall not to fall.

'Which woman?' I asked, my voice as shaky as my knees.

'"Wherever you go, I will go; wherever you live, I will live." Esther or Naomi or . . .'

'Ruth,' I said. 'It was Ruth.'

'You always knew the Bible better than I did,' Dalena said. 'Hello, Mart.'

'Hello, Dalena.' When Simon heard her name, something happened to his face. Like a balloon slowly deflating, or a fist opening. 'Well, can I see you?'

'Do you really think it's necessary?'

'"Wherever you live, I will live,"' I reminded her.

'No ways, Mart!' she laughed in my ear. 'At the moment I live in the Daisy Home for Unmarried Mothers – better known as the House of the Rising Sin – and the only way it can become your home too is if you've got a bun in the oven since I last saw you.'

It was four months ago, I realized, as I slowly sank down against the wall. We hadn't seen one another for four months. I sat down on the wooden floor and stretched out my shaky legs in the pyjama trousers.

'How are you, Dalena?'

'You don't want to know, Mart.'

'Yes, I do.'

'I'm eight months pregnant. I'm as heavy as a hippo, my feet are so swollen I can't get them into shoes and I have trouble sleeping because my stomach is in the way. I have backache and varicose veins and indigestion. And when I went to the loo yesterday, I discovered that I've developed piles as well.'

'It sounds . . . terrible,' I stuttered.

For the first time it really hit me that things were happening to my best friend in which I could never have a part.

'They say the worst is yet to come,' Dalena said. 'The next few weeks.'

Simon had gone to fetch a sweater and a cigarette in his room and now nervously edged closer while pulling the sweater over his head. I looked up and tried to smile reassuringly but my lower lip trembled when I opened my mouth. He sat down on the floor opposite me, shivering with cold, and passed me the cigarette like a consolation prize. I took a deep drag – and started coughing when I realized that it wasn't cigarette smoke I was inhaling.

'And by the way,' Dalena said when she heard me coughing, 'I'm not allowed to smoke or drink because it'll make the baby stupid.'

I blinked my eyes against tears and looked in confusion from the cigarette between my fingers to Simon but he only stared at the floor, his arms tightly wrapped round his body. I raised my hand and smelled it. Unmistakable.

Was this how my brother wanted to thank me because I had managed to get hold of Dalena? By offering me a joint for the first time? Or had the call upset him to such a degree that he didn't know what he was doing?

All I had to do was to hand it back to him. But I didn't. Curious, I lifted it to my lips and sucked carefully at it. Inflated my cheeks and allowed small amounts of smoke to escape. The way he always did.

'But everyone always carries on about how wonderful it is to be pregnant . . . shiny hair and rosy cheeks and –'

'They lie,' Dalena said. 'The whole thing is a Communist plot to keep the West over-populated.'

'Surely there must be *something* good about it?'

It felt as if the words weren't issuing from my mouth but drifting towards me from a distance.

'Well, for the first time in my life I've got a decent pair of boobs,' Dalena admitted unwillingly. 'I wear a size 36C bra now! But it's a helluva price to pay for bigger tits.'

I sucked on the joint again. Maybe the headmaster was right, I thought fearfully, maybe pot did peculiar things to your head straight away. As if your mind changed into a disturbed hive and all rational thought milled around like angry bees and nothing but a stupid vacuum remained in your head.

'I'm coming to see you, Dalena,' I said before my mind became so befuddled that I forgot why I was there.

'No, please don't, this place is too depressing,' she said. 'But I suppose we could meet somewhere.'

'Just say where and I'll be . . . I'll make sure . . .' Whatever I'd wanted to say disappeared into the air with the smoke of the joint.

At the end of the sentence I could no longer remember where I'd started or where I wanted to end. 'Just tell me where.'

'I have to go to town tomorrow. If you like, you could meet me off the train, then we can have coffee somewhere.'

'What time?'

The shorter I kept my sentences, I realized, the smaller were the chances of sounding like a stoned idiot.

'It gets in around eleven.' Her boy's voice was suddenly nervous. 'You'll be on your own, won't you?'

'Of course.'

I sucked loudly and audibly on the joint, the way my brother always did, and started coughing again.

'What's the matter? Have you got a cold?'

'It's probably the Cape weather,' I said, still coughing.

'OK, then, eleven o'clock at the station. Don't worry, you won't miss me – not with this belly. But I'm warning you, Mart, if you laugh, I'll clock you one!'

'I won't laugh, Dalena,' I promised and started laughing slowly. Too slowly, I realized. Just like my brother.

'Come on, tell me everything that's happening in Black River!' Dalena leaned eagerly across the table, her eyes green and clear as glass, her brown hair shinier and shorter than four months ago. 'I want to hear the lot.'

'First I must give you something from Suna.' I dug around in my handbag and took out a pair of knitted yellow bootees in a torn plastic bag. 'She knitted them herself.'

She shrank back when she saw the bootees sitting on my palm like two chicks.

'I know it's bad luck to bring clothes for the child,' I explained hurriedly while she stared at my hand as if she was afraid that the present was going to bite her. 'But Suna was so excited and it was so hard for her to knit them, it was something awful. She drove me nearly mad moaning about it. But for some reason or other she wanted the baby to have something from her . . .'

My voice stuck in my throat when I saw her stretch out a hesitant hand, pick up the plastic bag and take out the bootees. Here and there the yellow wool bore the smudges of Suna's sweaty hands. 'Black River will never be a knitter's paradise,' I said apologetically. 'It's too hot . . .'

'Tell Suna I said thank you very much. Tell her I know how difficult knitting is — I tried it myself.' She laughed when she saw the expression on my face. 'Can you believe it! It was supposed to be a little jacket but the one sleeve is so narrow that you can't get your little finger into it and the other is wider at the bottom than at the top. I think maybe I sewed it together wrong. But I wanted the child to have something . . . something I'd made myself . . .' Hastily she thrust the bootees into her handbag and took a greedy bite of the cheesecake in front of her. 'Hmm, this is unbelievably good. I don't know why. So that when he's grown up he'll know something about his mother? Even if it's only that her knitting would never have been sold at the local church fête.'

If I closed my eyes, I thought longingly, I could pretend we were back in our hostel room. She sounded exactly the same as before, and with her stomach hidden under the table, she didn't look very different either, except for the breasts. Even under the wide denim dungarees I could see her new size 36C boobs shaking when she laughed.

We were sitting in a café as ugly as the one next to the Plaza in Black River. Dalena's feet were so swollen that she had refused to walk another step when she saw the cheesecake in the dirty display window. From where I sat I could look past the cheesecake and a pile of doughnuts in the window at Table Mountain, which today also looked like a large cake with a white icing of cloud. I gave an admiring sigh.

'You Capetonians all suffer from mountain sickness,' Dalena mumbled, her back to the mountain and her mouth full of cheesecake. 'Every morning you carry on as if you can't believe it's still there! As if someone might've stolen it during the night!'

'Well, it's impossible to imagine the city without the mountain.'

'Like imagining Black River without mosquitoes?'

'You can't compare Black River with —'

'Come on, tell me what's happening in my valley! It's much more interesting than your swooning over the bloody mountain!'

'I don't know where to begin. So many exciting things happen every day that I could write a book about them.'

'Leave the sarcasm to Mr Locomotive.'

'It's not sarcasm, it's irony. Old Locomotive says there's a difference.'

She cast her eyes up to the ceiling, the same dirty-yellow colour as the walls, almost like Suna's bootees.

'The most important event in the hostel is that Miss Potgieter has acquired a new dressing gown.'

'Genuine?' Without a trace of sarcasm or irony. If only the newspaper reports I'd read to her last year had elicited so much interest!

'Yes, with red and white stripes. Now she doesn't look like a huge bird of prey any more when she creeps around the passages at night. More like a gigantic tube of toothpaste.'

'If you make me laugh I'll wet my pants,' Dalena warned. 'The baby presses on my bladder. I'm practically incontinent.'

'Well, if you want to hear a sad story I can always tell you about our rugby first team. They played their first friendly game of the season the other day against a farm school so small they don't have enough players to make up a team, so they used two girls as forwards. Not the kind of girls you'll ask about make-up. Anyway, Pine accidentally touched one's tits – it might have been deliberate, you know what he's like – and she socked him. Lights out!'

'I don't believe it!' Dalena laughed.

'Genuine! You should've seen old Locomotive's face! His best player knocked unconscious by someone wearing a bra! And without Pine the team lost, of course. But they always lose in any case.'

'And Pine? What happened to him?'

'He survived. Only the good die young.' Don't start blushing now, I thought apprehensively. I took a few sips of coffee and wondered whether to tell her more. 'But you can imagine the teasing.'

'Is he still lusting after Jolene's body?'

'No, evidently it's all over. He must've got what he wanted.'

'And what might that have been?'

I stared at the plastic tablecloth as if I hadn't heard her mocking question. Next to the plastic menu stood a plastic carnation in a plastic bottle. Even the coffee tasted plastic.

'I think he . . . I hear he . . .' My hands felt so slippery that I had difficulty in holding the cup. 'Suna says he's lusting after my body now.'

'What!'

A piece of cheesecake on her fork fell back on to the small plate while she looked at me in amazement. A bit too amazed I thought, mortified.

'Well, you're not that unattractive,' she decided.

'Thanks.' I'd hoped that it would sound sarcastic but it merely sounded . . . grateful.

'Or maybe he's one of those weird guys who has a thing about virgins.' I choked on the cold plastic coffee. She looked suspiciously at me. 'You *are* still a virgin, aren't you?'

'Of course,' I said with wet eyes.

'I'm pleased to hear it,' she said – as if she were my mother – and forked up the piece of cheesecake again.

'But what do you think . . . I mean, what should I do? If he makes a move.'

'What do you want to do?'

'I don't know.'

'Do you like him?'

'I don't know.'

'Let's make it easy,' she said, her mouth full of cheesecake. 'How do you feel when you look at him?'

'Well, he's quite well built. In a rugby-playing kind of way,' I added hastily. 'I think he's quite –'

'I don't want to know what you think,' she said with irritation. 'I want to know what you feel.'

Fear, I thought. An exciting kind of fear.

'I don't know what goes on in his head, Dalena.' With my eyes on the great, grey mountain. 'It frightens me.'

'If you want to wait until you know what goes on in a guy's head, you'll stay a virgin for the rest of your life,' she said, and tucked her hair behind her ears. I hadn't realized how much I'd missed that gesture. 'All I can say, Mart, is that if you decide to sleep with him –'

'I'm not talking about sleeping with him!'

'Well, whatever you're talking about.' She leaned back and folded her hands over her big stomach the way pregnant women always do. 'Just keep this image of your roommate's condition in mind. It should be a better contraceptive than any FL.'

I looked past her head at the mountain. Would it spoil everything if I mentioned Simon now?

'Suna is going on the pill.'

'Suna!'

'For her skin. She says it can prevent acne.'

'Hmm.' Dalena put the last piece of cake in her mouth and licked off the whipped cream on her lips. 'It could prevent a great many other things as well.'

I traced finger patterns on the plastic tablecloth, round and round the big yellow flowers.

'Dalena, have you thought about what you're going to do . . . when it's over?'

'Yep.' She sat with her chin in her hand and stared at the dirty-yellow wall. 'And the more I think about it, the more I realize that it'll probably never be over.'

For the first time that day I could see the yellow flecks in her eyes. But it might have been a reflection from the tablecloth.

'When's the baby due?'

'End of May, beginning of June – somewhere around there.'

'And then? What are you going to do for the rest of the year?'

'I've decided to go overseas. Perhaps for a few years.'

I looked up in astonishment from the yellow flower under my finger.

'Where to?'

'Oh, I don't know.' Now she was staring at the tablecloth. 'It probably doesn't matter where I go. Somewhere where it's always warm. Greece?'

'And what about . . . don't you want to go to university next year?'

She shook her head, still looking down at the tablecloth. 'I feel too old to be a student.'

'But where will you get the money to go abroad?'

'I've already asked my father.' Elbows on the table, hands folded like a shield over her face. 'He sent me a huge cheque by return. He can't wait to get rid of me. After all, if I'm living overseas, the neighbours can't gossip about me!'

Unexpectedly a teardrop fell on the tablecloth between us, exactly in the middle of one of the yellow flowers.

'Dalena . . .'

'I would so much have liked to spend some time on the farm before I leave! I don't know when I'll ever get there again!' She wiped her face with an open, impatient hand. 'I can't believe I'm sitting here, snivelling in public about my stupid pa and my stupid ma!'

I looked helplessly at her.

'It's quite funny, isn't it?' She smiled but her eyes were still grey with tears. 'I've never really had a burning ambition to travel. You were the one who always carried on about it. You and Pierre.'

His name fell like another astonishing teardrop between us.

We hadn't spoken about Pierre yet. There were so many things we hadn't spoken about.

'Dalena . . .' I swallowed with such difficulty that I wished there was still cold coffee in my cup. 'Simon asks if he could please . . . if he could just talk to you. Before the baby is born.'

'There's nothing to talk about,' she said firmly. 'I have to do what I have to do.'

'No, it's not that. He doesn't want to change your mind, he just wants to see you.'

She folded her hands on her stomach and looked down, frowning as if she felt something under her fingers she didn't understand.

'This isn't easy for him, Dalena!'

'Nobody said it was going to be easy, Mart!'

And she laughed as bitterly as Simon had laughed in his cramped room a few nights ago. They had both learned to laugh like Pierre.

London, 20 September 1993

My Dearest Child

Three news reports have stayed with me during the last month, longer than all the others that flash past my eyes every day.

More than fifty civilians died during Unita shelling of the besieged central Angolan city of Cuito, Angola radio said. It is reported that powerful shelling continually rocks the city, to the extent that Unita's shells are cracking the ground open and pushing dead and buried people into the open again.

It has literally become a *danse macabre*, that thirty years' war. But in your own country, believe it or not, things are nearly as bad.

With the exception of Angola, South Africa now has the bloodiest conflict in the world. Since August 1990, when 720 people died after the Pretoria Accord was signed, four other months also saw high death tolls, all occurring just after important political developments. In March 1992, 437 people died shortly after the referendum; in July 1993, when an election was announced for next year, 604 people died . . .

Etcetera, etcetera, *ad nauseam* . . . But hang on, don't stop reading, there is a spark of hope in this picture of despair. The report ended like this:

In the space of three years, South Africa has lost four and a half times the number of people who have died violently in Northern Ireland. But students of revolution believe that South Africa presents a better future scenario than Northern Ireland because ongoing negotiations are taking place in South Africa.

And now from the political to the personal. The third report was the one my mother sent me two months ago. The one I didn't see my way clear to writing about before.

The owner of a well-known Lowveld game farm, Miss Magdalena van

210

Vuuren, 34, was found dead in her bedroom on Thursday, apparently having taken an overdose of sleeping capsules the previous evening.

Miss van Vuuren was the youngest daughter of a respected farmer of Sunstream, near Black River, the late Mr Christiaan van Vuuren, and of Mrs Tossie van Vuuren who is well-known for her work with local charities. After her father's death in 1989, Miss van Vuuren turned part of the model farm which she inherited into a luxury game reserve, Enkosi, which attracted mainly foreign visitors.

According to a shocked Mrs van Vuuren, her daughter had previously been treated for clinical depression but in the past few months she had been in excellent mental health.

'She was excited about the growing tourist market in South Africa. She was busy with plans to extend the game reserve. I'm convinced that Dalena's death was simply a tragic accident,' Mrs van Vuuren said.

That was the core of the report. I've carried it in my handbag for so long, I've taken it out, unfolded and re-read it so often that it is becoming fragile from handling, like those letters I received from the Daisy Home long ago. But it still doesn't make sense.

My first thought was that Tossie van Vuuren was still just as worried about what the neighbours would say. Perhaps I simply wanted to keep the next thought on ice, the almost unthinkable possibility that my former roommate might have committed suicide.

By this time I've absorbed her death, however difficult it's been, but not the manner of her dying. Even if I look back to a few signs which I can only now decipher with hindsight, suicide makes no sense. It's as if I'm constantly hearing her voice, as deep and remote as it sounded over the telephone that evening, almost twenty years ago: *But don't you think it takes more guts to go on living?*

Love
M.

Hello, Darkness, My Old Friend

'*Summer!*' Suna threw her pen down with such force that it fell off the bed and rolled as far as my feet. 'When I heard the name of our next set book I though, aah, fabulous! It sounds like an enjoyable story about a seaside holiday! I should've known . . .'

I threw the pen back to her without looking up from the newspaper.

'Who's ever heard of an enjoyable set book!' She read out Mr Locomotive's instructions, her voice as deep as his and rolling each 'r' sarcastically: ' "Discuss the concept of trransience in the novel, *Summerr* by C. M. van den Heeverr." What the fuck does that mean?'

She clapped her hand over her mouth and looked at me with startled eyes. It was the first time I'd ever heard her using a swear word.

'It's all the stuff that passes, man. All the things that change, the seasons and the corn ripening and people getting old . . .'

I had written my essay the day before yesterday only because us hostel kids were forced to spend a few hours in the study hall every day. If I'd had Suna's freedom, I would probably have postponed it to the weekend as well. But now I was pleased that it was done – that I could read the newspaper with pleasure while she had to struggle with transience. Not that pleasure was the right word, exactly. The fluttering I felt in my stomach wasn't the soft butterflies I usually had before a party. It was more like a mass of insects swarming over a piece of rotten meat. And it owed more to the newspaper than tonight's party.

With the firm intention of dying rather than falling into the hands of the enemy, a South African Army officer held his cocked pistol against his head while the enemy tried to force open the hatch of his armoured car.

I looked at Suna sitting cross-legged on her bed, her head at an angle as if she was listening intently to the droning of the lawn mower out in the garden, her hair thrown over one shoulder like a pale yellow velvet curtain. The smell of newly mown grass hung heavy and sweet in the air, heavier than the scent of a frangipani flower, sweeter than my mother's hairspray. But it seemed as if I smelled something else under the heavy sweetness, something sour and salty.

After the ammunition in his armoured car was exhausted, a young lieutenant, his right hand temporarily out of action, pulled out his pistol with his left hand and killed eleven attacking Cubans. The driver killed the remaining two by running them down.

'Running them down?'

Surely the black gardener had been pushing that lawn mower for hours, back and forth, back and forth as if there was going to be a tennis match in the garden this evening instead of a party in the garage. As if the kids who wanted to stand outside necking would care about the state of the lawn! When the droning was silent for a moment I heard the high-pitched singing of a vacuum cleaner in the garage where a servant had been busy for almost as long.

According to the newspaper there had been an official TV programme broadcast the previous evening about the heroic acts performed by South African soldiers in Angola last year. (The same soldiers, by the way, who *weren't* in Angola last year, according to the government.) That was why the press could today, for the first time, reveal what had actually happened there. But the more I read, the more confused I became. Since when had it been an heroic act to kill someone by running him down?

The enemy had the dreaded Stalin organ with its red eye – but no matter: the 5.5 cannon with its slightly shorter range, played havoc with the enemy.

'Does it have something to do with Wynand's death wish?' Suna chewed her pen, her head still at an angle. 'This transient stuff?'

'Wynand? Please! It's *Hannes* who wants to die,' I said brusquely. Suna drove me crazy. How on earth was she going to get the essay written if she didn't even know the names of the main characters? 'And he doesn't really want to die, it's just that one part where he –'

'It sounds as if the whole lot are so depressed they want to die!'

Impatiently Suna threw the velvet curtain back over her shoulder. 'Except the Coloureds who behave like clowns all the time.'

'Well, why don't you write that?' I said quickly.

'What?'

'That it sounds as if all the white people are depressed and all the Coloureds are jolly?'

'Are you *insane?*' Suna asked, her eyes wide.

No, I wasn't insane but I was about to become despairing. Suna's mother had said that she had to finish the essay before we could start decorating the garage. And after we had decorated the garage with candles and crêpe paper, which could take a couple of hours, we still needed lots of time for putting curlers in our hair, bathing, dressing and doing our faces. Oh, and we were also supposed to lie down for fifteen minutes with cool slices of cucumber on our eyes. According to Clitoria Ferguson, this would ensure bright eyes in the evening. (She should know. Her eyes even shone when she showed us, early on a Monday morning, how to dissect a frog.) But if our pretty biology teacher had suggested that we lie with burning cigarette ends on our eyes, Suna would probably have been just as keen to follow her advice.

'Well, Mr Botha always says we must be original. It's certainly an original view of *Summer.*'

'But what does it have to do with transience?'

'Perhaps you could say that the white people in the book sound more transient than the Coloureds?'

'Because they don't laugh as much?'

Suna bit her pen, her blue eyes sceptical but I could see that she wanted me to convince her.

'Because they're more depressed,' I assented.

I felt doubtful all over again about the long, black dress I'd bought for the party. Suna said it made me look sexy, the black trilobal tight across my bottom, then falling in loose folds around my legs. Like that song, she said, 'Long Cool Woman in a Black Dress.' But I still wasn't sure that it had been the right choice. Suppose all the other girls were wearing jeans? And maybe I wouldn't even look sexy in my long black dress. Maybe I'd look like someone's grandma.

'Oh, well . . .'

Suna took the pen out of her mouth and started writing on the clean page in front of her. I felt so relieved that I imagined I was already hearing the party music playing in the dark garage: 'A Whiter Shade of Pale', 'Stairway to Heaven', 'Sounds of Silence', 'Simone' . . . Until a small report in the back pages of the newspaper caught my eye.

A spokesman of the Cuban Embassy in London yesterday denied that 150 to 200 Cuban soldiers had been killed in a single battle, as the South African government claimed. 'It is generally known that fewer Cubans died in the four months of fighting in Angola than during the American-supported invasion of the Bay of Pigs in 1961,' the spokesman said. Cuba claims that it lost fewer than 200 men in 1961.

The music had stopped. I knew what Pierre would've said. Somewhere someone was lying – that was about all one ever could be certain of.

Suna was dancing like Salome doing her number for the king. Her body rocked wildly to the beat of 'Sorrow', her head thrown back and her eyes closed, the lashes a shocking blue and stiff as starch after she had applied about ten layers of aquamarine mascara some two hours ago. If the headmster could see her now, he would say that this was why pop music was evil. It changed shy schoolgirls like Suna into shameless Salomes.

She wore a long, shiny halter-neck dress in the same pale blue as her eyes, and her writhing shoulders shone like copper against the thin straps around her neck. Her skin looked much better than it had last year but I was still too embarassed to ask whether it was due to the pill.

I didn't look half bad either, I'd decided earlier in the evening in front of the long mirror in Suna's room. When she unrolled her mother's electric curlers from my hair, I'd felt like a wild butterfly slowly emerging from a warm, electric cocoon. Perhaps a bit too wild, I'd thought, but Suna assured me the windswept look was just what my hair needed to make me look ten years older. Combined with the sexy black dress, of course. And lipstick which was so dark that it looked as if I'd rubbed mulberries on to my mouth.

'Ten years?' I'd asked the unfamiliar young woman in the mirror. 'Isn't that a bit much?'

'Okay, five years,' Suna said quickly. 'Don't worry, Mart, you look fabulous. Old Pine won't know what's hit him.'

I'd seen myself blushing in the mirror, even under the blusher which Suna had applied to my cheeks with such a lavish hand. But now I was grateful that I had been brave enough to wear the black trilobal dress. The party was well on its way and this was the first dance I was sitting out – and only because I didn't feel like dancing with Ben again. Tonight I realized that I was finished with him. When he'd touched me on the dance floor earlier, I didn't even feel a spark in my body. Then I knew. Once a fire had died, it couldn't be made to flare up again by dancing around it.

When Mick Jagger started singing 'Angie', Pine Pienaar unexpectedly touched my shoulder and his hand burnt a hole right through my new black dress. And when he led me on to the dance floor without saying a word, the hole became so large that the dress melted right off my body. Then I knew. You got cosy little fires in the hearth and you got dangerous bush fires. And the glow I felt didn't come from any cosy little fire.

He'd wanted to ask me a long time ago, he murmured, his breath hot against my ear but he'd been waiting for a slow dance.

I wondered what my roommate would say if she could see me now, reckless in a melted dress with a head of wild electric curls resting on Pine Pienaar's warm chest. His arms were as tight as clamps around me but I didn't mind. Do you know, Dalena, I would rather have smothered painfully slowly than tell him not to hold me so tightly?

His shoulders and his chest were as hard and as hot as a piece of corrugated iron which had been lying in the sun. But the hardest and the hottest was the lower half of his body. It wasn't that he was deliberately rubbing it against me, Dalena, but we were dancing so closely I could hardly not feel it.

When 'Angie' ended, we danced another slow dance, and another, and when the tempo changed we ignored it and clung to one another and swayed in one spot as if we were trying to stay upright in a high wind. By that time the music no longer mattered. It wouldn't have bothered me if they'd played 'Roll out the Barrel'. We swayed to another record, and another and another, until I stopped counting and started wondering if the big, dangerous Pine Pienaar only wanted to *sway* all evening.

Until he eventually asked, in an unfamiliar, hoarse voice: 'Would you like to go outside?'

I tore my head away from his chest with some difficulty and looked at him. In the candlelight his eyes were as black as my dress and his skin as dark as Pierre's had been. Not that he reminded me of Pierre, Dalena. He didn't have that kind of lean duskiness or those high cheekbones or those eyes that shone right through your head like searchlights. (Pine's eyes could probably also have been compared to searchlights but he definitely wasn't interested in my head. These searchlights were playing lower down on my body.)

Outside in the garden he gave a rather superior look at the kids cuddling in dark corners and, holding my hand, pulled me past them, over the lawn the gardener had spent so much time on that morning, on to the pavement in front of the house. There he casually strolled on, keeping to the shadows cast by a small avenue of jacaranda trees, his arm lying like lead across my shoulders. And the softer the music of the party became, the louder my own breathing sounded. It was only about ten houses further that my voice returned.

'Where are we going?'

'To Sparks's house. Just round the corner.'

I didn't know Sparks but I knew about him. He'd been in matric two years ago, a guy with a reputation as long as a river. Wild and reckless.

'He isn't there,' Pine said. 'Neither are his old people.'

'But why . . . what are we going to do there?'

My voice sounded more excited than scared, I realized with amazement.

'I have a key. I'm looking after the house. I'm sleeping there tonight.'

I looked uncertainly at him, with something that felt like a heavy stone dropping in my stomach – but still sending little bubbles of excitement to the surface. Then Pine Pienaar put out his hands, with the timing of a born rugby player, and caught the stone just before it caused a hole in my stomach. He folded his arms around me and kissed my mouth.

And it was truly a kiss that would have satisfied even you, Dalena. I'd thought the heroes of the rugby field would know the inside of a scrum better than the inside of a girl's mouth. I'd thought their large hands would fit more expertly around a hard rugby ball than a girl's soft body. I'd thought . . .

But by then I wasn't thinking at all, Dalena. All I could hear was the hammering of my heart in my chest and the rush of blood in my veins. I didn't know what was happening to my body but it felt as if all my hormones were waking up simultaneously.

When he unlocked the front door of the strange house, I saw that his hands were shaking. Was it possible that the big, dangerous Pine Pienaar was just as scared as I was of what might happen? But I didn't want to think about what might happen.

In the dark entrance hall he kissed me again. Now I had to keep my head as never before in my life. But it was difficult to remember that I had a head at all, with his warm hands stroking my body all over, a hand in the hollow of my back, a hand rubbing my stomach, a hand caressing my thighs, a hand – how many hands did he have? – unexpectedly slipping down the top of my dress.

And I wasn't wearing a bra, I thought, panic-stricken. The dress fitted too closely, I'd thought, the bra strap would show too clearly on my back. Or maybe I'd just wanted to be as daring as Jolene. But now I didn't feel daring, merely helpless, as my nipples hardened under his fingertips.

'Hang on.' He was trying to get me down on the floor, I realized rather anxiously. 'Pine, hang on a minute.'

Was this how it was going to happen? Was this how I was going to lose my precious virginity? Pulled down on the floor in the entrance hall of a strange house, overwhelmed by a rugby player?

'No, Pine, hang on!' I pushed him away, suddenly so frightened that I felt the strength of a rugby forward in my arms. 'Wait a moment!'

He staggered back slightly, caught unawares, and stared at me with unseeing black eyes. *They say a man can't think once his thing is hard.*

They say it's your own fault if you let him go too far. Help me, Dalena, please help me tonight. *He goes quite crazy. He'll rape you just like that.*

What now?

'Not here,' I whispered.

'Do you want to go to Sparks's room?' His voice was still hoarse but more hesitant than in the garage earlier in the evening.

'No,' I said quickly, 'not there.'

Through the open door of the living room I could see the weak circle of light cast by a lamp on a low table. I took his hand as if I knew what I was doing and led him to the light. It was one of those formal living rooms, I saw immediately, full of Persian rugs, dark, draped curtains and stiff armchairs covered in velvet. It was too grand, I thought, too formal. He wouldn't dare do it here.

I knew what you would say, Dalena. Once a chicken, always a chicken. But it wasn't that I was scared. OK, of course I was scared as well, but it wasn't only fear that was stopping me. I simply knew, then, that I didn't want to do it with Pine Pienaar. I didn't even like him very much.

But my nipples had hardened again under his fingers which were thrust into the top of my dress once more. I didn't want to do it but my knees betrayed me when he kissed me in the neck. I didn't want to but I actually sank down on the nearest sofa with him. My body simply refused to listen to my head.

I lay back on the uncomfortable sofa with his body heavy and hot on top of me, too heavy and too hot. He had managed to pull my dress down completely over one shoulder. My bare breast looked almost transparent in the weak light of the lamp, the nipple like a dark bruise. He drew a sharp breath when he saw it, like a child taking a toy out of gift wrapping. He put his open mouth on my breast, his avid hands stroking my legs so that my dress moved up higher and higher. His lower body constantly rubbed against me, so hard and hot by this time that I felt as if every particle of resistance in my lower body would either be rubbed away or scorched away.

But when he slipped his hand into the top of my bikini panties, I struggled up with the last bit of willpower left to me. Because then I knew – instinctively, even though it was my first time – that if I didn't say what I had to say at once, I wouldn't say it at all.

'No,' I said breathlessly, as I wriggled out from under his body. 'I can't, I won't, Pine, I won't . . .'

He stared at me, utterly taken aback. Had no one ever said no to him before?

'I'm sorry,' I said without knowing what I was apologizing for.

'You can't leave me like this, Mart,' he said, still in that hoarse voice, but now I could swear it had a pleading sound.

'Leave you how?' I asked before I could consider what I was saying.

He took my hand and put it down on his open fly. It didn't feel like frozen sausage at all, Dalena. It felt more like something alive, as if he kept a mysterious pet under the thin material of his underpants.

'What . . . what do you want me to do?'

I got no further because the pet suddenly burst out of his underpants like a furious watchdog wanting to bite me. I jerked my hand away in fright and stared. Why do they call it a *cock*? That was my first stunned thought. The thing didn't have anything nearly resembling feathers or wings. Nor characteristic sounds, as far as I could gather.

Pine folded his large hand over mine without saying a word and showed me how to hold this improbable cock. He started moving his hand back and forth – carefully at first, as tentative as finger exercises on a piano, and then gradually faster, more passionately, harder. The skin under my fingers felt as supple as the skin around a puppy's neck. Why didn't they rather call it a *dog*?

Pine closed his eyes and sank his head against the back of the sofa while our hands still moved rhythmically together. And then, unexpectedly, he dropped his own hand bonelessly next to him.

Now I was on my own. As nervous – and as excited! – as the first time my father allowed me to take the wheel in my mother's Cortina. After a while my hand started getting tired. The excitement started changing to panic – as it had when I couldn't get Ma's car into the right gear – but now I had to carry on, even if it felt as if my hand was about to drop off. I became more and more panicky. Surely something had to happen sooner or later? Or was I expected to carry on like this for the rest of the night? Then the body next to me jerked and I realized that the end was in sight. A few seconds later my fingers became wet and sticky, and the tense body as relaxed as a sleeping child's. I gave a sigh – of relief and amazement.

I did it, I thought, almost indecently proud of what I'd achieved. With the big, dangerous Pine Pienaar. Or with Pine Pienaar's *penis*, at any rate.

It was the first time I could think of the word without blushing. And when I looked at his penis again, Dalena, it didn't look like a dangerous watchdog at all. More like a cute little lapdog curled up and sleeping.

'Not bad, Norval,' Mr Botha said and handed back Ben's essay book. 'But you can do better. Or are you also love-struck these days?' Poor Ben looked as if he wanted to crawl under his desk with embarrassment. 'Like most of your classmates?'

I straightened in fright until I realized Mr Botha was looking past me at Pine who sat diagonally behind me.

'Pienaarr, this is a pathetic piece of work. If you'd taken the trouble to consult a dictionary to see what "transience" means, you would've realized that it has nothing to do with any character's transport.'

But Pine wasn't as easily embarrassed as Ben was. He rubbed his head the way Mr Botha always did, but made it look like a baboon searching for fleas. A few of the children in the class giggled but Mr Botha was blind and dumb to all this as he moved among the desks handing out the rest of the essays.

'Good work, Mart,' he murmured, not really interested as he handed mine to me. Already his attention was on the next book in his hands. 'But this time a dark horse won this particular race.' He gave a broad smile and handed Suna's essay to her. 'It was a pleasant surprise, Miss van der Merwe. I don't agree with everything you had to say but I gave you the highest mark because you at least voiced your own opinion.' Suna didn't know whether to glow with pride or duck her head in embarrassment. So she did both and glowed with her head bent low over her desk. 'Most of the others simply wrote down all the nonsense I threw off in class.'

It was my idea, I thought resentfully, the ridiculous theory that white people were more transient than Coloureds.

'It was the last part, especially, where you speculate on Hannes's death wish which struck me, Suna.' Mr Botha clutched the rest of the essay books to his chest with one hand while he rubbed the bald patch on his head with the other. 'Would you mind if I read those few sentences to the class?'

Speechlessly, Suna shook her head.

'Listen carefully, those of you who wonder why you have to read a book as old-fashioned as *Summer*. Yes, you too, Pienaar. Very well. I quote: "'A dark nostalgia burns in his blood for other worlds, other countries ... perhaps death ... He is shaken by the terrifying thought.' When Hannes has these thoughts about death, we know he doesn't really want to die because many of us have also had such thoughts. Many modern teenagers know the feeling. He could have been one of us."' Mr Locomotive surveyed the class and gave Suna an encouraging smile. "'' But the dark night clamped itself to his heart, the night that falls on the world like a dark giant and over-powers us all.' That's why we feel sad when Hannes does die at the end of the book. It's as if we had known him, as if he had been one of our friends. That's why *Summer* is a timeless book, even if its theme is the passage of time."'

For a few seconds the class was shocked into silence. Even Pine stared uncomfortably at his knuckles. It seemed as if Heinrich Min-naar's name had exploded like a stink bomb in our midst.

I was the only one who realized that Suna had also been thinking about her father when she wrote the essay. While she was sitting on her bed, her blue eyes unseeing and her head at an angle as if she could already hear the music at her party: *Hello, darkness, my old friend ...*

London, 30 October 1993

My Dearest Child

That small news item my mother sent me three months ago managed to achieve what five years in a foreign country couldn't do. It was the shock I needed to drive out the worst of the darkness in my imagination. The mirror is still not bright, but no longer is it wholly dim.

I know the time has come to say goodbye to some of my characters. Naturally I would prefer to keep all of them up to the last page of the story, writing a Shakespearian final act with the entire cast on an overcrowded stage but probably only Shakespeare could get away with that.

For example, I no longer need Pa or Niel or Lovey in the final scenes. I would like to have them there – I've become attached to them all over again, I must admit, even if they sometimes irritated me all over again – but I can do without them. And someone has to be dropped if I want to avoid that unwieldy Shakespearian ending. Eeny, meeny, miney, mo?

I can probably make it easier by saying goodbye to all three at once as I described them next to the swimming pool the last time. Lovey, a little sex bomb in a bikini as small as a flower; Niel, misusing his brother's Border experience to try and impress a girl while his uncontrollable voice threatened to run away with him like a wild horse; Pa with a swinging beer mug in his hand and a silly student song on his lips . . .

No, they haven't improved over the years. Lovey became a bigger sex bomb in an even smaller bikini; Niel a bigger braggart with an attorney's voice as controlled as a trained pony; and Pa . . . well, he doesn't drink more than he did before but the older he gets, the less liquor he needs to sound silly.

Lovey studied drama – what else? – and for a few years, as it should be, only wore second-hand black clothes and lived on cigarettes and black coffee while devoting her talents to Protest Theatre and Experimental Theatre. We could perhaps call them her Seven Lean Years although it was actually less than seven and she was never really hungry, not while she could seek comfort in Ma's kitchen at least once a week. In any case, a few Politically Correct years of Struggle before she, like so many others, was seduced by the glitter and the financial reward of the television screen.

These days she's famous as the sexy bitch in a melodramatic soap opera which makes millions of viewers forget all the political problems and social differences in the country at least once a week. (And that takes some doing! As Ma exclaimed in her last letter.) She has even shone on the covers of a few women's magazines. She has stopped smoking, drinks only *rooibos* tea and apparently perspires every day under the watchful eye (and stroking hands, if I know my sister) of an attractive Personal Trainer in her own private gymnasium.

And Niel, who looked at Simon with such younger-brotherly adoration, in the end became everything Simon never wanted to be. A successful attorney in Pretoria, married to a small, blonde woman with one of those hyphenated names which are supposed to sound French and are always spelled incorrectly. The proud owner of a dream house which has appeared in *Garden and Home* and *De Kat* magazines, two blonde children (Ruhanne and Tio), two Airedale terriers with equally pretentious names which no one can remember, a BMW and a four-wheel drive Suzuki for those weekends when, like his father before him, he wants to play at farming.

Pa is fairly bald these days – and still vain enough, on occasion, to hide the baldness under a cap – but he has achieved a measure of wisdom to make up for the loss of his hair. He still hasn't stopped thinking up wild and improbable schemes but has realized that he can't act on every impossible dream. But he had a narrow escape two years ago. Ma finally persuaded him to accompany her on an overseas tour. After they had 'done' a few European cities – and visited their lost daughter and grandson in London – they also made a lightning visit to Japan. (Ma wanted to go to Japan; Pa said no more than three nights.) Ma flew home with three new blue kimonos, Pa with another unbelievable scheme. He saw a chain of fast-food outlets arising all over the New South Africa, he told her on the plane – *suki* and *sashi* and karaoke from Cape Town to Komatipoort. *Sake* and *sushi*, Ma sighed, and all he would see with such a stupid scheme was his asshole. Luckily he listened to her that time.

Ma hasn't managed to get to Russia or Egypt. Pa always said he wasn't interested in Russia, the place was full of Communists, but now that there are apparently more Communists in South Africa than in Russia, Ma hopes she'll be able to persuade him. Egypt will be a bigger challenge. Pa still believes that the Republic of South Africa is the only civilized country in Africa and not a single one of Ma's hints about pyramids and papyrus have helped her at all. But Ma's hope is still as endless as her stock of hackneyed axioms.

Do you know, that's what I wish for you in the New South Africa? Not the hackneyed axioms (may the gods protect you!) but the endless hope of your hopeful grandmother.

And what of love and faith? You may well ask. Let me tell you how I see the matter. You're old enough to hear it.

Some people are apparently born blessed, the chosen, perhaps just lucky, call it what you will. Love lands on their bodies like the brazen pigeons of Trafalgar Square, faith ignites their minds like heavenly flames, hope bubbles in their hearts like wondrous hot springs – but for most of us it doesn't happen that way. Most of us have to search for these things every day. And even if we're lucky enough to find one of the three, there is still a life-long struggle ahead to retain it. And that takes guts, that attribute your mother admired above all others, and of which you've almost certainly inherited a great deal.

M.

Everyone Must See What's Happening Here

When I saw the little standard six girl standing in my bedroom doorway, just before the lights-out bell, it felt as if I was wearing a shirt buttoned too tightly round the neck.

I was sitting on my bed reading Dalena's latest letter. Before the child could tell me there was a telephone call for me I had jumped up, pushed past her and was running down the passage. With the letter still in my hand, I realized when I was halfway down the stairs.

'I really don't know what's happening any more,' Dalena wrote from Cape Town. 'The child should've been born a week ago but he seems to be having such a good time in my stomach that he's decided not to risk the cruel world. I suppose I should see it as some kind of compliment to my hospitality and all the healthy food I'm giving him but I'm really getting a bit pissed off! I remember that when my sisters and I went to play with other children my mother always said: *Don't overstay your welcome.* (As only my mother can say it, in her heavy Afrikaans accent, her mouth in that bloody decent pleat.) But that's exactly what her indecent grandchild is doing. It's so awful that I'm almost looking forward to the birth, even if I'm more scared of it than . . . Jeez, Mart, I'm scared.'

'Hello?' I gasped when I reached the telephone.

'Hello, Mart,' Simon said, his voice almost inaudible, as if he were speaking from another galaxy. 'Listen, I just wanted to let you know that Dalena is in labour. She phoned me just before they took her to hospital.'

I was too breathless to say anything. I'd begun to wonder whether the child was refusing to come out because it knew it was going to be given away.

'She said her waters had broken, but the pains were still far apart.'

'It sounds OK,' I said, still breathless, grateful for everything I'd learned from my mother's medical book during the past six months.

'She said it might last the whole night. But I'm going to the hospital in any case.'

'But they won't allow you near her!'

'I know.' His voice sounded as dull as it did on the day of Pierre's funeral. 'But what else can I do?'

'They don't want your brother to see the child,' Dalena had written. 'They say it only makes the adoption more difficult if the father is involved as well. (Probably scared he'll crack completely, grab the baby and run away or something like that.) But he got the social worker on his side (and that takes some doing!) and she said she'd see if she could arrange a visit. Her name is Miss Louw but we call her Miss I-Know because she always knows everything, no matter what you say to her. She reminds me of Clitoria Ferguson, the same way of discussing sex and genitalia as if there's no difference between humans and animals. (And these days I wonder whether they might not be right.)

'Anyway, your brother went to see her and charmed her off her feet, as he does only too well. (As I know only too well, otherwise I wouldn't be sitting in the House of the Rising Sin right now.) She said she'd see what she could do but she couldn't promise anything and it definitely wouldn't be a "contact visit". (In other words, he'll have to make do with looking through the window of the baby room.) But he was so grateful, Mart, he was so bloody grateful that my heart broke, not for the first time in the past nine months. For one entire night I couldn't stop crying. *Contact visit*. It sounds as if he wants to visit a convict!'

'But you can't spend the night in your car in front of the hospital!'

'Why not? If I don't freeze to death, I'll probably enjoy it.' He laughed jerkily, like a nervous little boy, my brother who had begun biting his nails again. It was winter in the Cape, it had been raining for days, and the Cortina's heater didn't work.

I looked through the window next to the telephone, through the wire mesh and the bars, at the cloudless sky where a full moon was slowly rising like a shining balloon over the roof of the dining hall. Here the weather was clear and warm, as it always was.

'I wish I was . . .' The lights-out bell rang so shrilly that I couldn't hear the rest of his sentence.

'I've got to go, Simon,' I said hastily. 'Can you phone me early tomorrow morning?'

'What time?'

'Around quarter to seven. I'll wait here at the telephone.' The shirt was tight around my throat again, so tight that my eyes shot full of tears and my voice sounded strangled. 'I . . . I don't know what to say, Simon.'

'Never mind,' Simon said, his voice so soft that I could barely hear him. 'Neither do I.'

It was going to be a long night, I thought in my dark hostel room. And it was going to be an even longer one for my brother, waiting in front of a hospital in a cold car. And for my roommate, who lay somewhere in that hospital in a labour ward, it was going to be the longest, loneliest, most unbearable night of her life.

I wished I were in my mother's bed, lying tucked against her back like that Sunday morning, two weeks ago, when I'd told her everything.

I hadn't planned it that way. It was one of those things that simply happen, which probably had to happen. Ma and I were alone at home over the weekend – Pa had gone to see a rugby match in Pretoria, Niel and Lovey were staying with friends – and I had decided to spoil her with coffee in bed. When I came through the door, she was lying curled up on her side. She opened one eye and immediately closed it again, as she had done years ago when it was her birthday or Mother's Day and we kids had tried to surprise her with breakfast in bed. I laughed and wriggled in behind her, embracing her body, still warm with sleep.

Then she sighed and said: 'I wish you were still small.'

'So do I, Ma,' I said and started crying.

She had tried to turn but I held her so tightly that she couldn't manage it. I'd pressed my face into the hollow of her back, between her shoulder blades, and dampened her pink nightgown with my sobs.

'Dalena is expecting a baby, Ma,' I'd wept. 'I wanted to tell you a long time ago but I couldn't because her mother doesn't want people to know – that's why they thought up that story of a good school in the Cape. But it isn't a good school, Ma, it's a home for unmarried mothers – and the baby is due any day now and Dalena is going to have him adopted because she doesn't know what else to do, Ma!'

All in one breath because I was afraid that if I stopped for a second I wouldn't have the courage to carry on. Under the thin cotton of my mother's damp nightdress, her back had become as rigid as an ironing board. I could feel her struggling to ask what she could not ask.

'It's Simon's child.'

Ma drew in her breath sharply, slowly moved out of my arms and sat up. Then I told her everything, sometimes crying so much that I couldn't utter a word while she occasionally asked me a question in a strange, cold, calm voice. When I eventually calmed down, wiped my eyes and looked at her, she sat with her back against the headboard and stared at the opposite wall without moving. Her eyes had never seemed so dark, or so large. Not even on the evening after Pierre's memorial service.

'So, at least Simon has seen her in the past few weeks?' she asked eventually.

'Yes. After I was there, during the holiday. At least they're talking to one another now.'

She started fiddling with her uncombed hair. I was so relieved to see this familiar gesture that my eyes started burning all over again. The cup of coffee I'd brought her stood untouched on the bedside table, as cold as tap water by now.

'I wish you'd told me earlier . . .'

That's what Simon had said.

'Ma . . .'

'Do you mean to tell me . . .' She'd looked at me, suddenly overcome, and bit her full underlip. Only then had her dark eyes filled with tears. 'Do you mean to tell me that I'm going to be a *grandmother* in less than a month?'

She got up hastily, walked to the bathroom with her head bowed and closed the door behind her. I could hear her opening the tap of the basin and letting it run for a long time.

I stood next to the telephone in the grey early morning of the hostel, tired and sleepy after a night harried by unthinkable thoughts and undreamable dreams. Suppose something had happened to the child? Suppose it was deformed or mentally retarded or something? Then no one would want to adopt it.

And what would I do if it hadn't been born yet? How could I sit in a classroom today, in my ugly grey uniform, like any other day, and concentrate on *Summer* and *A Midsummer Night's Dream* while my roommate was having a baby?

When eventually the telephone rang, my brother's voice sounded so different that I didn't recognize it for a moment.

'It's a girl.'

'A *girl*?'

'A girl.' (Did all men sound like this when their first babies were born? So surprised, stunned, overcome?) 'She was born just after five this morning. Healthy and normal.' (What could I say? 'Congratulations'?) 'And very beautiful.'

'You've seen her, then?' I asked, dazed.

'Half an hour ago. I spent the last couple of hours sitting in the entrance of the hospital. I couldn't stand it in the car any longer, I was getting frostbite and going mad. Then one of the staff took pity on me, a simple old guy pushing a trolley, probably saw I was falling off mine . . .' He gave a tired, forced laugh. It was one of the saddest sounds I'd ever heard. 'Anyway, he gave me a kind of running commentary on what was happening in the labour ward every time he passed through the entrance. So I knew, more or less, when she was born.'

It sounded as if he was too exhausted to say another word. I wanted to say something but the lump in my throat felt like a plug preventing speech. I couldn't stand and weep next to the hostel telephone!

'It was weird, Mart. I felt as if . ... as if I'd die if I didn't see my child! I hadn't expected . . . I thought it would be different. I didn't think it would be that bad! In the end I phoned Miss Louw – I think I got her out of bed. She sounded really pissed off, but when she heard the state I was in, all she said was, "Hang on, I'll be there in a minute." Then she came to the hospital and took me to the baby room . . . and then I saw her . . . through a dim window . . .'

Now I didn't give a damn, I decided. Now the entire hostel could see me crying next to the telephone.

'What does she look like, Simon?'

'Like me!' As if he couldn't believe it. 'The way I look in my baby photos, remember? A white skin and a wild mop of black hair.'

'Ma always said you could've been Snow White's baby brother,' I said sniffing, and wiped my nose with the side of my hand. *Hair as black as ebony, a skin as white as snow, cheeks as red as blood* . . . 'She still says you were her prettiest baby.'

'And I always thought she only said that because I was the first. Because she didn't know any better. But after seeing this child . . . I've never seen such a beautiful baby, Mart.'

'What are you waiting for?' Suna asked.

'I'm afraid of sounding soppy if I hear her voice. And you know what she's like. She'll put the phone down in my ear.'

'Do you want me to do it?'

I nodded but didn't take my hand off the phone. Suna swept her blonde hair over her shoulder with an impatient gesture and tapped her bare foot on the carpet. Her toenails were painted a strange green. It looked as if her feet had mildew.

We were sitting in her mother's pink bedroom on a bed with a padded pink headboard and a matching pink satin spread. A score of little cushions were arranged on the bed like a bouquet, covered in the same pink floral material as the curtains, which had the same pattern as the wallpaper. I felt as if I couldn't breathe, as if I were trapped in a huge cocoon of pink spun sugar. Even the carpet was pink.

231

'Why don't we phone her?' Suna had suggested at school in the morning. 'She'll have a phone in her room, won't she? When my mother had her boobs pumped up last year, I phoned her every day.'

I looked at Suna. Surely giving your child away had to be different from having a boob job?

'I don't know whether it's such a good idea, Suna. Perhaps she doesn't want to speak to anyone now . . .'

'We're not *anyone*!' The indignation stretched her voice like chewing-gum, a little thinner with each syllable until it reached breaking point on the *anyone*. 'Why don't we just try? If she doesn't want to speak to us, we can –'

'I don't think I could bear it if she won't speak to us.'

'Well, if she doesn't want to, Mart, at least she'll know we're thinking of her.'

'And the rest of the school will be too, Suna. You know how hard it is to make a phone call in this place without the world and her husband listening.'

'It's your free afternoon, isn't it? You can come to my house. My mother is having her hair permed. It takes hours. We'll have more than enough time to phone!'

I'd allowed myself to be persuaded. I was petrified of hearing Dalena's voice, scared of crying, scared that she would cry, scared that we wouldn't know what to say to one another, scared that it would feel like the end of our friendship – but in the end the longing overrode the fear. I even began to believe that she might be pleased if we phoned her.

Our first attempt ended in failure.

'I'm sorry,' said a friendly nurse's voice on the maternity ward, 'Miss van Vuuren isn't taking any calls.'

'She's not taking any calls!' I whispered to Suna.

'Miss van Vuuren doesn't wish to speak to anyone,' the nurse had said, still friendly but just a trifle more firmly. 'She asked us to remove the telephone from her room.'

'Oh,' I said, defeated. 'Oh . . .' I couldn't find anything to say.

Impatiently Suna had grabbed the receiver. 'I'm sure she'll want to speak to us! Just tell her that Mart and Suna are phoning from Black River!'

'I'm sorry.' With every word, the voice on the telephone had become firmer and less friendly. 'She said she wanted to speak to no one.'

'Only because she wasn't expecting us to phone her.' I'd listened to Suna with growing admiration. What had happened to the high little-girl's voice? She sounded as self-confident as a prefect! 'I'm sure that if you . . .'

'Look, I'm sorry.' Now there was no trace of friendliness, only suppressed impatience. 'I'm a nurse, not a messenger. Miss van Vuuren expressly –'

'Please, Sister?' Suna's voice had become thin as a reed. 'Please just tell her that Mart and Suna will phone again in half an hour, then she can think about it? Mart and Suna. *Please?*'

That half-hour took a lifetime to pass.

'Do you want me to do it?' Suna asked again.

I shook my head, drew a deep breath, dialled the number.

'It'll be OK,' Suna said consolingly. 'Now that she knows it's us.' But she sounded as if she was trying to persuade herself.

Again I asked if I could speak to Dalena van Vuuren. Again I waited with a heart hammering against my ribs, even more wildly than the first time, until I heard the same maternity nurse's voice. This time she made no pretence at hiding her impatience.

'Miss van Vuuren sends her apologies but, as I said before, she doesn't with to speak to *anybody*.'

Suna, whose head was bent as close as possible to mine, looked up in consternation.

'She said she was sure you'd understand.'

'Didn't she say anything else?' I had difficulty in keeping my voice under control.

'No.' The impatient voice softened a little. 'Nothing else.'

I put the receiver down and stared at my grey school uniform. Suddenly I felt as out of place as a muddy dog on this pink satin bedcover among all these little pink flowers, in this absurd spun-sugar pink bedroom. I could hardly wait to be alone in my bare hostel room.

'It was a stupid idea in the first place,' I said to Suna, my voice unnecessarily biting.

She didn't seem to hear me. She sat with her legs drawn up, her chin on her knees, her eyes on her green toenails and pulled at a thread in the hem of her tight jeans.

'Oh, well,' she sighed. 'Better to have loved and lost than never to have loved . . . or what's that line again?'

But I hadn't the faintest idea what she was talking about.

It was on days like this that I wished I could go home after school – even more so than on other days – so that I could be aware of what was going on in the rest of the world. All I knew at the moment was that something important was happening somewhere in the country. During recess the teachers had all gathered round a portable radio in the staff room, their faces grave. (Even Miss Potgieter, who normally thought needlework was more important than the news, and Clitoria Ferguson who usually drank tea on her own because she thought herself a cut above the other teachers.) Not one of the schoolkids could remember anything like this happening before.

'Apparently an Uprising has taken place in one of the Locations outside Johannesburg,' Bull's-Eye Pretorius had told us in history class, his eyes blinking nervously behind his thick lenses. 'But everything is under control. There's no need to panic.'

'It has something to do with Afrikaans,' was Mr Botha's only remark while he rubbed his head with a distressed expression. 'The black children have problems with Afrikaans.'

'Soweto is an acronym, class,' Miss Muffet had informed us excitedly, a long, pink fingernail aloft. 'Does anyone remember what an acronym is?'

'Something to do with NATO, Miss?' one of the boys had asked uncertainly.

'That's correct!' She spread her hands so that we could admire all ten beautiful nails. 'Yes, class, NATO is an acronym for the North Atlantic Treaty Alliance. Soweto is an acronym for South Western Townships.'

'Miss, can't we please listen to the news on your radio?' Pine asked in an Afrikaans accent which dragged at his tongue like an iron cuff. 'The English news, of course, Miss?'

Miss Muffet had looked longingly at the little radio between the piles of books on her desk. She listened to *Radio Today* before school every morning and occasionally – wearing earphones – to an English serial or a book reading while the children in her class struggled with English grammar.

'I don't think so, Petrus,' she'd sighed. Pine's face contorted as if she'd slapped him. No one, not even the headmaster, ever called him Petrus. 'We're not even half-way through *A Midsummer Night's Dream* . . .'

Hastily I combed my hair, grateful that it was our free afternoon, that I'd be able to reach a café in town. I wondered whether there would be anything in the afternoon newspaper by now. But when I studied my face in the bathroom mirror, I completely forgot the crisis which had hit the country. My skin was in a more serious crisis.

Never mind, Pa had said consolingly the previous weekend, they're just petting pimples. I'd thought about Pine – the big, dangerous Pine Pienaar who wanted to eat out of my hand like a hungry puppy every time he came near me these days – and felt my face growing hot. I couldn't help it. Since that evening on the uncomfortable sofa, he constantly reminded me of a puppy.

I quickly turned away from the mirror, determined not to pick at my face again. Maybe I should follow Suna's example and start taking the pill, I thought on my way out. For my skin.

I kept my eyes on my dusty school shoes while I walked through the garden. To think that in a few months I would never have to wear these shoes and these dirty-white socks and this ugly grey uniform again! It was almost time for the matric farewell – I wondered whether Pine was going to ask me – and next year I would be a student. *Miss* Vermaak. If only I could persuade Dalena to come to Stellenbosch with me.

On the pavement in front of the hostel I blinked my eyes against the sharp light as I always did, and looked round in total bewilderment when I heard my brother's voice behind me.

'Mart?'

He stood next to Ma's Cortina, his hand on the open door, his eyes hidden behind dark glasses. An apparition, was the first thought that crossed my mind, a mirage caused by the heat.

'Aren't you going to say hello to your brother?'

'Simon!' When I hugged him, I immediately felt the tension in his stiff shoulders. 'I thought you weren't coming home for the winter holidays! Didn't you have a job somewhere in the Cape?'

'Get into the car,' he said. 'I don't want to talk in the street.'

Which meant he didn't want Niel and Lovey to see him. My shoulders became as tense as his.

'What's wrong, Simon?' I asked. 'What's happened?'

He started the engine without saying a word. His suitcases were still on the back seat. Which meant he hadn't been home yet. The rest of my body became as tense as my shoulders. He'd come straight here to talk to me.

'What's happened?' I asked again.

He drove towards town as if he didn't hear me, his eyes still hidden behind the dark glasses. I realized where we were heading. Where else? I thought when we stopped next to the deserted, neglected park.

'She's gone,' he said the moment he switched off the engine, his hands still on the steering wheel. 'She's disappeared.'

'Gone? What do you mean, gone?'

'She disappeared from the hospital a few days ago. I thought she was hiding somewhere in Cape Town but I can't find her anywhere. No one knows where she is. Or no one wants to tell. She's simply . . . gone.'

'Perhaps she's come home?'

He shook his head, his eyes on the swings and the rusted slide behind the barred fence, his hands clenched so tightly around the steering wheel that his knuckles looked transparent.

'I've already spoken to her parents.'

'How do you know they're not lying to you?'

'No, her mother was totally stunned when I asked her what had become of Dalena. I could hear the old bitch wasn't lying. In fact, she sounded close to tears when she put the phone down on me.'

Absently he put out his hand to switch on the radio. Someone was sobbing a song about a dying boy and a cowboy. On any other day he would've looked for another station immediately. My brother found Country and Western almost as bad as *Boeremusiek*. Now he simply sat there as if he didn't even hear the music.

'But I put my pride in my pocket – the little I have left – and phoned again to speak to her father. Just to make quite sure. She's not on the farm, Mart.'

I rolled down the window. It was unbearably hot in the car. The plastic covers felt as sticky as syrup against my legs. But it would have been even worse to sit in the neglected park again.

'I think she's left the country,' Simon mumbled.

He took off the dark glasses and wiped his hand over his face. When he looked at me, his eyes were bloodshot.

'Just like that?' I couldn't bear the expression on his face. I looked away and stared through the open window at a row of palm trees in the park. 'Without saying goodbye to anyone?'

'She's not exactly one for dramatic farewell scenes, is she?' When the cowboy gave his horse to the dying child, my brother gave the radio a disturbed glance. He started twiddling the knob, got *Women's World*, swore inaudibly. 'She didn't say goodbye to any of us before going to Cape Town.'

'But that was different! She didn't know . . .'

'Perhaps she simply didn't see her way clear to doing it.' He was still fiddling distractedly with the radio. 'Maybe she's not as brave as you think, Mart.'

'Don't you think she's brave, Simon?'

'Sure. But Pierre always said . . .'

He stopped when he heard an excited reporter's voice on the radio.

'. . . Soweto, where some ten thousand black teenagers caused almost unbelievable destruction today. The mutilated body of one of the white victims lay in the sun next to the wreck of his burnt-out car. Initially a part of the noisy crowd wanted to throw the man's body into his burning car but others screamed: "Leave him! We want everyone to see what's happening here!"'

'What's going on?' Simon asked, stunned.

'I was hoping you'd be able to tell *me*. Didn't you listen to the radio earlier today?'

'Not yesterday, either,' he said, shaking his head. 'I needed quiet; needed to think. I've got to find her, Mart. I can't simply carry on with my life as if nothing has happened! There are still too many things we have to discuss, too much unfinished business. Everything can't just be left hanging in the air.'

'Only Romeo and Juliet discuss everything all the time,' I muttered.

A black woman and a blond toddler had appeared in the park, seemingly out of nowhere. The child ran to the same swing on which the ghostly grey-headed woman had sat a few months ago. The black woman helped him on to the swing and carefully pushed him to and fro.

'The first signs of trouble in Soweto became apparent about five weeks ago,' the reporter on the radio explained, 'when pupils of Phefeni Junior Secondary School refused to be taught in some subjects through the medium of Afrikaans.'

'Five weeks ago?' Simon looked even more staggered. 'And this is the first I've heard of it?'

I was still looking at the toddler on the swing. He threw his head back and the sun glinted in his blond hair. If Pierre had been here, I thought longingly, we would have known what was happening in Soweto.

'What did Pierre say?'

'Pierre?'

'You mentioned something Pierre had said. About bravery.'

'Oh, yes. He believed that the guys who were truly scared often behaved like the bravest ones – in the Army, in any case – to try and hide their fear.' He smiled Pierre's crooked smile, which didn't suit his face at all. 'He was very brave the day he died.'

I refused to cry. I was never going to cry again. I had cried enough in the past few months to exhaust a lifetime's tears.

'And you think Dalena is only pretending to be brave?'

He shrugged his shoulders in a helpless gesture and the crooked smile quivered.

'I don't know. I only know I can't pretend it's all over! For the rest of my life I'm going to pine for a child which I saw only once through a dim fucking window!'

He rubbed his eyes angrily. And I started crying again. Can you believe it?

'I must look for her, Mart. Where the hell ever she might be hiding. I think she's gone abroad. I'm going to find her, even if I have to sell all I own to afford the airfare.'

'Are you out of your bloody mind?' I was so startled that I stopped crying. 'You can hardly walk through the streets of Paris or Rome asking whether anyone's seen Dalena van Vuuren! You don't even know which country to start looking in, Simon!'

'Somewhere where it's always warm?' Again that crooked smile which didn't belong to his face. 'At least that eliminates Scandinavia.'

He leaned forward until his head rested on the steering wheel and closed his eyes as if he wanted to go to sleep like that. On the radio a politician was discussing the situation in Soweto in a sombre voice.

'In any case,' Simon said after a while, his eyes still closed, 'it sounds as if the time has come to get out of this country.'

My Dearest, Dearest Child

Your mother's disappearance opened a seam in my life which I have never been able to stitch up again. I'd always hoped that I would see her again one day, that perhaps she would help me to trace you.

Not to turn your life upside down, simply to know what had become of you and to keep a watchful eye on you from a distance. I saw myself as some kind of guardian angel – in a shiny, white gown with a cigarette burn on the bum – who could help you, should you ever need help some day. Now you'll have to do without me, and I without you.

My parents moved away from the Black River area shortly after I wrote my matric exam, because my father had grown tired of the struggle to get a health farm going. (His partners, who patiently waited for the health-conscious eighties, are all millionaires today.) I studied and worked in Cape Town and gradually lost contact with everyone who had been at school with me. (Even with Suna, who married Pine Pienaar, believe it or not, and was the proud mother of four black-haired sons when last I heard from her.) While still in South Africa, I hopefully posted a Christmas card to Dalena at her parents' farm every year. But I never received a reply. And during the past five years in London, my last links with Black River were finally severed.

Simon, however, I saw a few months ago. He was on his way between somewhere and nowhere and unexpectedly had to spend a night in London. We talked until morning, the way we had when we were young. I even smoked a joint for the first time in years. I can't help it. My brother always releases all my suppressed rebelliousness.

Each time I see him I become an angry seventeen-year-old again. Fortunately I very seldom see him.

Probably because he never turned into a conventional adult. Definitely not conventional, Ma and Pa say, and not really adult either, I have to admit.

In the end, he did go overseas in 1976, ostensibly to look for Dalena, but Pa still thinks he was only looking for an excuse to live like a bum for a few years. When he eventually returned, he refused to study law again (a severe blow for my father) and entered an English university (another grave disappointment) and in the end took a degree in 'all kinds of useless social subjects' (according to Pa). But the worst blow of all, for my father, was that he became involved in 'Communist' student politics.

In the eighties Simon left the country again, this time without a noisy family gathering at the airport. This time the family didn't even know he was leaving. We learned later that the Security Police were looking for him. Many of his friends didn't manage to escape in time and landed in prison. This was during the dark days of the first State of Emergency.

After many wanderings, he finally settled in the US where he now works for some human rights organization which no one has ever heard of. (There are a great many of those in the US.) He's regularly sent to the Third World and other trouble spots where he always stays in the best hotels and preferably drinks only gin and tonic.

No, he hasn't been an angry young man for a long time. A cynical, almost middle-aged bum might be a better description.

'You've probably heard of the lost generation,' he muttered that night while he rolled joints for us.

'You mean all the black kids who never had any proper education after 'seventy-six?'

'Them as well.' He moved the pips to one side with his small finger and carefully divided the remaining dope between the two Rizla papers. 'But the problem is actually far larger. It wasn't only black children who were lost.'

He was greying at the temples, I realized with astonishment. All at once I wondered what Pierre would have looked like by now. For the first time I tried to picture him at the age of nearly forty. Would his thick black hair have started to thin, his taut body become slack, his tight stomach turned into a flabby paunch? I closed my eyes and shook my head. I couldn't do it.

'Many of us whiteys who started using our minds in the seventies, are just as lost.' He lit one of the tightly packed papers with an antique silver lighter and sucked at it deeply and gratefully. 'Everything we were brought up to believe has disappeared. Or is busy disappearing.'

'But isn't that what you wanted? I mean ... the Struggle and all that? The whole idea was that everything had to change, wasn't it?'

'Sure. But that doesn't make it any easier.' The small John Lennon glasses behind which he hides these days reflected the light so that I couldn't see his eyes. 'I mean, there's nothing that keeps me from going back to South Africa, except for this feeling that I've lost my way – that I lost it so completely that I'll never find it again.'

I know, I wanted to say, I've felt like that, too. But my head was buzzing from the dagga and my tongue lay lifelessly in my mouth.

'Sometimes I feel as if I'm floating in a spacecraft in the outer darkness with no landmark to help me find the earth again!'

He's still a good-looking man, I thought sadly, but I doubted whether any young girl today would refer to him as a dish. I didn't know whether any young girl would still use the word 'dish' to refer to anything except crockery. While Pierre, like James Dean and Marilyn Monroe on those posters in my bedroom, so many years ago, would always remain young in my memories. I would never have to face the reality of what he might have become, or not become. It was probably better that way.

'And even if I managed to reach it, one way or another, I wouldn't know what to do there.' He started laughing slowly, too slowly, as he'd done long ago. 'Or what to believe in.'

'Maybe it has nothing to do with the seventies,' I said. I heard my voice coming from a great distance, like long ago. 'Maybe we feel alienated simply because we're older.'

'I'm not speaking about alienation, Mart! I'm speaking about being lost!' He let out a heavy sigh along with the smoke. 'We're fucking *lost*, man . . .'

Yep. When my brother gets stoned, he still sounds like the poor man's Bob Dylan.

I didn't want to get as lost as my roommate. I had another flash of clarity – a moment of light in the darkness – when I folded that newspaper item for the twentieth or maybe the two hundreth time to put it back into my handbag. I had started reading the advertisement on the back with no particular interest – a perfectly ordinary ad for a sale in a department store – when I noticed a date. It allowed me to work out, for the first time, precisely when Dalena had died.

Then I knew. Your mother committed suicide on the night of your seventeenth birthday. That's the age she was when you were born.

I saw it as a final message from my lost roommate.

I started writing this story because I had to take a decision about our future – mine and my son's – but the more inevitable the decision seemed, the more frightened I became. Until your mother's death reminded me of guts again. It's an absurd thought, isn't it? That a bossy, know-it-all teenage friend could still influence my life twenty years later. Even after her death.

Do I hear you laughing somewhere, Dalena?

'Why are you smiling, Mummy?' my inquisitive son asks next to me.

'Because I'm thinking . . .'

But at this moment the pilot announces that Flight 605 from London is about to land at Cape Town and my heart's beating constricts my throat so that I'm incapable of further speech.

'Why are you *crying*, Mummy?' he asks, bewildered.

I shake my head and help him to fasten his safety belt.

'Because we're almost home, Pierre.'

Yes, I have decided to come home. I want to cast my vote in the first democratic elections in the history of my heartland. I have made up my mind in favour of hope.

So, let me say goodbye to you for the last time, my dearest child. It's time for me to stop writing and start living anew. I can't be your guardian angel but I console myself that at least I'll be closer to you.

And who knows, maybe one day, somewhere in this country, we'll walk past one another, look into each other's eyes and briefly wonder: *Where have I seen her before? Something about her looks familiar. I wonder who she is?* And then our attention will be diverted and we'll forget about one another again.

And never know that for a brief moment we saw face to face, looking at a bright image in a mirror.

Love

Mart Vermaak